Kyra turned the spigots of the big porcelain tub and poured a small amount of bath salts under the steaming water. She left the water running as she unfastened her riding habit and stepped out of its cumbersome folds.

She had just finished lathering her body and had submerged her limbs under the warm water when she heard the pass key in the door, followed by the rustle of silk as Alma walked across the room to lay Kyra's dress on the bed. "Alma," she called out, "could you come back in half an hour and help me with my hair?"

The maid's footsteps approached the bathroom door, which was almost directly behind Kyra's back. She began to turn, to see what Alma wanted, when a towel was thrown over her face, stuffed roughly into her mouth, and wound around her whole head with an expert twist. . . .

Another Fawcett Gold Medal Title
by Teona Tone:

LADY ON THE LINE

FULL CRY

Teona Tone

FAWCETT GOLD MEDAL • NEW YORK

A Fawcett Gold Medal Book
Published by Ballantine Books

Library of Congress Catalog Card Number: 85-90697

ISBN 0-449-12747-8

Manufactured in the United States of America

First Edition: August 1985

For
W. T. S., M. F. H.

CHAPTER 1

Race Day—
April 20, 1907

KYRA felt a flash of irritation when she heard the crunch of carriage wheels on gravel coming down the driveway to the barn. It was only eight o'clock in the morning— and it was her day to be together with Gerald. Since she'd married Senator McMasters and formally dismantled Keaton Investigations, Kyra jealously guarded what little time her husband had with her after his official obligations were met. Today was the beginning of his spring break from the Senate and also the first day of the Daisy Hill Hunt Club's Race Day Weekend, which they had looked forward to for months.

Kyra glanced quickly at the barn. Gerald had gone in to check on his favorite mare, which was due to foal any day. He hadn't heard the carriage, so perhaps she could avert the impending interruption. Her view of the buggy's occupant was obscured by a row of trees, but she was all too certain that it would be one of her husband's aides or some other messenger from the capital with an urgent request for Gerald's personal attention to a matter of national import. It seemed at times as if Gerald were the only competent member of the Senate—certainly the only one capable of handling the wide range of problems he fielded continually. It was not unusual for

President Roosevelt himself to call Gerald in to ask his advice on some matter under consideration, such as the recent negotiations with Japan and China. But today Kyra wanted her husband for herself.

"Just a minute, Diana," she said, patting a large chestnut mare she had been about to mount. She handed the reins to the groom and walked toward the driveway, ominously tapping her crop against the skirt of her riding habit, a superbly tailored green worsted that set off her slim figure and golden-blond hair.

Her flashing tiger eyes indicated that she was well prepared to send a mild-mannered aide back to the capital empty-handed. Then she recognized the carriage. It was the ostentatiously elegant barouche belonging to Edna Harding, the widow of Perseus Harding, who had been murdered in connection with the attempted nationwide telephone company take-over that Kyra had exposed almost eight years ago—it hardly seemed possible it had been that long a time, but a lot had happened since then. For one thing, Edna Harding had moved from Philadelphia to Washington, to be close to her son Oswald when he got a job at the Library of Congress. Gerald had recommended Oswald for the job and sometimes chuckled about the havoc he had wreaked through that simple recommendation: Edna Harding had quickly become one of the capital's most officious busybodies. Her sharp features became well known in most social circles and her even sharper comments were a constant source of irritation, annoyance, and embarrassment to everyone she met. Kyra generally defused Edna's invective with humor, but she was not amused by this early morning visit. She stopped, tempted to turn and walk away, but Edna's shrill voice cut through the morning air.

"Mrs. McMasters!" she almost screeched as she climbed out of the carriage, holding her voluminous skirts in one hand and her copiously plumed hat with the other. "Tragedy has struck! Absolute tragedy! I knew you'd want to know, so I got up at dawn to be the first to tell you. I didn't want to trust the telephone lines, you know. I never have since poor Perseus . . .'' Her voice trailed off and she dabbed a handkerchief theatrically at the corner of one eye, a habit she affected every time she mentioned her departed husband. Kyra sometimes irreverently thought that if there was an afterlife, Perseus must be enjoying it fully, knowing that he had escaped his wife for at least a little while.

"So what is this tragedy?" Kyra asked impatiently, catching a glimpse of Gerald emerging from the barn. "We're just mounting up to ride over to Hopsworth for the races, so tell me quickly or not at all."

"Well, it *involves* the races, which is why I thought you'd like to know before you got there. It's absolutely terrible! And it's too late to call things off—some of the *very best* people will already be . . .''

Kyra turned on her heel and began to walk away, exasperated. She would *not* let that infernal busybody ruin her morning with trivial hunt gossip. She had gone about three paces when Edna's voice penetrated her anger.

"Senator Howard's son is dead!" Edna announced with an air of satisfaction. "He was riding that stallion the senator set so much store by and they went down over a fence. The dear young man broke his neck. The horse came limping in without him after dark and they had to send out a search party. They found Nathaniel in the middle of the night, dead where he'd fallen. Nadine was with the search party and she's heartbroken, of course, poor dear. At least she *seems* heartbroken—I know she's your friend and all of that, but last Sunday she didn't act like she'd be so sorry. . . .'' She paused for a moment to see what effect this had on Kyra, then added, "Well, I suppose all young married couples do have their little squabbles, but . . .''

Kyra stared at Edna, wondering if she'd gone stark raving mad or if what she was saying could possibly have some basis in reality. The older woman continued unabated, "Oswald was at Hopsworth when it happened,

3

so he told me everything as soon as he came in, which was almost dawn. He was going to ring you up on the telephone, but I offered to come in person and break the news. He was greatly relieved, the poor dear—his nerves have been so *delicate*, you know, ever since his father's death.'' She then leaned forward and whispered with a self-important flourish, ''And there's a possibility of foul play involved here, too! I thought you'd like to know *that* in particular!''

''You're telling me that Nathaniel Howard is dead and someone killed him?'' Kyra asked incredulously.

''Yes,'' Edna answered with a nod that made the plumes on her hat bobble and sway like some fantastic sea plant. ''He went out late yesterday afternoon to practice a bit for today's steeplechase, and his horse tripped on a wired fence in Farmer Ingleson's pasture.'' Edna gave an affected shudder, which Kyra echoed with the real version as she pictured the horse catching his legs on the wire, then crashing to the ground. It was one of the most dangerous falls possible, because the horse was jerked to a sudden stop midair, then somersaulted over the fence, while the helpless rider was catapulted out of the saddle by the force of impact. It was not unusual for both horse and rider to break their necks in such falls, and foxhunting clubs in Virginia had gone to great lengths to persuade farmers not to run wires along the tops of their fences, as they were difficult to see until the last minute, even under the best of conditions.

''But Ingleson wouldn't wire his fences,'' Kyra exclaimed. ''He was friendly to the hunt—he even provided a hunt breakfast once last season.''

''Precisely!'' Edna agreed with a note of triumph in her voice. ''I think that if you checked with him, you'd find that he didn't wire his fence—someone else did. And I think I know who,'' she added smugly.

''Who?'' Kyra asked. ''Who would possibly want to hurt Nathaniel? He's one of the most likable people I've ever known—everyone likes him.''

''Well, perhaps *some* people knew him better than

others, such as your friend Nadine," Edna responded tartly. "But *you* figure it all out—you're the famous lady detective. You don't need *my* help, certainly!"

"Whatever you wish," Kyra answered evenly, her good breeding preventing her from making a curt reply. "If you'll excuse me, then," she added as she picked up the train of her habit and walked toward the barn as quickly as her skirts would allow.

It had been almost five years since Nathaniel Howard had married Kyra's best friend and former assistant, Nadine. As far as Kyra knew, the couple's happiness was marred only by their inability to have children. This was a particularly sore point for Nathaniel, who by nature loved and was loved by children and animals alike. Not having any offspring of his own, he lavished affection on his friends' children, his hounds, and his horses. He enjoyed being called "Uncle Nat" by the children who continually followed him around Hopsworth, but it was not enough; he wanted one of his own. Besides, as the old senator often pointed out, Nathaniel needed an heir. Nadine, on the other hand, had lost her mother in childbirth and was nervous at the idea of becoming pregnant herself. She had confessed to Kyra that she and Nathaniel had more than once had bitter scenes during which he'd accused her of taking measures to prevent herself from conceiving. Nadine swore that she hadn't, but as the years passed with no children, even Kyra began to wonder. She herself had three, the eldest of which was already learning to ride a pony under Nathaniel's tutelage.

Otherwise, however, Nathaniel and Nadine seemed perfectly happy. Although Nadine had a hot temper, Nathaniel's easygoing nature kept things on an even keel most of the time. In addition, Nadine was a better rider than most men and helped Nathaniel enormously in training and hunting his pack of hounds. Together, they also managed Thurston's extensive thoroughbred breeding and training program, as the elderly senator was too busy with his official duties to do much more than glance over the paperwork and take an occasional stroll through the barn.

Kyra had not talked to her friend in several weeks, because all three of her children had been down with the grippe and their nanny had thrown up her hands in despair at the thought of tending to all of them without Kyra's help, even for a few hours. But Kyra was certain that if there had been some major problem between Nadine and Nathaniel, Nadine would have rung her up on the telephone to talk.

When Kyra reached the barn, Gerald was already mounted. The groom held Kyra's mare as she quickly stepped from the mounting block to the stirrup and settled herself into the sidesaddle. For the first time in a long while, she missed the freedom she'd had in California to ride astride; she could have covered the distance to the Howards' much faster with the use of two stirrups and her legs encased in britches instead of the cumbersome folds of her riding habit. But there was no time now for regrets of any sort as she touched the mare forward with her crop, simultaneously explaining to Gerald, "Nathaniel Howard's been killed in an accident on Truly Fine. They went down over a jump and his neck was broken. I need to get to Nadine as fast as possible."

About an hour later, Kyra and Gerald cantered their lathered horses up the winding driveway toward the white-columned mansion that dominated Hopsworth, Senator Thurston Howard's estate. Clearly, something was terribly wrong. The rolling green lawns were dotted with small groups of people in hunting attire, huddled together, speaking in hushed voices to each other. In spite of, or perhaps because of, the men's festive scarlet jackets and the women's rich satin riding habits, they looked deflated, wilted, like expensive cut flowers that had been left in the sun too long without water. And they looked frightened. From the partially opened windows of the house came the sound of Senator Howard's voice, howling in anguish and agony. Over and over he cried out, "My son! My son! My son is dead!" followed by heart-rending groans and sobs.

Oswald Harding emerged from the house as Kyra and Gerald approached. "I'm so glad you're here!" he exclaimed. "My mother told you?"

"Yes," Kyra answered. "Thurston doesn't sound very good."

"No, he's much worse than he was last night, even. Dr. Whitley's with him now, but he refuses to allow himself to be sedated," Oswald explained, wringing his hands in agitation. "Perhaps you or Senator McMasters can talk some sense into him."

"We'll see what we can do," Gerald said reassuringly as he helped Kyra from her horse. "In the meantime, perhaps you could get the servants to bring these people some coffee and refreshments—I'm sure there was a breakfast planned, and it would be better for everyone to have something to keep themselves busy for a while."

"Of course," answered Oswald. "That's an excellent idea." He seemed relieved to have something constructive to do as he went off to give instructions.

When he had disappeared around the corner, Gerald said to Kyra, "I doubt we'll have any luck getting Thurston to allow himself to be sedated, considering what happened to Sarah."

Sarah had been Thurston's wife. She had died several years earlier after a long battle with morphine addiction. Howard was convinced that his wife had been killed by the drug, which she had initially taken in the form of a patent medicine for a stomach ailment. Since Sarah's death, the senator had become one of the most outspoken members of Congress in favor of government regulation of morphine, heroin, and other opiates. Just over a year ago, he had been instrumental in legislating an increase of the import tariffs on opium, which he considered a major step toward his ultimate goal of getting opiates banned altogether. He had sworn repeatedly that he would rather suffer agonies of pain than use any of the opium drugs.

"I think you're right," answered Kyra, pulling off her riding gloves and picking up her train to walk up the steps into the house. She was stopped midway by the approach of a small group of people with various degrees of concern, alarm, and fear showing on their faces. It was a delegation of some of the key members of the Daisy Hill Hunt, people Kyra had known for six years now and Gerald much longer than that. The delegation was headed by Sir Randolph Roseberry and his wife, Lady Pandora.

Sir Randolph was tall, broad-shouldered, and beefy, with a red face from too much port and a full head of distinguished gray hair which now only peeped out from under his top hat. He carried himself so stiffly that he always reminded Kyra of an aging toy soldier in his scarlet hunting jacket, white breeches, and tall black boots with brown leather tops. He was, in fact, a retired officer of the Royal Army. He had spent a number of years in India, where he had developed a taste for polo and hunting. He loved to tell tales of chasing jackal and black buck with English foxhounds in the "shires of India" near the Peshawar Hills. Upon his return to England, he had scandalized British society by turning his ancient family castle into a hotel. In the next few years Sir Randolph had proved his wisdom by expanding the original hotel into an international chain of vacation spas designed especially to please affluent British travelers. Then his wife of twenty years died under somewhat suspicious circumstances and he suddenly turned his business interests over to a manager and left for America. A short time later he was joined by Pandora, who was rumored to have been a chorus girl in a cheap London opera house. She was younger than some of his children—but that had been over twenty years ago and age had evened the difference as it rounded her figure and grayed her hair. Her face was still pretty, though, and Kyra had always liked her cheerful, bustling manner. She looked rather like a plump little elf in her riding habit, and she rode with surprising grace, no doubt because of her background as a dancer.

"Ahem!" Sir Randolph cleared his throat, as he always did before addressing Gerald, as if he felt he had to enunciate especially clearly when speaking to a U.S. Senator. "We've been awaiting your arrival to decide what action should be taken concerning this terrible tragedy. The race meet must be canceled, of course, but since you are Thurston's fellow senator, we thought it would be best if you were to decide for him what everyone should be told."

"And we supposed, dear," chimed in Lady Pandora, addressing Kyra, "that it would be best if you were to talk to Nadine, since you're old friends."

"Ahem! Yes," agreed Sir Randolph. "We thought that would be best, considering the rumors. . . ."

"We understand that the senator has called in detectives," contributed the third member of the group, Tobias LaFarge. Tobias was a hail-fellow-well-met promoter, who had made a great deal of money selling useless western desert to immigrants who thought they were buying farmland. Kyra had never liked Tobias, with his slicked-back red hair and glib tongue, and couldn't understand why Nathaniel had made him Field Master. Nevertheless, he seemed to do an adequate job of getting the other members of the hunt over fences and streams with the least number of spills. And he was quite popular with the Field, most of whom did not know about his shady dealings. They just appreciated him for his ready wit and camaraderie.

At the moment, however, Tobias was not smiling or joking. His brow was furrowed with an expression clearly intended to convey his concern as he said, "Nathaniel and Nadine *were* having some problems recently, as I'm sure you're aware. I'm not saying that every couple doesn't have problems once in a while, but considering the circumstances, I think we should find out what really happened before things get out of hand, if you know what I mean."

"Are you saying that you think Nadine killed Nathaniel?" Kyra asked bluntly, noting the immediate looks of consternation that greeted her remark. None of these three were given to saying anything directly. Like Edna Harding, they dealt almost exclusively in innuendos and hints, a characteristic that usually amused Kyra but which she now found infuriating. If they were going to implicate her friend in a murder, they could at least do so openly.

"Oh, no! Not at all!" protested Tobias immediately. "We simply want to do everything possible to keep her from falling under suspicion."

"Oh, yes, the poor dear," chimed in Lady Pandora's high-pitched voice. "We feel so sorry for her, don't we, Randolph?" Sir Randolph answered this with an equivocal "Uhmmm," which could have been either assent or denial. He wasn't about to stick his neck out for Nadine yet.

"Well, it seems she's already come under suspicion," answered Kyra tersely. "So our job will be to clear her of suspicion by finding out who really did it."

"Of course, dear," Pandora readily agreed. "That's absolutely right and you'll have our full cooperation. We just don't want there to be any more scandal than absolutely necessary. We're Nadine's friends and we'll do everything we can to help her, within reasonable limits, of course. Isn't that right, dear?" For answer, Sir Randolph moved uncomfortably from one foot to the other and flushed redder than ever.

"I don't think there's much more we can do out here," put in Gerald, who had been listening to this exchange in silence. "My wife and I will go in and find out what we can, and if we need your help, we'll let you know."

"A jolly good idea!" expostulated Sir Randolph with a look of relief. "I see the servants are bringing out some food and drink, so I think we'll retire to the refreshment tent for a glass of sherry. I daresay we could all use it."

"I daresay," agreed Tobias, unconsciously mimicking Randolph's British phraseology.

Gerald and Kyra proceeded on up the steps to the front door, where they paused again briefly as she handed her gloves and crop to the liveried doorman and lifted her veil so that she could see the darkened interior. The heavy draperies had been left drawn because of the death, although the windows themselves had been partially opened to allow some air circulation. The weather was unseasonably warm for April, and the house was already muggy.

"Th' sen'tor's in th' liberry," the doorman volunteered. "Y'all knows th' way, don't ya, suh?"

"Yes, we do, thank you very much," Gerald answered as he took Kyra's arm and guided her down a hallway to the left. As they walked he said, "Would any of those three out there have had a motive for killing Nathaniel?"

Kyra knew immediately which three he was referring to and answered, "Not that I know of yet, but if they did, I wouldn't trust them further than I could throw them."

Gerald continued reflectively, "You know, when Nathaniel first started this hunt almost eleven years ago, it was a small, local thing. Almost all of the members were landowners who had been here for generations, some of whom even remembered when Thurston's father had hunted hounds here before the Civil War. I used to come out sometimes, because I was a friend of Thurston's—that was my first year in the Senate and he had become my mentor. Those early years were great fun, but lately the membership has changed a great deal."

"How is that?" Kyra wanted to know.

"Well, there's too many new people from the city. They've made their fortunes fast and dirty, bought up a bit of land, and now want to pass themselves off as gentlemen farmers, but when it comes right down to it, they have neither breeding nor scruples—my feeling is that any one of them would just as soon cut your throat as not, if they thought it would be to their economic or social advantage.''

"I agree that they *are* a bit uncouth at times," answered Kyra, ''but I really don't think they'd go that far.''

"I think they would, if they thought they could get away with it," Gerald maintained. "Tobias in particular. I hadn't mentioned it before, but he's been giving Nathaniel a big sales pitch for the past year or more about some scheme he has to divide Hopsworth up into five- or ten-acre parcels and sell them as 'estates.' ''

"Nathaniel would never do anything like that," said Kyra with disbelief.

"Not unless he were forced to," Gerald said. "I've suspected for some time now that Thurston lost a great deal of money in an investment bubble last year—he may have to sell Hopsworth."

Kyra did not have a chance to react to this piece of information, as they had arrived at the solid oak door to the library, which they opened softly.

They were immediately engulfed by the sound of Senator Howard's groans. The white-haired and usually dignified man paced the floor with a wild look on his face, while Dr. Whitley sat on a chair helplessly looking on. The latter rose when he saw the McMasterses and crossed the room toward them. He motioned for them to go outside again with him before his anguished patient saw them.

"I've done everything I can for Senator Howard," he said wearily. "As you're probably aware, he won't allow himself to be sedated, so I've done all I can. And I'm glad to see you here. The presence of good friends at a time like this can make all the difference in the world. I need to go tend to some other patients now, but I'll be back in a couple of hours to check on Thurston and the young widow. She's asleep and probably won't wake up before then, but in case she does, I've left some medication with her maid. Can you two take charge until I return?''

"Certainly," answered McMasters after glancing briefly in Kyra's direction and noting her almost imperceptible nod. They had come to know each other so well that often words were unnecessary to communicate their desires. Senator Howard had been almost like a father to Gerald and they would do anything they could to help him.

As soon as the doctor left, Kyra and Gerald went back into the library. This time Thurston noticed them immediately. His face crumpled as he met Gerald's eyes and a wave of agony swept over his body, prompting the younger man to step quickly across the room and grasp Howard by the arms to keep him from falling. The bereaved father responded by laying his head on Gerald's shoulder and sobbing with renewed force, although with perceptible efforts to stop so that he could talk. After several minutes he succeeded.

"M-m-m-y f-f-riends," he finally managed, his voice coming in barely controlled jerks. "Y-y-you heard what happened?" he added, gaining more control with every word.

"Yes," answered Gerald, "but perhaps you're better off not talking about it right now."

"What the hell else am I going to talk about!" exploded the older senator with a surprising amount of his usual vigor. "Some bastard kills my only son and you say don't talk about it! I'll tell you how I'm not talking about it! I'm not talking about it by getting the best man Pinkerton has out here on an express train—I'm not leaving this matter to the Virginia Sheriff's Department. Oh, no! I'm not leaving one stone unturned until I've found who's responsible and seen justice done!"

Kyra knew exactly what Thurston was feeling—she had felt that way when her own father had died and later when her Cousin George was killed. She felt her breath rush in with the force of her sympathy for Thurston, who heard her gasp and turned to look at her.

The senator gazed at her for a moment, reading the thoughts that clearly showed on her face, then he started talking as if he were in a dream—or, in this case, a nightmare. "Ah, yes!" he said. "Gerald's lady detective. You've been raising babies for so long now that I almost forgot you ever did anything but preside over a teapot. I would be honored if you would lend me your assistance in this time of trouble. I always was of the opinion that ladies made much better detectives than men, anyway. And you confirmed my opinion of that with the telephone company case—a pretty little piece of work that was, too. And you did a right smart job of clearing my name afterward. I would have been in a real pickle, through my own stupidity, if it hadn't been for you." With that, Howard gazed away from Kyra and wandered toward the other end of the room, as if he had already forgotten what he was talking about. He clearly did not expect an answer from Kyra.

Kyra and Gerald exchanged glances. Already their presence seemed to be having a beneficial effect on Howard. At least he had stopped ranting and raving. But Kyra was also anxious to see Nadine. She signaled to Gerald that she would be back soon and tiptoed out of the room as Howard sat down in an armchair, recollecting to McMasters about how close he had come to ending his political career as a result of being falsely linked with the conspirators of the telephone take-over.

As she closed the door Kyra heard Howard say, "Your little wife did such a good job of clearing my name that my constituents sent me back to the Senate with a landslide vote! An absolute landslide, that's what it was!" She knew he would be busy with his recollections for at least half an hour.

Kyra headed up the beautiful old curving staircase to the suite of rooms on the second floor that Nadine and Nathaniel had shared. She found Nadine's personal maid, Sobie, seated in a chair by her sleeping mistress's bed. Sobie raised a finger to her lips and whispered, "Dr. Whitley said to let her sleep, but she wants to talk to you as soon as she wakes up. She's real concerned about something—was almost hysterical, in fact. I've never seen her that way before, but everyone takes death differently."

"How soon do you think she'll wake up?" Kyra whispered back.

"The doctor gave her an injection that he said would make her sleep most of the day. And he left some other stuff in case she was still hysterical when she woke up. But she wants to talk to you as soon as possible. She wanted to telephone you during the night, but our lines were out again."

"Does that happen often?" asked Kyra.

"About every other week or so, I guess," Sobie answered. "It's always on a night when the hounds are howling to beat the band, too. Then, in the morning, everything's okay. The phone company just can't figure it out. They say it must have to do with the weather."

"Yes, when anyone can't figure something out, they generally blame it on the weather," Kyra said dryly. Sobie grinned in appreciation. Then, remembering where she was, she glanced guiltily at Nadine's sleeping form.

"Had you noticed any particular problems between Nadine and Nathaniel recently?" Kyra inquired, watching Sobie closely.

"No ma'am!" Sobie said too quickly and emphatically. "They never had *any* troubles. They were the happiest couple I've ever known. Why?" she added suspiciously.

"I heard that they might have had a bit of a disagreement last Sunday."

"Who told you that? Was it that pesky Edna Harding? Don't ever believe anything she says," Sobie retorted with gunfire rapidity, not even stopping for Kyra's replies.

"Sobie, Sobie," Kyra soothed. "I'm Nadine's friend. You don't have to protect her from me. It would be best if you told me what the problem was, so that I can deal with it from the first."

The tension in Sobie's face relaxed a bit and she said, "I don't exactly know what the problem was. They had a fight Saturday night about something and Nadine was still all riled up Sunday morning when they went out hunting. She apparently made some remark, though, and that Harding woman is spreading it all over that she killed her own husband.''

"Yes," mused Kyra. "She implied as much to me. But you and I both know that Nadine wouldn't do that, so it really doesn't matter what the others think for a while."

"But what about the detectives and the sheriffs? What's going to happen when they hear that?" objected Sobie.

"We won't let anything bad happen to Nadine," Kyra reassured the woman, patting her on the shoulder. "But I need to talk to her the minute she wakes up. I have to go take care of some things now, so you send one of the houseboys in search of me when she starts to stir."

"Yes, ma'am!" said Sobie, visibly more cheerful.

Kyra walked into the large and airy barn Thurston Howard's father had built nearly one hundred years earlier to house the hunting and racing horses he bred. He had designed the structure himself and it was still used as a model for horse barns wherever people wanted maximum efficiency combined with a graceful elegance of style. Kyra breathed in the fragrance of timothy hay and leather as her eyes adjusted to the semigloom inside the barn. The air was also several degrees cooler and the sounds from outside dulled to a low murmur. Slowly she made out the forms of horses in their stalls and identified Truly Fine in an extra large box stall at one end. She reached in and stroked the stallion's velvety nose through the bars that composed the top half of the double stall door.

"What have they got you behind bars for?" Kyra said to him gently. "You're one of the victims, not the criminal." The horse nickered softly and nudged her hand, looking for a sugar lump, which Kyra promptly produced from a pocket in her riding habit. "You're a smart one, aren't you?" she murmured, chuckling as she opened the lower half of the door and ducked into the stall.

Truly Fine was a much larger horse than Kyra had realized. In the past, she had always seen him from the saddle of her own mount, but now she stood beside him on foot and he towered over her, at least seventeen hands high at the withers. His shoulders and legs were massive and she was thankful for his gentle temperament as she knelt to look at the wire cuts on his shanks.

"You had a bit of a surprise, eh, fellow?" Kyra said as she finally stood up and ran her hand along his neck and shoulders. The pattern of scrapes and bruises indicated that he had taken the brunt of the fall on his right shoulder. Kyra tried to form a mental picture of what had happened but knew that she would have to visit the spot itself in order to do so fully. She gave the horse a final pat and said, "If you could talk, I wonder if you would have anything to tell me?"

"Ah don' knows 'bout that ole hoss, but Ah 'spect t' have som'thin' t' tell you real soon," said a familiar voice just behind Kyra.

"Benny!" exclaimed Kyra, whirling around to face the red-haired, freckle-faced young man who still looked like a street urchin in spite of his height and age. "How did you know? I was just about to send someone for you."

"Waal, this mo'nin', befo' you ev'n got up, Ah already done herd theah wuz som'thin' terr'ble wrong at Hopsworth. So when Ah saw Mrs. Hahdin' cum up in her big carriage, Ah slipt in 'hind it real quiet an' Ah lissened t' what she said."

"You really miss detective work, don't you?" Kyra responded. Benny Mulchanney had been a street boy until Kyra had recruited him to work for Keaton Investigations in the late 1890s. When she had closed her little agency and moved to Virginia, Benny had chosen to come with her and learn how to train horses from Gerald. He had worked hard and had become a very good hand with a horse, but Kyra always suspected that he missed sleuthing more than he admitted. He now confirmed her suspicions by his half-embarrassed, half-anxious grin.

"Y'all will let me help, won'tcha?" he pleaded. "Ah kin larn lots o' thangs from th' other stable boys—an' th' ladies' maids." The latter he added with a devilish sparkle in his eye.

"That's a wonderful idea, Benny," Kyra answered. "You can be the undercover agent on this case." Benny looked at her hard for a moment, unsure whether she was pulling his leg, but finally decided to accept her statement on his own terms.

"Sho' 'nuff!" he exclaimed. "Whether it's unduh covuh o' on top o' th' haystack, Ah'll gits th' info'mation y'all needs!"

"Okay," agreed Kyra. "But don't get yourself into any trouble—and bring me a report each evening. I'll be sending for some clothing so that Gerald and I can stay here for a few days. I'll let you know which room we'll be in."

At that moment a boy in his early teens, wearing hunting attire, strolled into the barn, leading a large pony by the bridle reins. He looked around with a haughty air until he saw Benny. "Boy!" he called out, accompanying his command with a snap of his fingers. "Come here!"

Benny rolled his eyes expressively and walked slowly toward the young gentleman, whom Kyra recognized as Hadley Turbot, Edna Harding's nephew. Kyra remained standing in the shadows next to Truly Fine's stall, interested to see what would happen next.

"Take my pony and put him in one of these stalls," Hadley commanded imperiously. "It seems as if the races have been delayed and I don't want to stand around holding him all day."

"Don'tch'all have y'own groom?" Benny asked, making no move to take the horse.

"Yes, but he's busy right now" was the curt reply. "So just do as you're told and take the horse."

"Waal, Ah don' knows if thass 'xactly right, seein' as

how mah own boss might need mah services,'' temporized Benny with exasperating slowness, rubbing his chin and looking Hadley up and down. " 'Sides, Ah don' knows if Ah takes orders from someone yo' size.''

"Oh, *please* help me!'' Hadley exclaimed, his haughty façade breaking down completely as he looked over his shoulder toward the crowd by the refreshment tables. "My pet skunk has escaped! Someone let him out of his carrying case, and my groom and Lord Roseberry's Indian fellow are helping look for him. If he makes trouble, my aunt will tan my hide! So I've *gotta* go look, too!'' The boy was jumping from one foot to the other in his impatience and made an attempt to thrust his pony's reins into Benny's hands, which Benny deftly avoided by putting his hands behind his back.

Kyra remembered several occasions on which Hadley had disrupted tea parties and other functions with his skunk and suspected that he had planned something of the sort for the hunt ball. He was one of the few young people she genuinely disliked, and she knew Benny felt the same way.

"Ah'll think 'bout puttin' yo' hoss away, but Ah don' want ta have nuthin' t' do with no skunk!'' Benny exclaimed, holding his nose.

"He has had his smell sacs removed,'' explained Hadley, his usual haughty voice returning. Then he added with a genuine note of desperation, "But my aunt says she'll have my skin if that skunk turns up in the wrong place—and you don't know what my aunt's like when she's angry!''

"Whut does that have t' do with me?'' asked Benny, nonchalantly leaning against a stall door with his fists jammed into his pockets.

Hadley appeared to think this over for a moment, then slipped one of his own well-manicured hands into his breeches pocket and pulled forth a large silver coin. "I'll give you this silver dollar if you'll help me! It's real silver. My father gave it to me for spending money while

I'm visiting my aunt, but I snitch money out of her purse, so I haven't needed it."

"Lemme see it," said Benny, stretching forth one hand. Hadley placed it in his palm with some reluctance, apparently only because he saw no other recourse. Benny examined the coin minutely, turned it over several times, then bit its edge while Hadley watched anxiously. Finally Benny said, "Okay, Ah'll show you wheah yo' skunk is!"

"You know where he is?!" exclaimed Hadley, forgetting in his excitement to retrieve the coin, which Benny pocketed while striding toward the door, followed by the skunk's anxious owner, still leading his pony.

"As Ah rode ovah heah, Ah saw a skunk cum scurryin' away from this place, cross th' path Ah wuz on, an' hide hisself in an ole stump," said Benny in his heaviest Southern accent. "Couldn't be none othah than yo' skunk, as wild'uns don' travel durin' th' daytime."

Kyra watched them go, wondering what exactly Benny was up to. He had clashed with Hadley before, and Benny was not above . . . No, Kyra thought, he wouldn't dare. She dismissed the matter from her mind. There were far more important things to think about.

CHAPTER 2

The Master Speaks

KYRA spent the next half hour interviewing Hopsworth's grooms and stable boys. Most of them were gathered in the tack room, speaking to each other in hushed tones about what had happened. A couple of them showed signs of heavy hangovers, and one was missing. When questioned, they confessed to having gotten hold of several bottles of brandy yesterday when unloading the liquor supplies for the weekend. Michael, who was the kennelman in charge of feeding and caring for Nathaniel's hounds, had apparently gone into town to continue with his bout once the brandy was finished. Although he had apparently left long before Nathaniel's accident, Kyra sent a couple of the men to look for him so that she could question him in person. He might just provide the clue necessary to solving the whole mystery.

Kyra emerged from the barn in time to see Gerald striding across the lawn toward her. In spite of her agitation, she couldn't help but admire how handsome he looked in his riding attire. His slim hips and long legs were naturally suited to snug breeches and tall boots. He had opened his scarlet—the correct term was pink— jacket and the slight breeze flattened his silk shirt against the muscles of his chest as he walked. His glossy black hair shone in the bright sun. He was one of the best-looking men Kyra had ever met and she always felt a surge of desire when she saw him unexpectedly like this.

"I thought I'd find you out here," he said when he saw her. "I talked Thurston into lying down to rest on the couch for a while and he dozed right off, even without a sedative."

"He's not a young man anymore," Kyra responded. "And he *was* up all night."

"Yes, and he didn't refuse a couple of shots of brandy, either," said Gerald with a smile. "But there's no telling how long he'll sleep and something has to be done about all these people. As Joint Master of the Daisy Hill Hunt, it's probably my duty to make an announcement, explaining what happened and canceling the races."

"Yes, I should think that would be best," agreed Kyra. "From the looks of it, everyone has arrived." As she spoke, Kyra glanced from the crowd on the lawn to the spur line of the local railroad, which ran up next to the barn. The tracks were now the scene of a great deal of activity as grooms unloaded skittish horses from specially designed boxcars and their owners stepped down from luxurious private Pullmans.

"Poor Nathaniel," said Gerald, following Kyra's glance. "He was so excited when he heard that members of the Newcastle Hunt Club would be coming all the way from New York State to ride in the Daisy Hill Race Days. He was like a child, looking forward to seeing their famous railway cars. He even believed the stories about gold spigots and sinks in the cars for both men and horses."

"The stories are true," Kyra commented. "I've seen them—the ones in the box stalls are mostly brass, but the sinks and spigots in the Pullmans are fourteen-carat gold."

"Whew!" whistled Gerald, but before he could say any more, the McMasters both caught sight of Melvin P. Dickey stepping down from one of the Pullmans, adjusting his tie and smoothing back his hair, with characteristic fastidiousness. Kyra and Gerald grimaced at each other, their distaste for Melvin winning over polite indifference. Nathaniel had been one of the few people who genuinely liked Melvin—but then Nathaniel liked everyone. He had staunchly defended the man to the rest of the family when his only sister, the apple of his eye, wanted to marry Melvin, who had begun his working career at the age of twelve, selling medical supplies and patent medicines to the poor of New York City. Even though he now ran a multimillion-dollar business that owned patents for several of the most popular nostrums of the day, he had retained certain mannerisms and attitudes typical of sidewalk hucksters. He also tended to drink too much.

For these reasons Thurston did not trust him and had reluctantly given his approval to Juliette's marriage only after he had arranged that her inheritance be held in trust in such a way that Melvin could not touch it.

Even at that, every time Thurston set eyes upon his birdlike little son-in-law he would shake his head and mutter, "Whatever in Cree-a-shun could a woman—any woman—see in a man like that?" In addition, Thurston had often been heard to exclaim, "I know my little Julie was never a great intellect, nor even the most beautiful belle at the ball, but you'd think she could do better than *that*!" Thurston had persisted in thinking of his daughter as "little," when in fact she was a large-boned, rather awkward woman who outweighed her husband by quite a bit. They made a rather odd-looking couple, and they were oddly matched in other ways as well. Juliette had always been a tomboy, riding to hounds with her big brother instead of dressing up with the girls. But Melvin was completely nonathletic and had a morbid fear of horses. He had tried to persuade her to give up riding after they were married, but, while surprisingly docile toward her husband in most matters, in this she had been adamant. She would not give up her horses. For a while their marriage had teetered with the force of the conflict, then Melvin had shocked everyone by announcing that *he* would take up riding. And he had. With grim

23

perseverance he had taken lessons and mastered his fears, even learning to jump, so that he could accompany his wife on foxhunts.

"I just don't think it's appropriate for a married woman to careen about the country in such a pursuit without her husband," Melvin often said in a voice that conveyed more than a hint of martyrdom. In time, however, he actually began to enjoy riding and also became active in the politics of the Newcastle Hunt, a foxhunting club just outside of New York City that Juliette, and then he, had joined. The members were mostly businessmen like himself—some of the newest, but richest, industrialists and executives in New York. They all found an element of escape in the tangible thrills of the weekend chases after the less palpable thrills of monitoring the stock exchange or other business interests Monday through Friday. Here Melvin was in his element and soon became one of the Newcastle Hunt's officers. In fact, although Juliette still rode with the Newcastle Hunt, she had been quite eclipsed by her husband's popularity and influence. The very mannerisms and attitudes that seemed crude to Juliette's father made him all the more popular among men who were considered robber barons by much of polite society.

Kyra had always liked Thurston's daughter and was concerned that Juliette had seemed increasingly unhappy over the past few years, though she never uttered a word of complaint to anyone. But each time the couple came to visit she was just a little more pale and a bit more subdued. Kyra knew that Nathaniel had been concerned about his sister, too. It had been one of his motivations for entering into a business partnership with Melvin to manage some property he had inherited in New York. The partnership gave him an excuse to travel to New York occasionally and he always stopped by to have a cup of tea with Juliette or arranged things so that he needed to spend the night at the Dickey mansion on East Fifty-fourth Street.

Spotting the McMasterses, Melvin walked toward them

with a self-satisfied smirk. He tipped his hat to Kyra with exaggerated politeness and extended his hand to Gerald. "Good morning!" he exclaimed in his high-pitched voice. "Isn't it a lovely day? And the cream of society are here to enjoy it! A day like this always makes me wonder what the poor people are doing. Not that I really give a damn, of course!" He chuckled at his own humor. Both Gerald and Kyra looked at him in silence, too taken aback at his crudity to say anything.

Apparently Melvin didn't know about Nathaniel's death, which meant that Juliette was equally ignorant. They had been on the train all night, traveling down from New York with the Newcastle hunters. Most probably, it had been too difficult to get a message through to them—or no one had thought of it in the midst of the crisis. But where was Juliette?

As if in answer, Juliette's tall figure filled the doorway of the railroad car for a moment. Almost falling forward in a leap beyond the steps, she landed heavily and ran at her husband, her face twisted with a mixture of emotions including grief, anger, and something else Kyra could not quite identify.

Melvin must have heard Juliette's running footsteps. He had turned halfway around before her body impacted against his, sending both down to the soft turf. His face showed surprise, consternation, and complete bewilderment as his usually docile and well-mannered wife beat on his chest with her fists and heaved great sobs, mixed with incoherent words. The sight would have been funny if the circumstances were not so tragic.

Kyra noticed Pandora Roseberry stifle an impulse to laugh, exclaiming instead, "The poor dear, I feel so sorry for her!" Tobias LaFarge stood at her side, opening and closing his mouth, as if he were about to say something. His perpetually red face and carrot-colored hair completed the impression of a giant red carp.

As usual, Gerald was the first person to take action. He straddled the prone couple and grasped Juliette firmly from behind, holding her arms to her sides as he lifted her away from Melvin. When she saw who was holding her, she collapsed in tears against his shoulder and allowed him to lead her to the house. Kyra went with them, leaving Melvin for someone else to pick up.

"Nathaniel!" the distraught woman wailed. "My brother! My brother is—" She stopped short and looked at Kyra with wild hope. "He's not, is he? Tell me he's not! He couldn't be! It's all some terrible joke, isn't it?"

Kyra looked Juliette full in the eyes and slowly shook her head, watching the hope drain from Juliette's face as she did so. It was one of the hardest things she'd ever done, but she knew it would be cruel to give her the smallest doubt, even for a moment.

It took some time and one of Dr. Whitley's powders, which Kyra borrowed from Sobie, to get Juliette calmed down enough so that they could leave her in the care of her maid. Then Gerald resumed his hunting jacket and top hat and they went outside to make the announcement. As they walked down the steps, Melvin Dickey came hurrying up to them, followed closely by Edna Harding.

"I had *no* idea!" the little man exclaimed, his hands fluttering in the air around him. "I thought she'd gone mad! Is she all right? Once I'd heard the news about Nathaniel I didn't *dare* come in—didn't want to upset her further, you know?"

"She'll be fine once she gets over the initial shock," Kyra replied, trying not to let her distaste for the man creep into her voice. "But you're probably wise to leave her alone for a while. Do you have any idea why she reacted the way she did?"

"None! Absolutely none whatsoever!" Melvin stated a little too emphatically, then added, "I sometimes thought she missed her brother a little bit more than a sister should, if you know what I mean."

"I understand," Kyra responded tersely, "and I suppose you told her so?"

"What's a husband to do?" he answered defensively. "She's talked about nothing but Nathaniel's race days for weeks—you'd have thought they were her own creation."

"Perhaps, in a sense, they were," answered Kyra, remembering how Nathaniel and Juliette used to talk about putting on just such a weekend. She suddenly wondered if Nathaniel had done it, in part, to put some zest back into Juliette's life.

"She wanted to come down here a week ago," Melvin continued through Kyra's thoughts, "to help Nathaniel get things ready. I put my foot down at that. We had entertaining of our own to do and I felt that coming this weekend was enough. Perhaps *that* is what she is so upset about—perhaps she feels that if she had been here, Nathaniel would not have been killed."

"Perhaps," Kyra said, unconvinced. She was certain that Melvin knew more than he was telling. He had clearly been jealous of Juliette's relationship with her brother, and he was a petty tyrant to his hapless wife, no doubt, but that did not make him a murderer. Besides, Melvin was on the train, far from Hopsworth, when the "accident" happened.

While Kyra had been talking to Melvin, Gerald had made his way through the milling crowd to the temporary podium that had been built for the judges near the finish line of the races. He rang a little bell he found there to get everyone's attention.

"Ladies and gentlemen," he began. "No doubt most of you have heard by now of the unfortunate death of Senator Howard's son, Nathaniel. He was killed yesterday evening in a regrettable accident while practicing for the races today. Our only consolation can be that he died doing something he enjoyed supremely, a pursuit to which he had devoted a large part of his life and energies. Let us hope his efforts were not in vain and that the Daisy Hill Hunt Club will continue to grow and prosper and provide the type of enjoyment for its members that Nathaniel intended. For this weekend, however, I, as Joint Master of the Hunt, feel that it would be inappropriate to continue with any festivities—"

"Wait a minute!" roared Senator Howard as he suddenly burst through the French doors of the library, banging them back against the walls with such force that several panes of glass broke. He charged across the lawn toward Gerald, his tousled mane of white hair giving him the appearance of an enraged lion. "Wait a minute now, young man! I never said a thing about canceling the race day, did I?"

"Why, no, sir!" uttered the surprised Gerald, looking so much like a guilty schoolboy that Kyra had to suppress a smile. "Do you *want* them to go on?"

"If you'll kindly let me have the stand, I'll explain the matter to these gentle people," answered the older senator, running his hands through his hair in preparation for speaking to the crowd. It was a characteristic gesture, a habit he had developed during his years of whistle-stop campaigning. Kyra felt a lump rise to her throat as she watched the indomitable old man climb the steps to the platform. He looked so old and tired. Gerald apparently thought so, too, and extended a hand to assist Thurston, but the old man brushed it aside almost angrily and moved to the center of the platform, where he could see and be seen by all.

"My friends!" he began. "Last night my only son died, riding a course in preparation for today. Hunting meant a lot to Nathaniel. It was not just a sport, but a means of providing pleasure for others. Above all else, Nathaniel liked seeing people enjoying themselves in God's great outdoors. He saw it as almost a form of worship—of getting closer to Creation and exercising the mind and body in a natural way, a way intended by the Creator when He made man and the lower animals." Here Thurston paused to wipe his eyes and clear his throat before continuing. Kyra looked around at the spectators, noting their puzzled looks. What was the senator from Virginia getting at?

"Certainly he isn't going to allow the race day to take place?" one young lady whispered to her escort, unaware that her words could be heard by almost everyone in the general silence.

"You're absolutely right, Miss Bridgette," Thurston said unexpectedly, pointing at the embarrassed young woman. "I'm *not* going to allow the races to take place, I'm going to *insist* that they take place. It's what Nathaniel wanted. I think he had some kind of premonition of what was going to happen, as one of the last things he said to me was, 'If anything happens to me, please see that the Daisy Hill Race Day Weekend takes place as scheduled.' I agreed to that, and I always keep my agreements." Thurston paused again and the crowd murmured in surprise.

"To this purpose," Thurston continued, raising his voice slightly until the buzzing subsided, "I would like to ask Senator McMasters and his lovely wife to take my place in seeing that things run smoothly, as planned. And I would like to ask Oswald Harding to take Nathaniel's place as Huntsman. You three can appoint others to assist you, as needed. My only request is that all participants wear a black band, either on their arm or their hat, in memory of my son, who made this weekend possible." At this point, two servants came forward, carrying trays of black strips of cloth which they distributed among the listeners. Watching them, Thurston broke down in tears.

"This is ridiculous!" exclaimed a paunchy, balding man. "It's practically indecent! I, for one, intend to go home immediately and I suggest that anyone with any sense of decency do the same. With all due respect to the senator, I think the strain has been too much. . . ."

"And what is your name, sir!" demanded Thurston, tears still streaming down his face.

"Paul William Fennimore the third" was the proud, though somewhat surprised answer.

"Will someone please make note of that name?" ordered the senator, his usual composure and sense of command returning. "I must warn all of you," he continued after clearing his throat, "that anyone who leaves these grounds before the official conclusion of the Daisy Hill Hunt Club Race Meet festivities will automatically become a prime suspect for the murder of my son!''

"You mean we're *imprisoned* here for the weekend?" a woman called out.

"No," answered Howard. "You're free to go, if you wish. But I'm letting you know now that if you do leave, I'll turn your name over to the sheriff's department and to the detectives I've hired, so that they can perform a full investigation on you. The same goes for anyone who failed to show up today. We have a registration list of participants—and I have reason to believe that one of you is responsible for my son's death. I intend to discover which one."

"So that's your *real* reason for continuing with the race day weekend!" pronounced Edna Harding with an air of gloating satisfaction. "I know we're *mere* amateurs, but can we help in any way?" she added.

"If you know anything that might be relevant, tell me or one of the sheriff's detectives who are around somewhere. . . ." He paused for a moment and Kyra was afraid he would mention her name, but Edna Harding interrupted.

"What about Mrs. McMasters?" her high-pitched, nasal voice intoned. "She's quite a famous lady detective, the former Kyra Keaton—won't *she* be taking part in such an *important* investigation? After all, the murder of a United States *Senator's* son . . ."

"Yes," Howard replied brusquely, clearly irritated by the woman, "Mrs. McMasters has volunteered to take part in the investigation. Are there any other questions?"

"What happens if the murderer is not discovered by the end of the weekend?" asked a young man wearing the very latest cut in hunting jackets. "Do you intend to keep all of us here beyond that?"

"No, of course not," the senator answered impatiently. "I fully expect to have at least a list of prime suspects by then, if not the actual murderer under lock and key. Any further investigation can be continued more easily then *without* a mob of people around.

"If there are no more questions," Howard continued, "I propose that the horn blowers be called out to officially open the Daisy Hill Hunt Club Race Meet." With that, he stepped from the podium with great dignity and walked toward the front door of his mansion, with the crowd of hunt coats parting on either side of him like the Red Sea.

As soon as the front door closed behind Senator Howard, the crowd surged together again and everyone talked at once for a few moments. Then the talking stopped as suddenly as it had begun, as if everyone realized at the same moment that they were *all* under suspicion, that anything they said to anyone could be taken the wrong way and . . . what might happen then? Slowly people began to move away from each other to stand alone or in small groups consisting of family members or close friends. Kyra could feel the tension in the air. Perhaps some of it would clear once the races began.

"Oh, *Mrs.* McMasters!" gushed Edna Harding. "Did I say the wrong thing? I'm *so* sorry if I did. I just didn't stop to think that you might want to work *incognito*, as the term goes. I *do* hope I didn't ruin anything for you! It's so terrible, what happened to poor Nathaniel, and I'm sure we *all* want to find out who's responsible. . . ."

Kyra was provided a merciful respite once the horn blowers, who had taken their place on the podium, began a "Call to the Races." Even Edna could not talk over their strident blasts, and Kyra took advantage of the moment to gather her skirts and slip back to the house. She wanted to check on Nadine and Juliette, not to mention Thurston, before she was needed outside again.

Kyra stood alone in the vestibule for a moment while her eyes adjusted to the semidarkened interior of the house. Thankful that the doorman had been called away to distribute black bands, she relaxed her body for a few seconds, leaning against a thick wooden pillar which was cool to her touch. It wasn't even noon yet, and she felt as if she'd been up all night—most likely because she had, she remembered. She'd almost forgotten that she had three children at home, two of them still recovering from the grippe. She'd been up and down all night for most of the last week. And now she had a case to solve. Probably the most difficult case she'd ever faced, if only because of the people involved. The "very best" people, as Edna Harding would say. Many of the people out there were government officials of one type or another, or powerful industrialists. Not the type to welcome an investigation for any reason, much less for suspicion of murder. She had watched the faces of several such men as Senator Howard made his announcements, and she knew that it was going to be a difficult weekend.

She was startled out of her reverie when she heard the clomp of riding boots on the stone steps outside. Instinctively, she slipped into the nearby coat closet, leaving the door slightly ajar, just in time to see one of the very men she had been thinking about, Jerome P. Cushing, a wealthy shipping magnate, walk into the hallway. He also paused for a moment for his eyes to readjust. After looking quickly around to make sure he was alone, he headed straight for a small alcove across from Kyra's hiding place, in which hung an early-model telephone which frugal Senator Howard had never replaced with a more modern version. Cushing cranked vigorously, almost viciously at the little handle on the side of the instrument's sloping wooden box.

"Hello! Hello, operator!" he shouted several times into the mouthpiece. "Hello! *There* you are!" He tried to shield his mouth with his hands to keep the sound from carrying beyond the hallway. He seemed terribly anxious and craned his neck to peer out of the alcove to see if anyone was coming. "Can you place a long line call for me?" Pause. "To New York." He gave the number and billing information, which Kyra jotted down on a little pad she always carried with her. More than once she had been grateful for that habit, formed during her detective days.

Cushing then replaced the receiver and, after looking around once more, seated himself on the edge of an armchair, the only other furnishing of the alcove. He took an envelope from his hunt coat pocket and wrote copiously on the back of it as he waited for the operator to get back to him with his call. He glanced nervously up and down the hallway every few minutes. The source of his nervousness was revealed when Kyra heard the sound of voices at the front door. Cushing leaped up, ready to abandon his call and flee, but the voices receded and he slowly sank back onto the chair.

Did he have an accomplice outside? Kyra wondered. Was someone watching the front door, ready to divert any intruders until Cushing got his call through? Kyra did not have time to wonder for long, as the telephone rang and Cushing snatched the earpiece up from the top of the box and gave a muffled bellow into the mouthpiece. "Hello! Yes, this is he! Yes, put it through." There was another pause, during which Cushing tapped his foot, then: "Hello! Thank God I caught you! Something terrible's happened here! The Howard boy's dead." Pause. "Nathaniel, the senator's son." Pause. "Yes. That's right." Pause. "Yeah, he was murdered. At least the old man thinks so, and he's probably right. But the point is that there's no chance of any future deals going through now, so you've gotta pull out. Understand? Or else find another way—" At this point the front door opened and a group of several women, accompanied by the gallant young man in the fashionable hunt jacket, entered. Cushing hung up without another word and strolled toward the group, which had been drawn to a window by a scream from outside.

"Ugh! Uuugh! Get it away from me! Eeeeeeeeew!" a woman's voice screamed, followed by a hubbub of other voices and screams. The party in the vestibule turned to look outside, and Kyra made use of the moment to slip out of the coat closet and away down the hallway. She didn't have to look to know what was happening on the front lawn. The pungent odor of skunk that wafted inside as the door opened again only confirmed what she already knew: Benny Mulchanney had wreaked his revenge on Edna Harding's snotty nephew. She felt a smile play at the corner of her mouth in spite of all the other things on her mind. Then she returned to the practical. At least the commotion would delay the beginning of the races long enough for her to check up on Nadine and Juliette, not to mention the senator.

The two women were asleep, but Kyra found Senator Howard at his desk in the library going through some papers. As she entered the room, a desk model telephone next to him rang hoarsely and he picked it up.

"Howard here," he barked, then paused for a moment before continuing in a tone that conveyed both reverence and respect, "Yes, Mr. President. Thank you. Yes, we think it was murder and we're doing everything possible to find the bastards!" He paused again, listening, and his eyes misted over. Then he said softly, with a catch in his voice, "Thank you, Teddy," and gently replaced the receiver. He sat for a moment, staring into space, then blew his nose loudly into his pocket handkerchief and looked toward Kyra, who still stood in the doorway.

"Please come in!" he exclaimed, rising to his feet as soon as he realized that his visitor was a lady. "Come in and have a seat," he added, pulling a chair forward for her. "You're just the person I wanted to see right now—but where is your charming husband?" As if in answer to Thurston's question, Gerald appeared in the doorway. "Ahh! There he is!" Thurston added, motioning Gerald to a chair next to Kyra and resuming his own seat.

He pulled a bell cord next to his elbow and a moment later his personal secretary entered the room through another door. "Alexander, would you please have my roadster brought around to the back door in ten minutes," Thurston said, and the young man left without having spoken a word. "I want to show you the jump," he added for the McMasterses' benefit. "But first I want you to see Nathaniel."

With that, he led the way down a private staircase to where the body lay in the cool basement billiards room. Ordinarily, the body would have lain in state in the best parlor, but because of the unseasonably warm weather, Thurston had decreed that it should be put in the billiards room, which had been built in the cellar when the rest of the mansion had been renovated. The room had been a special present from Thurston to Nathaniel, who had a passion for billiards. He would often play until well past midnight with anyone who would join him, but most often with Oswald or the kennelman, Michael.

At the thought of Michael, Kyra wondered if he had been found. She had sent some men after him earlier, when she'd talked to the grooms about what had happened yesterday afternoon, and had been told that he had probably gone off on one of his periodic drunks. Kyra decided that if Michael had not shown up yet, she'd send Benny in search of him as well, although she didn't have much hope that the groom would be in any condition to help.

"Not a pretty sight, is he?" Thurston commented with a look that wrenched Kyra's heart. "His neck was broken and he died instantly, thank God. But the horse must have kicked his face as it tried to get up." Thurston covered his own face with his hands at the thought and groaned. But he quickly regained his composure and continued, "I want to show you exactly how we found him, and how the fence was wired."

"Are you sure you want to put yourself through that? We were planning to ride over there a bit later, anyway," Gerald said gently. "And I think we can reconstruct the scene from the sheriff's report and from talking to the others who were with you."

"No," Thurston insisted. "I *want* to show you myself." The three of them went to the back entrance, where Thurston's shiny black Panhard and chauffeur were waiting.

Within a few minutes, they were well away from Hopsworth and moving with surprising smoothness along the back roads. Thurston pulled a piece of paper from his pocket and said, "This is a map we found in Nathaniel's coat pocket—clearly his projected course for the race and the course we presume he was following when he fell." Gerald and Kyra looked at the pencil-marked piece of paper and nodded. It was one of Nathaniel's typical maps—the kind he drew up for paper chases or the occasional drag hunt during the off season. Thurston had circled one spot with a red pencil, which they assumed was the scene of Nathaniel's fatal fall. The fence was not far off the road they were on, and in a few minutes Thurston ordered the driver to stop.

"Wait here for us," he said as they disembarked.

"And please make a note of anyone who goes by," Kyra requested politely. Thurston gave her a quick look, then smiled grimly.

"Do you think we might have been followed?" he asked when they were out of earshot.

"It's possible," Kyra responded. "It's something we all need to keep in mind over the next two days."

"Yes, of course," agreed Thurston. "The culprit or culprits would be particularly anxious to know what you're doing. You have quite a reputation. Quite a reputation . . ." he repeated, then lapsed into a thoughtful silence as they walked across a cow pasture toward Farmer Ingleson's fence.

They could see plainly where Nathaniel had attempted to jump the fence—bits of skin and hair from Truly Fine's legs were still stuck to the wire and the soft soil on the other side was trampled and gouged. Kyra was thankful for her training in detection methods, which would enable her to decipher the tangle of marks before her. Some were from Nathaniel's fall. The rest would be evidence of his would-be rescuers, the Virginia sheriffs, and the Howard servants who came to take the body back to Hopsworth.

The marks of the servants' shoes were easy to make out. Not only were they topmost, they were all identical, except for size. Kyra knew that the Howard family had traditionally kept the village shoemaker busy supplying shoes for the servants as well as the family. The pattern for the servants' shoes had been the same for over a hundred years, the men's slightly heavier than the women's, but both were high-quality, sturdy shoes that offered good support. Thurston's grandfather had the servants' shoes specially designed by a European surgeon, on the premise that comfortable feet made for happy people. Whether he was right or not, the specially designed shoes made Kyra's job considerably easier that day.

There was one other set of prints on top of the servants' prints that puzzled Kyra. They were thin-soled city shoes, somewhat run-down at the heels. Kyra carefully measured them and jotted the measurements on her pad, noting that they went around the complete perimeter of the scene and tiptoed up to the spot where the body had been. The latter puzzled her. She could understand someone tiptoeing up to the body itself—that was an almost instinctive reaction—but up to an empty spot?

Next came the Virginia sheriffs' bootprints, which were also easy to decipher, as they were standard-issue police boots with very characteristic stitching on the bottom. Two sheriffs had been sent to the scene, one a considerably larger man than the other. They had tramped over the area almost as if they were purposefully trying to obliterate evidence. Were they? Or was it just the usual incompetence found in so many public law officers?

Another thing that puzzled her was that there were too many pairs of riding-boot prints on the first layer surrounding the body. Thurston had said that there were four people in the rescue crew—himself, Nadine, and two grooms. But there was a third set of male bootprints in the area surrounding the body. She almost asked

Thurston if he could possibly be mistaken about the number of people who had been with him, then decided against it. She could ask him later, if she needed to.

The marks that Truly Fine had made in falling had been almost completely scuffed out by the footprints, except for several deep scores in the earth made by his iron-shod hooves. But that was enough for Kyra to reconstruct how he had probably fallen and how his hooves might have thrashed out to hit Nathaniel's face as he lay on the ground nearby.

Lastly, too many horses seemed to have visited the scene. In the area on the other side of the fence, where the riders had dismounted and tied their horses, there were six sets of hoofprints in addition to Truly Fine's. That was two sets too many, since both the servants and the sheriffs had come by automobile, parking near where the chauffeur had parked Thurston's Panhard.

There were several possible explanations that Kyra could think of right away. One was that Thurston was simply mistaken about the number of people in the search party. There could have been five, or even six, if one had stayed mounted on the other side of the fence, presumably to keep an eye on the horses. Or one or two riders could have visited the scene shortly before or shortly after Thurston and the rescue crew. Again, one of them might have stayed mounted while the other examined the body, which would account for there being only one extra set of riding-boot prints. But whose prints were they?

Thurston and Gerald waited patiently while Kyra completed her examination of the area. When she straightened up and put away her notepad, Thurston could no longer keep quiet. "Did you find any clues? Anything to tell us who's responsible?" he asked with pathetic urgency.

"I can't tell yet," she responded. Then, seeing his face fall, she added, "There may be something, but I need to think about it for a while."

"You'll let me know as soon as you come up with anything?"

"Of course," she reassured him. "Now I need to look at that fence a bit more closely." With Gerald's assistance, she climbed back over the fence the way they had come. Followed by the two men, she walked first up and then down for about a quarter of a mile, examining both the wiring job and the ground near each post. The wire had been put on the pasture side of the fence, where the ground was covered with springy grass that had been cropped to almost bowling-green smoothness by a flock of black-faced sheep. Footprints disappeared almost immediately on such a surface, so there was little to be learned about the culprit in that way. But several times Kyra stooped and picked up small objects, which she slipped into her pocket.

"You spoke with Farmer Ingleson and he denies having wired this fence?" Kyra asked Thurston.

"Yes, he telephoned of his own accord when he heard about the accident—but I knew it wasn't him before that, because we'd talked about wiring just a week or so ago. He was dead set against it."

"I just needed to make sure," explained Kyra. "Whoever *did* wire the fence tried to make it look like a routine wiring job."

"You mean by going all the way to the end of the fence on either side, not just covering the obvious jumping area?" Gerald asked.

"Yes, and by using exactly the type of wire and staples that every farmer in the area has in his tool shed for repairing fences, even if he doesn't use it along the top."

"Yes," agreed Gerald, fingering the wire. "I do believe I've seen some exactly like this hanging in our barn."

"You're right," said Thurston, looking at the wire more closely himself. "Robert's Farm Supply had a big sale on this very wire a year or so back, and we bought half a dozen rolls ourselves—galvanized steel wire, guaranteed to hold a thousand pounds or more, made by U.S. Steel. But what does that prove?"

"It proves that whoever did this is familiar enough with the area to know what kind of wire would be most common, but probably does not know Farmer Ingleson very well."

"Yes, I can see that," said Thurston gravely. "But what else? I can tell you're thinking something else, too."

Kyra smiled at the old politician's uncanny ability to read people's faces. "You're right," she agreed. "Take a look at where the staples were pounded in to hold the wire."

"What about it?" said Thurston with his nose practically on the post. "I don't see anything special."

"Don't most small farmers do the majority of their own carpentry and repair work?" Kyra asked rhetorically. "Does that look like it was done by someone with a lot of practice using a hammer?"

"No . . . no, it doesn't," said Thurston. "Whoever did it missed the staple about half the time, I'd say."

"And dropped a lot of staples, without bothering to pick them up," Kyra added, reaching into her pocket and pulling out a handful of the little horseshoe-shaped metal objects. "No farmer that I know would be that wasteful."

"Yes, especially in *this* area. They're the tightest bunch I've ever known—you'd think it was Scotland!" agreed Thurston.

"So you think the person who wired the fence was familiar with the area, but was not himself a farmer?" summarized Gerald.

"Yes," said Kyra. "I think it was someone like us—a landowner, or frequent guest of a landowner, but not someone used to handling tools."

"Someone like one of the Daisy Hill Hunt Club members?" Thurston asked. "Just what I thought in the first place! But *who* would want to kill Nathaniel?"

"That's what we need to find out," said Kyra as

gently as possible, noticing that Thurston was looking anguished again. "Did you know anything about his business dealings?"

"Nathaniel didn't do much in the way of business," Thurston said. "Other than a little deal he had going with Melvin, I can't think of anything else. He just didn't have the head, or the hard nose, for business. He was too nice. He'd give away the shirt off his back if someone asked for it, which is no way to be if you're trying to negotiate a deal. No, he spent most of his time training his hounds and playing with his hunt. He was also an excellent horse trainer, of course, the best in Virginia, but he never took that too seriously, either. I suppose he never needed to take anything very seriously, which was probably my fault, but I liked to see him happy. . . ." Here Thurston broke down in tears again and the McMasterses led him back to the motor car. Kyra had seen all she needed to see, anyway, and it was time she and Gerald got back to the race meet.

CHAPTER 3

A Different Race

SOFT Oriental footsteps approached the blond Foreign Devil reclining on a little cot at the far side of the room. The man was so tall that his feet dangled over the end of the mattress, but he didn't seem to mind. His eyes rolled back into his head and he sucked rapturously on the mouthpiece of a long tube ending in a burbling water pot.

A second Oriental figure squatted by this pot, rolling a small, grayish ball between his fingers. When the Foreign Devil relinquished his hold on the tube and rolled over to dream, this second figure carefully grasped the little ball between two dirty fingernails, placed it on the end of a wire, set it on fire, and plastered it into a small cup at the top of the pipe. Then he in turn sucked up the pungent smoke as he slowly eased himself onto an identical dirty cot a few feet away from the other.

The room was filled with these cots, each holding a man in some state of opium intoxication. The air was close and warm, mixing the odor of the burning pipes with sweat, grime, and dirty socks. It was not the most pleasant smell, but the dreamers didn't seem to notice. Their faces wore smiles of bliss, transcending their immediate surroundings—their drug-induced dreams provided an escape from all ugliness.

All of this was taken in by the aging Oriental man in flowing silk robes, who carefully stepped across the room to where the tall blond one lay. He smiled approvingly at the other dreamers, nodding his head above his folded hands. He felt himself a great benefactor. When he went home at night, he was fond of telling his wife and children, "Foreign Devils in Bowery work just as hard as coolies, need escape just as badly. Some go to Coney Island, some come to me. I give them much better deal!" And he would laugh, clapping his hands together in glee, so that his wife would laugh, too, demurely and hesitantly, as befitted a woman in the presence of her husband.

Huy Ching was a good man who meant well. Many of his patrons, both Chinese and Caucasian, had come to him for years, once a week or once a month, some only a few times a year, as they could afford it. He never forgot a name or a face and welcomed each man personally, making him feel at home. He sometimes sat down with them for a cup of tea and tender rice cakes while they waited their turn at the pipes. For some, Huy Ching's opium den was the closest thing to a home and a family they could hope for. They were among the thousands who had grown up on the streets of New York City or had emigrated to the United States from unspeakable poverty abroad.

An occasional dandy or thrill seeker found his way through the labyrinthine streets of New York's Chinatown to Huy Ching's, but was generally discouraged from returning again. Huy Ching did not feel such people were good for business. They made his usual patrons uneasy. Besides, he'd had one bad experience with a high-strung poet who began coming every day until he literally dried up and faded away, in spite of Huy Ching's attempts to get him to drink nourishing broths and refrain from smoking so much. When he read of the poet's death in the papers, he shook his head mournfully and was saddened for weeks. There were some who just could not follow the path of moderation.

Huy Ching was concerned about the tall, blond Foreign Devil for the same reason. Most of his clients did not have the money to be anything other than moderate in their smoking, but this man seemed to have an inexhaustible source of income. He had started by coming occasionally, for binges of a day or two, then more frequently, until recently he rarely left. In fact, he only left if Huy Ching insisted, which he was beginning to do with some regularity, for the man had become alarmingly gaunt and unhealthy-looking. Huy Ching knew what that meant, and he did not want to read another notice in the papers.

He had fed the man a nourishing supper of noodles and vegetables in broth last night and had then sent him away, saying, "You go home now, rest for a while. Takee trip, see parents, visit girl friend, stay away from smokee, smokee. You need vacation."

And here he was, back again. Huy Ching had gone out to take care of some business and the tall one had returned during his absence. The elderly Chinaman sighed heavily as he looked down at the gaunt, prone figure. It would be hours before he awakened and could be induced to leave. But what then? If Huy Ching refused him admission the next time, he would just go to one of the other opium dens. From the looks of him, he may already have been doing that for some time.

Huy Ching's thoughts were interrupted by a ruckus at the door. He made his way quickly but silently back through the rows of cots, to see what was going on.

"My old man's in there!" shouted a young boy with a battered hat pulled down over a mass of tangled blond hair, so that the rim shaded but did nothing to dim a pair of piercing blue eyes. "I demand to see him!" he continued, still shouting in an attempt to make Huy Ching's assistant understand him. But the assistant, who spoke only Chinese, nodded and smiled and refused the boy entry.

Huy Ching did not sell opium to children, as some of his competitors did, even though it was perfectly legal.

"What is problem?" Huy Ching asked, motioning for his assistant to stand aside.

"My old man's in there," the boy repeated in a slightly lower tone. "Mom's sick and he's gotta come right away!"

"I think he not be able to," answered the Chinaman. "He, he—"

"I know," interrupted the boy. "He's drunk from smoking that stuff again. But I've woke him up before, when he was drunker than all get out. Let me in and I'll have him up in a minute."

Huy Ching hesitated. He doubted that the boy could wake the man, no matter what he did, and it was against his policy to disturb a patron until he woke of his own accord. But this new development might solve the larger problem—it might keep the man away from Huy Ching's long enough for him to regain his health. Still, he did not want the boy's efforts to awaken his father to bother any of the others in the room. He stood perplexed for a moment, then a solution flashed into his mind and he spoke rapidly in Chinese to his assistant, who bowed deferentially and departed.

"You wait here one minute," Huy Ching said to the boy. "We bring father to you."

"How do you know which one's my father?" asked the boy. "Ain't there a lot of guys in there?"

"Only one who look just like you," Huy Ching smiled, patting the boy on the head. "How old you?"

"Ten" was the answer. "But I can beat up any twelve-year-old that messes with me, and some that's older." He held up his fists in fighting position as he talked, and the Chinaman had no doubt that he was telling the truth. His own son was rather a disappointment, and for a moment he envied the Foreign Devil. If *he* had a son like that, he'd see that he was trained in all of the martial arts. In fact, he suddenly wondered why the man was spending so much time away from his family.

Huy Ching had assumed that he was a loner, like so many other of his customers. He shrugged philosophically: one never knew what motivated a man to do anything.

There wasn't time for further thought anyway, as the assistant had returned. Accompanying him were two beefy Chinese guards carrying the cot with the tall, blond man on it. Huy Ching gave more orders in rapid Chinese and they deposited the cot in a small anteroom to one side of the front door. The man snored softly, oblivious to everything. Huy Ching dismissed the others with a motion of his hand and said to the boy, "This is father?"

"Yeah, that's my old man, snoring like a turkey—but not for long!" The boy walked to the cot and shook his father vigorously, then gave him three sharp raps on the forehead with his knuckles. To Huy Ching's amazement, the man opened his eyes, albeit somewhat blearily. The boy flashed a triumphant smile at the Chinaman and said, "You see? It's easy, if you know the right combination." Then, turning back to his father: "Mom's sick and you gotta come home, 'cuz the doc's on his way an' she wants you there. She had me call the priest, too, so you better sober up quick-like."

"Ooooooooh," groaned the man, holding his head as it rolled from side to side. He sat up with obvious effort. "Tea," he mumbled. "Gimme—cup—tea."

Huy Ching left for a moment to give orders for tea to be brought. When he returned, the tall man was sitting on the side of the cot, his head between his hands. Over the course of the next fifteen minutes, he gulped down cup after cup of strong, black tea and regained control of his faculties with a speed Huy Ching would have thought impossible if he had not seen it with his own eyes.

But the boy was not impressed. He shifted impatiently from one foot to the other, urging his father to hurry. "Come on, Pops," he repeated several times. "Mom's not gettin' any better with you sittin' there holding your head!"

Finally the man put his hand on the boy's shoulder and raised himself from the cot like a creaky old man. Once he was on his feet he walked quite steadily, although a bit like a sleepwalker. He headed for the door and passed within inches of Huy Ching, as if he weren't there. The son, however, tipped his oversized hat and said, "Thank you, sir, for gettin' my old man for me. My mom will be real appreciative."

Huy Ching watched the pair until they rounded the corner—had he watched them further, he would not have slept as soundly as he did that night. As soon as they were a block or so away from Chinatown, the tall man began to walk briskly, with no hint of his former lethargy.

The boy laughed heartily, slapping his hat against his thigh. "You're the greatest actor I ever saw! You should be on Broadway!" He slapped his thigh again. "Damn, you're great!"

"You're not so bad yourself," complimented the man. "But next time don't be quite so realistic—my ears are still ringing from the way you knocked my head around!"

"I couldn't pass up a chance like that, now could I?" the boy joked. "I may never get another."

"I sure hope you don't," answered the man, rubbing his head. "Now tell me what this is all about. Why did you break in on my game, just when I was starting to get somewhere?"

"All I heard was that the boss wants you to do something else. Something more important."

"Well, well. It must be pretty important, then. Let's go find out."

CHAPTER 4

The Wild Goose Chase

NADINE and Juliette were still asleep, and Senator Howard had lapsed into a grieving silence in the wake of his visit to the scene of Nathaniel's death. While Gerald went to see how the races were progressing, Kyra took advantage of the opportunity to ask some questions of the Hopsworth servants, most of whom were gathered in the servants' hall for a haphazard meal. Their usual schedules had been hopelessly disrupted by the events of the past two days, and they were experiencing their own grief and shock over Nathaniel's death. They had loved him like family and were eager to help in any way they could; they answered Kyra's questions thoughtfully and promised to report anything that might be relevant. Even so, she couldn't help but be a little disappointed after the interviews. On the whole, what they had to say did not appear to be of much help.

Kyra was just heading back to the races when a groom came in with a message for her.

"Mr. Oswald and your husband are looking for you, ma'am," he said politely. "They would like you to meet them at the judges' stand."

"Thank you, George," said Kyra as she adjusted her veil to go outside. Then she turned to Corrie, the head housekeeper, and said, "Please keep an eye on things in here and let me know if I'm needed."

"Yes, ma'am," said Corrie with a curtsy. "And I'm sure I speak for all of the servants when I say we'll do whatever we can to help find whoever killed the young master."

"Thank you," said Kyra softly. "Thank you."

The day had grown even brighter outside and a few horses just beginning a race were already lathering in the unseasonal heat. Kyra stopped at the top of the steps for a moment to watch the field of seven horses clear several jumps near the judges' stand, then head away for the cross-country part of the course, which had been marked with little flags that fluttered in the slight breeze like brightly colored spring flowers. She felt a wave of regret and grief that Nathaniel was not there to take in the beautiful scene. He would have enjoyed it so much. Her eyes swept the panorama. Farmers' wives in plain dark dresses were sitting elbow to elbow with large-hatted millionaires' wives on a homemade grandstand; the farmers themselves were perched along the tops of Hopsworth's fences, chatting amiably with city dudes in top hats; horses and riders were warming up for the next race or saddling up, attended by servants and well-wishing family members; there were even people still milling around the refreshment tables. Near one of the tables, Kyra saw Jerome Cushing, the man who had made the phone call to New York, huddled in conversation with two other men she did not recognize. Closer by, Lord Randolph Roseberry was talking to a group of young ladies. From his gestures and their looks of admiration, Kyra supposed that he was telling them tales of his hunting adventures in India, the only time Roseberry ever became expansive. As if to lend credence to his stories, Roseberry's Indian groom chose that moment to obsequiously approach his master, turbaned head held low and hands folded reverentially.

"What is it, Jawan?" Roseberry asked, evidently irritated at having been interrupted.

"Sire, your horse is prepared for you to mount for your race," the groom said, bowing low as he spoke.

"I'll be ready in a moment," Lord Randolph said imperiously. Without dismissing Jawan, he turned again to the young ladies and added, "Jawan Singh here is a cousin of the Maharaja of Ajodhya and one of the finest horse trainers in the world. He used to be in charge of the Maharaja's royal stables and personally taught all of the royal children to ride, including the young ladies. Eh, Jawan?" he said with a wink. "But you liked the ladies too well, or at least one of them, and got yourself into trouble, didn't you?"

Jawan bowed his head even lower but said nothing to refute this, and Lord Randolph continued, "That's how I was lucky enough to get the rascal in my pay—he was willing to do anything to get out of India at that moment, and I could give him official British protection. He's been very grateful ever since, haven't you, Jawan?"

"Yes, sire, my extreme gratitude shall always be yours," muttered Jawan, with his head still bowed. He spoke with a controlled resentment that made one or two of the young ladies glance inquisitively at him. But Lord Randolph did not seem to notice anything out of sorts.

"But I suppose I should go mount my beast." Roseberry sighed, adding, "Not that I care for these races at all, but one *must* support one's hunt, don't you know." With that, he excused himself to the ladies and departed with the groom in his wake. Kyra watched the two retreating forms for a moment, then walked toward the judges' stand.

"Mrs. McMasters," said Oswald Harding as soon as he saw Kyra. "I have a favor to ask of you. I have already asked your husband, and he has consented on the condition that you agree."

"No promises," responded Kyra with a smile, "but tell me what you want."

"As you know, Nathaniel was to have led the Wild Goose Chase, which is the last race on the program.

You and your husband were entered as contestants in it, but I would like to propose that you lead it instead. There are only a few people who know the country as well as you do, and none of them have horses fit for steeplechasing."

"You want us to lead the race together?" Kyra asked.

"Yes," answered Oswald. "That was Senator McMasters's suggestion. He pointed out that although you know the country better than he does, some of the gentlemen contestants might take umbrage at following a lady. Since the rules Nathaniel set out state that the contestants must ride in pairs for the sake of safety, and some of them will be riding with female partners, it seemed reasonable to have a couple lead the race." Oswald stopped for breath and added, "It really would be a great help."

"Well, I guess we'd best go mount up, then, Gerald," said Kyra with a smile of resignation. "We'll need to ride out and plan our course a bit beforehand, won't we?"

"Thank you, Mrs. McMasters!" exclaimed Oswald, and for a second Kyra thought he was going to hug her out of sheer relief. But instead he turned back to the race, as yells from the grandstand proclaimed that the first horses were already in view, galloping toward the last cluster of jumps. As soon as the race was over, they settled the details of the steeplechase and agreed that Gerald and Kyra should ride out and plan a course beforehand. As they were about to turn and go, Oswald stopped them and asked Kyra, "You were in the house just now?"

"Yes," Kyra answered.

"How is . . . how is Nadine taking . . ." He stopped, unable to continue, but Kyra knew what he was asking.

"She's still asleep," she answered. "Dr. Whitley gave her a sedative, but Sobie has orders to let me know as soon as she wakes up."

"When you see her, will you tell her I'm sorry?" Oswald asked with tears in his eyes. "And let me know if there's anything I can do. . . ."

"Of course," Kyra said comfortingly, putting her hand briefly on Oswald's arm. "Of course I'll tell her." Oswald's face flushed through his tears and suddenly Kyra remembered that he had been in love with Nadine eight years ago in Philadelphia, but his mother had threatened to disinherit him if he married her, so the romance had died. At the time, Kyra had thought it a great pity, but Nadine and Nathaniel had seemed such a perfect match that Kyra had almost entirely forgotten about her friend's brief engagement to Oswald. She wondered if perhaps Oswald hoped that Nadine might someday return his affection—now that their circumstances were changed. . . . But there wasn't time to worry about things like that now; she and Gerald had a race to get ready for.

Gerald held Kyra's arm protectively as they walked back across the lawns toward the stables. She liked the feel of his tall, strong body near her and realized how much the stress of the day had already affected her. Years of quiet country life had made her unused to dealing with the ugliness of murder—it seemed so unreal and out of place in the midst of the beautiful spring day, with blue skies and green hills and scarlet-coated riders on gleaming horses. But it *was* real and it had to be dealt with. She squared her shoulders and took a deep breath. Sensing her mood, Gerald squeezed her arm and smiled encouragingly.

"I'm glad we'll have a chance to get away from here for a while," he said, voicing her feelings exactly. "I don't think there's much else we can do at the moment, anyway."

"No," agreed Kyra. "I don't think there is." Then she told him about the strange phone call to New York. "I wonder where Benny is," she concluded. "I would like to have him keep an eye on that fellow."

"It would also be nice to have some help tacking up our horses," added Gerald tersely. "All of the stable boys seem to be out watching the races." At that moment, Edna Harding came bustling into the stable.

"Have you seen my nephew?" she gasped. "I was told he came this way, and when I find him I'm going to ring his little . . . Are you riding in the next race?" she asked, suddenly noticing that Gerald was saddling his horse. She didn't wait for an answer, however, and continued, "If you're looking for your groom, I'm told he is with little Hadley and if *I* were you, *I* would punish him *severely*, most severely, for the nasty trick he played on the poor boy. Not that Hadley didn't call it on himself by bringing that *beastly* animal along. Nevertheless, one just can't have servants doing things like that, don't you agree?"

Kyra turned away to hide a smile, while Gerald looked completely bewildered. "I'm sorry, I don't have the faintest idea of what you're talking about," he said. "But if you see Benny, please ask him to wait here for us."

"I'll send one of my own grooms, if you'd like," piped Edna with fatuous generosity. "I've permitted them the liberty of watching the races, but *that* can easily be revoked. Servants should be happy with whatever crumbs are left at table, don't you think?"

"Thank you for your kind offer," answered Gerald through clenched teeth, "but I'm sure that won't be necessary. We're just going out to set a course for the Wild Goose Chase, then we'll let our horses rest until it's time for the race. They'll be quite warmed up enough on a day like this. If Benny's not here, we can tend to them ourselves."

"Oh, *you're* going to lead the Wild Goose Chase!" exclaimed Edna. "And *Mrs*. McMasters as well? My, my! Some of us have been wondering who would get that job—the rumor is, you know, that Nathaniel was setting a course for that very race when he met his unfortunate fate. Of course, no one actually knows for sure, but still . . . they say lightning always strikes twice, and all that. But I'm certain you know what you're doing. Good luck, and I'll send Benny in if I see him." She picked up her riding skirts and bustled off, the complete and perfect busybody with a juicy tidbit of gossip to tell.

"There'll be no need for Oswald to make an announcement about who's leading the Wild Goose Chase now," Gerald observed with a wry expression.

"Edna certainly knows how to wheedle information out of a person, doesn't she?" observed Kyra just as wryly.

"I know, I know, don't rub it in," Gerald groaned. "I'd rather deal with the most wily of politicians for an hour than Edna Harding for ten minutes."

"Then let's get away from here before she comes back!" exclaimed Kyra as she stepped unaided from the mounting block to her horse and settled herself once more into her sidesaddle. Gerald quickly followed suit and the two of them rode off toward the woods without a backward glance. Had they looked back, they would have noted that their departure was followed by several unfriendly pairs of eyes.

Edna's news spread like wildfire throughout the crowd. As Oswald had predicted, not a few took umbrage at the idea of a woman leading, even as part of a couple, a race that until recently had been the prerogative of reckless young men. Steeplechases had originally been called "pounding races," because the leader would set the most difficult possible course across the countryside, with the stiffest obstacles, in an effort to put down or "pound" the pursuers. There were of course a great many injuries to both horses and riders in these races, and they had recently been outlawed by the fledgling Masters of Foxhounds Association of America, which had set down some sensible rules for cross-country chases. Since then, the Wild Goose Chase and other cross-country events had become generally safe enough for even a woman in sidesaddle to ride, provided she was a competent horsewoman to begin with. But a woman *leading* such a race was quite another thing. Before Gerald and Kyra were completely out of sight, a group of men had gone to the judges' stand to protest to Oswald.

Kyra and Gerald were happily oblivious to the fuss at the stand as they entered a shaded wood and slowed their horses to a walk. They had already determined a general direction for the race, which would include at least twenty difficult jumps and another ten that were somewhat easier.

"We can also cross the river and make a loop around Winter's Hill," suggested Kyra. "There are half a dozen double walls to go over, which should prove a challenge."

"Yes, it would sort out the unfit horses all right," mused Gerald. "And it would also set us back in the general direction of Hopsworth. Let's do it."

"All right," said Kyra. "The race is planned. Should we head back?"

"In just a moment," said Gerald, moving closer to Kyra. "This may be the only time I have alone with you all day, and I want it to last as long as possible." With that, he halted his horse against hers and leaned over to kiss her. His lips conveyed a passion that she had feared was gone from their marriage, and she felt her body tingle in response as his arms enveloped her and gently pulled her from her saddle to rest in front of him. There they kissed for long moments, until Kyra felt as weak as water and totally at Gerald's command. She was already breathing raggedly, through parted lips, when the horse began to shift nervously.

Gerald slipped off the animal, pulled Kyra down after him, and carried her in his arms to a pile of last year's dried pine needles. He left her there for a moment, dizzy with desire, while he tied the two horses to a tree. Then he was back at her side, kissing her cheek, her neck, and following his fingers with his lips as he unbuttoned the front of her riding habit all the way down to her silk drawers, which he slipped off over her boots. Gerald sat back and let his eyes run slowly over her body, his face glowing with admiration.

"Even after three children," he said softly, "you're

still the most beautiful woman I've ever seen.'' She felt herself flush under his gaze as she suddenly remembered how he had gloried, too, in her pregnant body, running his hands again and again over the swollen belly that she had feared would repulse him. But she was not pregnant now. Her figure was once more as slim as a boy's. But lately they had made love less frequently, no doubt because of the demands of his busy schedule and her preoccupation with their children. Nevertheless, Kyra had been worried about it, and relief now flooded her— Gerald was still hers. His passion had not died.

Their moans of ecstasy mingled for a time with the cooing of two wood doves in the tree above until the moans became cries and they finally lay panting in each other's arms. They lay there for some time, slowly recovering, their hands playing softly over each other's bodies and their lips meeting for gentle kisses. They would have stayed there for hours, oblivious to all in their escape from the ugly realities of the day, had not one of the horses stamped its foot and snorted loudly, recalling them to the task at hand.

"They'll soon start wondering what happened to us," Kyra said, continuing to twiddle her fingers in Gerald's hair.

"But they'd never guess, not in a million years." Gerald laughed. "Those sticks-in-the-mud would never guess that I seduced and ravaged my wife of seven years under a tree in the woods, practically within earshot of the Daisy Hill Hunt's Race Day celebration."

"I do believe"—Kyra giggled like a young girl—"this is probably the first time a steeplechase course has been set in quite this way!"

"And probably the last." Gerald laughed. "Unless you'll consent to setting it with me again next year."

"I'd never let you set it with anyone else!" responded Kyra as she rose and began to restore her disheveled clothing to some semblance of order. Gerald finished his lesser restorations first and retrieved her hat from where it had rolled under a bush. He brushed a smudge of dirt off and tenderly placed it on her head. Then he gave her a kiss on the cheek and cupped his hand ever so briefly over her left breast before he turned to untie the horses. His message was clear: To the world, Kyra was his wife, properly dressed, coiffed, and behatted. In private, she would always be his wanton mistress, his passionate harlot, whose object was to please and be pleased. There were no limitations other than those they set for themselves.

Restored by their brief escape, they remounted and rode sedately back toward Hopsworth, glowing inwardly from their interlude in the woods. As they neared the rolling lawns, they could see that the racetrack was empty and people were clustered again in little groups.

"They must be having a break between races," commented Gerald. "And look at that crowd of men around Becky Hollingshood! Like bees to honey!"

"Yes, quite," said Kyra dryly, feeling an uneasiness in the pit of her stomach. Rebecca Hollingshood was a tall, dark beauty with a brazen forthrightness that only the very rich could get away with. She had inherited millions from her father's steel foundry and lived a life devoted to foxhunting and other outdoor sports, the more challenging the better. Just the previous year, she had been the first woman to drive an automobile over the Alps, and rumor had it that she was planning an expedition to Alaska to hunt polar bears and arctic wolves. She had already gone on several African safaris. Kyra had always rather liked her, and Becky had been a frequent guest at the McMasterses' home until Kyra noticed, or thought she noticed, that Gerald seemed to like her a little too well. That was during Kyra's last pregnancy, and although she had never said a word about her suspicions to either Gerald or Becky, she had noticed that neither one had said anything when the friendship between the two women suddenly began to cool.

The sight of Becky at that particular moment chilled Kyra's postcoital contentment like a dash of cold water.

She was abruptly brought back to a world in which ugly actions and feelings not only existed, but often seemed to dominate benevolence. Although Becky's family had married her off at age nineteen to a rich industrialist twice her age and half her size, she was rumored to have been the cause of several scandalous divorces since then. One of them had even resulted in the death of the man, supposedly at the hands of his estranged wife.

Suddenly Kyra wondered if Becky could possibly have had anything to do with Nathaniel's death. He had been spending a lot of time with her recently, as she had been considering starting her own pack of foxhounds and thereby becoming the first woman Master of Foxhounds in the United States. Nathaniel had been teaching her everything he knew about the sport and the training and working of the hounds. He'd often claimed that she learned faster than any man he'd ever known, and once Kyra had thought she'd heard more than mere admiration in his voice. Then there were Edna Harding's innuendos to consider. The woman *was* aggravating, but there was no doubt she was also smart, in her own way. Could she be right that Nadine had . . . Kyra shook her head to rid herself of the thought, yet it lingered there like a black worm. She knew how she herself had felt when faced with the possibility that Gerald was more than merely friendly with Becky. And Nadine was a much more impulsive person. There was also the possibility that Becky herself had . . .

But there was no time to think of such things now. Kyra and Gerald had delayed in the woods so long that it was already time for the Wild Goose Chase to begin. Fortunately, their horses were perfectly warmed up, so they were ready to go. They had only to wait for the contestants to gather near the starting line and listen to Oswald repeat the rules, reading in a monotone from a sheet of paper.

As he read, Kyra looked over the small group in front of him, seated on horses eager to be off, stamping and snorting and fidgeting in their impatience. The riders looked nearly as impatient as their mounts. Most of them were young men, haughty and clean-shaven; a few were middle-aged men; fewer still were women. Becky Hollingshood was one of them. She rode a large bay stallion that would have been difficult for most men to control. Her partner was a man Kyra had never met, but she was willing to wager he was a professional horse trainer. Although he was dressed in gentlemen's clothing, he seemed as if he would be more comfortable in the ancient tweed coat and gaiters favored by trainers—and he handled his own high-strung mount with telltale expertise. Becky clearly intended to win the race.

Before Kyra had much more time to think about Becky, the starting gun had gone off and she and Gerald departed at a canter toward the first fence. They were to have a minute's head start before the contestants took off. They had just cleared a tall wooden panel, and were galloping across a grassy pasture, when they heard the second gun and a whoop from the crowd indicating that they were now being pursued. They increased their speed slightly and jumped a coop into a copse of willows that bordered a stream. Slacking their speed only slightly, they slid down the muddy bank, crossed the little rivulet, and clambered up the other side, where they cleared a rock wall into another pasture and their horses once again stretched out to a full gallop.

By the time they had covered half the course they'd set, Kyra's breath was coming in gasps as the wind whipped against her face, and she could feel that her hair had slipped from its pins and was streaming from under her hat—but she felt wonderfully alive and completely, exhilaratingly in tune with the powerful mare under her. Diana loved to race and seemed to fly over the fences, as if Kyra's weight on her back were nothing at all. Gerald and his mount seemed to share the same exhilaration, and he grinned at Kyra with boyish enthusiasm as they cleared a fence together and headed up a steep hill.

At the top of the hill they paused for a moment to let

their horses catch their breath and to survey the country below. Becky and her hireling were just emerging from the stream bed, well ahead of the others, as expected. A bit farther back, one horse had already come to grief at a tall fence and was limping off without his rider, who sat on the ground on the far side of the jump, blocking the contestants behind him from coming over. The latter were gesticulating wildly with their crops, and Kyra could imagine their oaths as they urged the hapless rider to get out of their way or be landed upon. He scrambled to one side as everyone but his partner leaped the fence and took off toward the willows as fast as they could.

After negotiating their way down the far side of the hill, Kyra and Gerald were confronted with a winding county road, bordered on both sides by rail fences too high to jump at such close quarters. About half a mile farther on, however, was a set of panels set just right for a horse to jump out of one enclosure onto the road and then off the road into the opposite pasture. Kyra and Gerald were familiar with these and headed straight for them, with Kyra taking the lead. She had cleared the first panel and her horse was bunching to take off over the second when she heard Gerald bellow, "Turn your horse!" Without a moment's hesitation, she yanked Diana's head mercilessly to one side, away from the jump and down the road, where she slowed and turned back to see what was wrong.

Gerald was off his horse, standing in the road, looking over the panel at something on the opposite side. Kyra rode up beside him and looked over his head. There was a large hole in the ground just where Kyra's horse would have landed. It was covered with brush to disguise it but had obviously been hastily done, as a mound of freshly dug dirt lay under the fence to one side of the jump.

"I saw the pile of dirt," Gerald said. "And I knew something was wrong. Thank God you were able to stop—your horse would have gone right over on top of you!"

"I wonder how many other of the jumps are rigged this way," Kyra conjectured.

"Probably not too many," answered Gerald. "There wasn't time. Whoever is responsible for this did it *after* we left to plan the course."

"Yes, and it had to be someone who knew which way we went and who knows the country well enough to have figured out that we'd have to cross this road to get back to Hopsworth, but that we probably wouldn't go that far while planning the course and discover the digger in action."

"There's at least half a dozen people who meet those qualifications—and all of them know that you're working to discover Nathaniel's murderer," Gerald pointed out.

"If it's me they were after," Kyra continued, "then they had to have known that I generally ride ahead of you."

"Everyone in the Daisy Hill Hunt knows that—but there wouldn't be too many others." As Gerald spoke, Kyra slipped off her horse in order to examine the hole and the pile of dirt more closely.

"There are footprints of two men here," she observed. "And tracks where a carriage pulled off the road and the horse stood waiting for a while—see the fresh pile of droppings and how the grass on the verge is trampled?" Suddenly she bent over and picked something off the middle rail of the fence—it was a small strand of gray homespun, of the type often used for sweaters.

"Someone squeezed between these two rails," she said. "And his sweater caught on this sliver, leaving behind a little memento for us."

"I thought *I* had sharp eyes!" Gerald said admiringly. "Now all we have to do is find the occupant of a ripped gray wool sweater."

"What bothers me," said Kyra, "is that this is all so sloppy. It's almost as if they *want* us to know who they are."

"Perhaps they were just in a hurry," Gerald suggested.

"They didn't have much time, after all. But I agree that they must be in a real panic over something. . . ."

Gerald was interrupted at that moment by the approach of Becky and her partner, who were sliding and bounding down the hill as if their mounts were goats instead of horses. When they reached the flat, they raced along beside the fence to the panel and leaped it in turn, coming to an abrupt halt in front of the McMasters.

"Don't tell me one of the *geese* has had its wings clipped!" she exclaimed loudly, but with a shortness of breath that attested to the hard race she'd been riding. When her eyes lighted on the hole on the other side of the jump, her expression changed. "Christ Almighty!" she swore like a man. "Someone tried to do you in for sure!"

"Yes," answered Kyra, "and the race is over. There might be other traps like this one. Would you two please stay here and warn the others, while Gerald and I ride on back toward Hopsworth?"

"Certainly," answered Becky in a greatly subdued voice, her eyes filling with tears.

For an instant, Kyra thought the woman was crying over not being able to win the race, but Becky's next words set her straight.

"I know some people think I might be responsible for Nathaniel's death—that Edna Harding keeps making innuendos—and I've been putting on as good a face as possible, but I want you to know that I didn't have anything to do with it. I might do a lot of things others wouldn't, but I'm not a murderer—and I liked Nathaniel. . . ." Here she paused and looked at Kyra and Gerald, tears streaming down her face, but her head still held proudly.

Kyra wanted to believe her former friend, but something niggled at the back of her mind, keeping her from trusting Becky completely. That something hardened to a resolute lump when Gerald offered his handkerchief to Becky and said tenderly, "That's all right, now, don't take on so—I'm sure you didn't have a thing to do with

Nathaniel's death, or this, either, and we'll do whatever we can to keep you out of it."

Becky cheered up visibly at this reassurance and, regaining some of her famous spunk, quipped, "Besides, if I killed someone, it would probably be by poison—I wouldn't do something that would hurt an innocent horse, too."

"Look," interrupted Kyra, pointing at the hillside, down which a few more horses and riders were careening. "You stay here and collect the rest of the contestants, Gerald and I need to go on ahead."

"Certainly," agreed Becky, her composure now fully restored. "And I'll volunteer Reggie here to fill in that hole before it does in some innocent minister on his way cross-country to visit a sick parishioner." Kyra noticed that Reggie did not seem overjoyed at being thus volunteered, but he obediently dismounted and went over to look at the hole. As Gerald and Kyra rode off, he had begun desultorily shoving the pile of dirt back into the hole with the side of his right boot. His whole bearing indicated that such work was beneath him, thereby strengthening Kyra's conviction that he was, in fact, a horse trainer: a gentleman would have thought in terms of safety to the others first, as Becky had. A true gentleman would have pitched right in, probably flinging the dirt back into the hole with his hands.

There was more to Becky than met the eye, mused Kyra as she watched the other woman riding back toward the next contestants to warn them about the jump. She would bear keeping tabs on, for more reasons than one.

CHAPTER 5

Casting

OSWALD Harding left the judges' stand and walked hurriedly across the lawn toward Kyra and Gerald as they rode back along Hopsworth's driveway for the third time that day. As he walked, he pulled his watch from his vest pocket and glanced at it nervously, a habit he had when upset or distraught.

"Senator Howard's awake and asking for you, Senator," he called to Gerald. "And Sobie just sent down a message that Nadine is beginning to stir," he added for Kyra's benefit.

"It sounds like we got back just in time," said Gerald. "We'll be in to see them as soon as we put away our horses—Benny appears to be missing still."

"I'll take them myself, if you'd like just to go on in," Oswald offered.

Gerald hesitated for a moment, looking first at the house and then at Oswald. "All right," he finally said. "But remember not to move too quickly around Charger, and don't go into the stall with him when you put him away."

"No problem," Oswald assured Gerald, rubbing Charger's neck affectionately. "I know this stallion well enough by now—a pussycat under saddle but a terror in the

barn, aren't you, old boy?'' He patted the horse again
and said, ''Don't worry, Senator, I'll take good care of
Charger and see that he doesn't get upset.'' Then he
stopped with a perplexed look on his face and glanced at
his watch again. ''But why are you back so soon? There
wasn't a problem with the Wild Goose Chase, was there?''

''Yes, there *was* a problem,'' Gerald answered. ''One
of the jumps was booby-trapped, so we canceled the rest
of the race. The others should be in shortly.''

''Was anyone . . . .'' Oswald began to ask, then stopped.

''No, no one was hurt,'' Kyra answered. ''But we
couldn't take the chance that another jump wouldn't be
similarly rigged.''

''No, of course not,'' the young man hastily agreed,
nodding his brown, curly hair so that it wobbled, reminding Kyra of the plumes on his mother's hat. ''You
did absolutely the right thing. Do you have any idea
who's responsible?''

''None at all,'' Kyra answered, glancing quickly at
Gerald. She was not about to tell Oswald, or anyone
else, about the carriage tracks or the bit of gray wool. At
least not yet. Not until she had a better idea of what was
going on. After all, even Oswald might have had his
reasons for getting rid of Nathaniel and consequently for
getting rid of her, too. He had been at Hopsworth on the
afternoon and evening before and had even ridden out to
check on some of the jumps not long before Nathaniel
had left on Truly Fine, according to a groom Kyra had
spoken to. He'd had every opportunity to wire Ingleson's
fence—and he was also in a position to know which way
Nathaniel was likely to go. In addition, he had been the
first to know that she and Gerald were leading the Wild
Goose Chase—there would have been plenty of time for
him to send an accomplice out in a carriage to dig that
hole. But who would that accomplice be? One of the
grooms? Then she remembered that Edna had recently
hired a gentleman's gentleman for Oswald—she'd made
her usual big to-do about it, as she did about anything
she did for Oswald.

Kyra slipped off her horse, handed the reins to Oswald, and said casually, "Speaking of Benny's being missing, I hear you have a new servant."

Oswald looked at her blankly for a moment, not following her abrupt change of topic, then flushed and said, "Oh, yes, Jones! My mother seemed to think I needed him, but he's been in bed with the grippe since the second day he moved in. I don't know what good he's going to be if he's sick all the time."

"The grippe has been particularly bad this season," Kyra commented sympathetically, watching Oswald's face closely. Something was wrong but she couldn't put her finger on it. She followed Gerald slowly up the front steps. For a moment she thought he had forgotten about her in his hurry to reach Thurston, but he stopped and held the front door open, saying, "I guess the doorman has been permanently requisitioned elsewhere."

"Yes, the whole world has gone topsy-turvy," Kyra answered as she took off her riding gloves once more and raised the veil of her riding hat. "And I'm finding that there isn't anyone I'm not suspicious of."

"You mean Oswald?" Gerald was quick to respond.

"Precisely. He always seemed like a good person, the salt of the earth, but since he inherited all that money from his grandfather a couple of years ago, he's changed. I never thought much about it until now, but he's developed just a hint of his mother's snootiness, an edge of something not very nice."

"I've felt the change, too," agreed Gerald. "Do you remember a few weeks ago when the son of one of Senator Howard's old army buddies came along on a hunt?"

"Yes, a nice young man—he knew a great deal about hounds, didn't he?"

"That's the one," Gerald answered. "After the hunt, he had a long conversation with Nathaniel about how the hounds hunted that day, especially the strike hound. Nathaniel was very impressed with his knowledge and invited him to come back any time."

"Yes, I remember that."

"What you probably didn't hear, however, was Oswald's comment to Nathaniel after the young man left."

"No, I don't think I did."

"If you had, you would have remembered it. As soon as the young man was out of earshot, Oswald said, 'I don't think he can *afford* to hunt with us, Nathaniel—he's only a minor clerk in Roosevelt's new National Parks Department.' "

"What was Nathaniel's response to that?" Kyra wanted to know.

"To his credit, Nathaniel said that anyone who knew that much about hounds was welcome to hunt with him any time he wanted to, rich or poor. He added that he'd provide him with a horse if he couldn't afford to keep one himself."

"Good for Nathaniel!" Kyra exclaimed. "At least *he* wasn't a snob, even if most of the other people in this hunt are."

"The sad thing is that I never thought Oswald was a snob, either," Gerald mused. "Even at the time, I chalked his comment up to jealousy. He'd been training under Nathaniel for some time and may have felt threatened by the young man's superior knowledge. But since then he's said and done some other things that have made me wonder—but let's talk about that later. I hear Thurston in the library, and I'm sure you're anxious to speak with Nadine."

"You're right, Oswald can hold till later." Kyra took one step toward the stairs but turned around to add, "I've had clothes brought over so that we can stay here for the weekend. All of the guest rooms were taken because of the race days, so I arranged for us to use Sarah's old suite."

"That will put us right between Thurston and Nadine, won't it?"

"And across the hall from Juliette and Melvin."

"Excellent!" exclaimed Gerald. "You haven't lost your touch, have you?" Then he added softly, as he stepped forward and brushed his hand against her cheek, "And I mean that in more ways than one!"

Kyra felt an almost schoolgirlish thrill of excitement at Gerald's compliment—and a surge of fully mature desire at the touch of his fingers. As she hurried up the stairs a few seconds later, she wondered how she could ever have had any doubts about her husband's constancy. She couldn't ask for a more loving, considerate man.

Sitting in a chair at the top of the stairs, his arms folded across his chest as if he were ready to wait forever, was J. Eldridge Cooper, chief investigator for the Virginia Sheriff's Department. When he saw Kyra coming, he unfolded his arms and slowly eased the great bulk of his body out of the chair. Kyra could hear him wheeze with the effort from halfway down the stairs. She had met him once before and had found him both offensive and unimaginative, ordinarily a disastrous combination in a detective. But he also possessed a tenacious cunning which had netted him quite a few successes. Nevertheless, Kyra did not like him, and if she had known he was there, she would have taken the back stairs to avoid him. There could be no graceful retreat now, so she smiled and nodded a greeting, hoping to walk past without a confrontation.

"Wait a minute, little lady, let's not be in such a hurry," Eldridge wheezed. "Mrs. McMasters, isn't it? Mrs. *Senator* McMasters." He made a little motion toward his forehead, clearly meant as a mock salute, which was accompanied by the leer that was his normal smile. "I want you to know that you're one of our prime suspects. In fact, we would have apprehended you by now if it weren't for the fact that you are a lady, and the laws are a little sticky about putting ladies in jail unless we have all the evidence together—but we'll get it, we'll get it. So don't you develop any notions about running off anywhere."

Kyra looked at the man's bloated face for a moment

in pure astonishment, then she said, "*I'm* one of your *suspects*?"

"Not just *one* of them, Madam Senator, one of our *prime* suspects, and don't make the mistake of thinking that your husband's position will get you off. In Virginia, a crime is a crime, no matter who commits it."

"You—you think *I* killed Nathaniel?" Kyra stammered, feeling her face go involuntarily hot then cold.

"Answer me this, young lady," he continued, ignoring her outburst. "Where were you late Friday afternoon?"

"Why, I was out for a ride," Kyra answered calmly enough, recovering some of her composure. "I usually ride in the morning, but one of my children had been ill during the night, so I slept in and rode in the late afternoon instead."

"An ill child, eh? Quite an excuse!" He snorted. "And in what direction did you ride, can you tell me that?"

"I started out toward Hopsworth, but then decided that an evening ride through the woods over by Sutter Creek would be nicer."

"A likely story. And did anyone see you riding 'over by Sutter Creek'?"

"No, I don't believe so. . . ."

"But *several* people saw you head toward Hopsworth, right across from the Ingleson farm. The way I see it, you would have had to go over the *very* fence that ended Nathaniel Howard's life. Imagine that. But if you were the one to *wire* the fence, then you certainly wouldn't have gone over it, would you? Oh, no, you would have circled back through the woods along Ingleson's stream— which leads, conveniently enough, right to Sutter Creek. What a coincidence!" The inspector's voice dripped with ugly sarcasm.

Kyra was tempted to brush him aside and to ignore the whole incident, which was what it deserved. But curiosity impelled her to ask, "What do you think my motive would have been for such an action?"

"Your motive! Ha!" Cooper crowed. "Everyone knows you're Nadine's best friend—what better motive could there be than to make her a well-to-do widow and split the proceeds? We know how the two of you used to work together. And we know all about the insurance policy, too."

"The *insurance* policy?"

"Yes, with Lloyds of London. Exclusively to cover 'accidents while hunting and jumping.' You and Nadine went to their Washington office and took the policy out less than two weeks ago. Their agent described you exactly and we have your signatures on the policy."

"But that wasn't a policy on Nathaniel. That was for the Daisy Hill Hunt Race Meet—Senator Howard himself insisted on it, and Nadine and I were only carrying out his orders. Ask him yourself."

"No matter who ordered the policy, the fact remains that the widow of the deceased stood to benefit by his 'accidental' death. But Mrs. Howard was too smart to be caught out riding while the deed was done. Oh, no, *she* stayed in her room with a headache while her accomplice strung the wire. And what a perfect accomplice—no one would possibly suspect a senator's wife of murder, especially do-good Senator McMasters' wife!"

"This is ridiculous!" Kyra cried out, feeling a twinge of very real alarm—the man actually *believed* what he was saying, and there was no telling what lengths he would go to to "prove" her guilt. He might even have her followed from now on, and she needed as much freedom as possible to locate the real killer or killers and clear Nadine of any suspicion. But there was no point in continuing the conversation, so she pushed on past him toward Nadine's room.

"You can act hoity-toity if you want, but it won't do you any good in the end," Cooper called out behind her. "You're going to wind up behind bars with the kind of social contacts you deserve." Kyra heard the stairs creak and groan under Eldridge Cooper's weight as he descended. She had fully expected that he would leave an officer as a guard upon her.

What did Cooper have in mind? she mused. Based on the evidence he had, she *could* see why he would consider her a suspect, but why tell her about it in such an abusive manner? Was it simply another case of the traditional antagonism between private and public investigators—or was it something more?

Nadine was in bed when Kyra entered the room. Her skin was so pale that her face would hardly have stood out from the pillowcase had it not been for her eyes, which were open now and very dark—her pupils, huge and more dominant than the irises, indicated that she was still heavily sedated. But upon seeing Kyra, she struggled to raise herself.

"That's all right, just lie still," Kyra soothed as she sat on the bed and took Nadine's hand in hers. "You just take it easy and I'll sit right here where you can see me," she added. She unconsciously spoke to her friend in the same tone she would have used for one of her sick children, and the usually spunky Nadine responded with passive acquiescence.

"I'm glad you're here," she said with childish simplicity. "Everything will be all right now—you'll find Nathaniel, won't you? Did they tell you he was lost? He went out for a ride, but he didn't come back. We looked and looked, but we couldn't find him in the dark. We found someone else, but it wasn't him, and that's when I got sick." In spite of the stale warmth of the room, Kyra felt a chill of fear creep up her spine.

When Kyra didn't answer immediately, Nadine tugged insistently at her hand. "You will find him, won't you?"

"I'll do what I can," Kyra answered, uncertain whether she should risk disillusioning Nadine so soon. Perhaps Dr. Whitley could advise her when he returned. In the meantime, she glanced at Sobie, who shrugged her shoulders, as if to say that this was something new, that

71

Nadine had not been acting like this when she went to sleep.

"What was Nathaniel wearing when he went out?" Kyra asked, deciding to go along with Nadine's fantasy, at least temporarily. "I'll need to know that if I'm going to look for him."

"Yes, I know," Nadine answered in a child's high-pitched voice. "He was wearing his gray tweed jacket, brown jodhpurs, and short boots with gaiters. He had on his plaid tam, too, the one I gave him for his birthday." A tear squeezed out of the corner of her eye.

Nadine's description matched the one in the sheriff's report Kyra had picked up earlier in Thurston's library. Kyra and Gerald had arrived too late to see the body before it had been cleaned up and prepared for the funeral, which would take place on Monday.

"Did Nathaniel say anything to you before he left to go riding yesterday?" Kyra asked Nadine in a matter-of-fact tone.

"He didn't say anything," Nadine pouted innocently. "He didn't even tell me he was going riding. He was mad at me."

"Oh? Why was that?" Kyra almost held her breath as she waited for Nadine's response.

"We'd had a fight. A *terrible* fight," Nadine elaborated with wide, guileless eyes. "I threw the poker at him, and he was mad at me. But I was mad at him, too," she added.

"Why were you mad at Nathaniel?" Kyra asked with trepidation.

Nadine opened her mouth as if about to respond, then closed it again with a surprised look. "I don't know," she finally said after puzzling for a few moments. "I don't remember why I was mad at him—but I was very mad, I remember that."

"Did it have anything to do with Becky Hollingshood?" Kyra ventured, remembering her own feelings that morning about Becky and knowing that the good-looking heiress had been spending a lot of time at Hopsworth.

"Oh, no! Becky is my *friend*. We ride our ponies together and play with the doggies. She is Nathaniel's friend, too."

Pausing, she pulled herself up closer to Kyra and whispered, "I found them kissing behind the barn, and they aren't supposed to, you know. That's one of the rules. 'No kissing behind the barn.' So I told Nathaniel that I was going to tell his daddy, and then he'd be sorry. He promised he wouldn't do it again, but I said I was going to tell his daddy anyway."

"So that's what you were angry with each other about?" Kyra suggested, although something didn't quite ring true.

"I guess so" was the simple reply. "Do *you* think that's what we were angry about?"

"Perhaps," Kyra answered. "Now why don't you lie down again and rest for a while, and we'll talk some more later."

"Okay," Nadine said with a sigh. "I *am* tired." Then she turned her head quizzically to one side and added, "Why am I so tired? Oh, yes, we were up all night, playing hide-and-seek in the dark on our horsies. But Nathaniel was very bad, he wouldn't come in when the game was over. . . ." And she drifted off into sleep, still murmuring inaudible words.

Kyra gently put Nadine's hand inside the light coverlet and rose from the bed, turning toward Sobie, who said, "She wasn't like that when she went to sleep. She was crying and carrying on, but she was *herself*."

"It could be the sudden shock of Nathaniel's death, or even the sedative Dr. Whitley gave her that's causing this," Kyra suggested to Sobie. To herself, she thought, Or an overwhelming sense of guilt. Was it possible that she had killed Nathaniel in a fit of jealousy? But then why would she talk so freely about finding him kissing Becky behind the barn? Unless she really had gone out of her mind.

"She might be better when she wakes up again," she continued out loud for Sobie's benefit.

"Do you want me to call you then?" Sobie asked.

"Yes, please," Kyra answered without hesitation. "And if she says anything clearly in her sleep, would you write it down? There should be ink and some paper in her writing desk."

"I'll do anything, if you think it'll help," Sobie said as she opened the top of the rolltop desk to get out the paper. She jumped back with a gasp and a horrified look on her face, letting the top of the desk slam down of its own accord. A second later, a putrid, rotting smell pervaded the room from the area of the desk. Sobie had turned ghastly pale and was retching into the wastebasket.

Kyra helped Sobie to a chair, then turned toward the desk and gingerly opened it. Inside lay the severed head of a large foxhound. Its purple tongue was huge and swollen, its lips drawn back in a death grin that revealed all its teeth, its eyes were open and staring—and the whole thing crawled with maggots. It had obviously been dead for several days and had decomposed rapidly in the unseasonal heat. Kyra quickly closed the desk again, before the stench became unbearable.

"I'll get one of the outside boys to come take it away," she said to Sobie.

"It's one of Nathaniel's, isn't it?" Sobie asked.

"Yes, it's Anthony, his best young stud hound."

"But who would *do* such a horrible thing—and put it in Nadine's desk?" Sobie wanted to know.

"I don't know, I really don't know," mused Kyra. "A few days ago a messenger came over from Hopsworth, asking if anyone had seen Anthony. I talked to the boy myself. He said that Anthony had wandered off during a roading session, but didn't come in that night."

"What's a 'roading session'?" Sobie wanted to know.

"Don't tell me you've lived here all this time, almost five years now, and you don't know even a simple hunting term like that?" said the astonished Kyra.

"I never did like dogs much," Sobie explained defiantly, "least of all hunting dogs, so I never paid much attention to all the hunting talk. It always seemed kind of foolish to me for rich people who had better things to do with their time than to dress up in silly outfits and go chasing all over the country on horseback after a poor little fox. But please, ma'am, what is a 'roading session'?'' she concluded with single-minded perseverance.

"It's when the huntsman and several assistants on horseback take the hounds out for exercise along the roads, to keep them fit for hunting," Kyra explained. "Once in a while, a hound slips away from the pack during such a session, and goes hunting on its own. It usually returns to the kennels by nightfall, tired out and penitent."

"But Anthony didn't return," Sobie said softly, looking at the closed desk.

"No," Kyra said. "Whoever did this must have killed him when he caught him or later. But the question is, why?" It struck her that there might be some clue in the desk, a note, perhaps, so she hurried down the back stairway to the kitchen to get some help to remove the head—it had to be removed immediately for sanitary reasons, anyway. A few minutes later she was back in Nadine's room with one of the gardener's boys, who carried a large covered bucket and a pair of fireplace tongs.

"Jeeezus Christ!" he exclaimed when Kyra opened the desk, but he quickly picked up the offending head with the tongs and dropped it into the bucket, slamming the lid into place and holding his nose. Kyra swabbed the area it had sat on with a rag soaked in sudsy water and disinfectant she had brought back with her. When she was finished, she emptied the basin and gave it to the boy to return to the scullery on his way outside with the head.

"What shall I do with the head, ma'am?" he wanted to know.

"Take it to the rear of the ice house, right by the riverbank, and bury the whole bucket, closed up, just the way it is. And mark the spot, so you can find it again," Kyra instructed. "We may need it as evidence, and it will stay cool enough there to keep it from rotting any further. And thank you for your help," she added, slipping a small gold coin into the boy's shirt pocket, since his hands were full. His eyes lit up and he exclaimed, "Thank *you*, ma'am!" and quickly disappeared.

Sobie had already opened the windows wide to air out the room when Kyra returned to the desk for a closer examination. She was relieved that Nadine had slept through the whole episode. The sight of that head wouldn't have done her any good.

Kyra was about to give up her search for clues when she noticed a pile of letters with recent postmarks. She flipped through them, noting that most were from Nadine's old school chums. One, however, was a good deal thicker than the rest and bore a New York postmark. Kyra thought she recognized the handwriting on the envelope and slipped the letter out. She was right. It was from Juliette. There was no reason that should be surprising, as the two women were sisters-in-law, but Kyra knew that they had never been close. They openly competed for Nathaniel's affection, and the only thing that kept them from being outright enemies was the distance between Hopsworth and New York.

Kyra raised her eyebrows in disbelief as she read the letter. It was in Juliette's best style, friendly and chatty, expressing excitement about the forthcoming race meet and complimenting Nadine on the excellent job she had done in helping Nathaniel organize it. At the end, in a postscript, she said, "I almost forgot that Melvin asked me to enclose some diagrams Nathaniel wanted back as soon as possible. I hate to think of Hopsworth coming to this, but I suppose it's impossible to stop 'progress.' Melvin said to tell Nathaniel that they could talk about the deal over the weekend, but that it seemed basically sound to him."

What deal? Kyra wondered as she folded the letter and smoothed open the enclosed papers. They were surveyor's maps of Hopsworth, detailing a plan for subdividing it into five- to ten-acre parcels. Stamped in one corner was the name and address of Tobias LaFarge's "investment company." She had heard mention of such a project before, but she had no idea that matters had gone so far. And she had thought that Nathaniel and Nadine were both staunchly opposed to taking such a step except as a last resort. Things couldn't possibly be *that* bad. Or could they? Could Senator Howard have lost even more money than they suspected? Kyra flashed on the man making the long-distance call to New York that morning in the hall—it seemed years ago already. Could the severed head have been a warning to pay up on monies owed or else? But why put it in Nadine's desk? Were they aiming to increase the shock value, or had it been a mistake? After all, Nathaniel and Nadine shared the room, and a stranger might have thought the desk was his, as it was a man's desk, not the usual feminine escritoire with spindly legs and inlaid rosewood designs. Nadine despised such furniture, preferring heavy, functional pieces that could take some wear and tear.

Kyra put the rest of the letters back in their place and slipped Juliette's into the pocket of her riding habit, which was designed large enough to carry a sandwich or other snack. She would discuss it with Gerald later. Perhaps he knew more about the matter than she did at this point, as he had become Thurston's confidant with regard to a number of things, both personal and political.

She made a quick search of the rest of the bedroom and the adjoining sitting room. She found nothing else of interest, so left Sobie to watch Nadine while she went to change out of her riding clothes and rest for a while before the evening festivities began. There were other things she could do, she knew, but she had had enough detecting for the day—and heaven only knew what the evening would bring.

On her way down the hall moments later, Kyra had to duck to keep from being hit in the head by an easel carried by a tall, exceedingly thin man with mousy brown hair and a very precisely trimmed mustache.

"Oh! So sorry!" the man exclaimed in a thick British

accent. "Damned awkward thing to carry, don't you know?" he added nervously, then set down both the easel and a large bag he was carrying and thrust forth his hand. "Paul Leonard Asquith, the Third, at your service, madam."

"Kyra Keaton McMasters," she responded, giving him her hand in return.

"*The* Kyra Keaton?" he said, his previously superior attitude disappearing abruptly. "Are you *the* Kyra Keaton who captured your father's murderer right in a London restaurant—the papers were full of it for a week! Even Lady Churchill had to make a comment to the press about spunky American women. She was one herself, you know, but then I guess you *do* know—you're friends or something, aren't you?"

"Jennie and I first met years ago when she was visiting her family in New York and I was there on a trip with my father. We've met several times since, and I admire her greatly, but we're hardly friends." As Kyra spoke, she examined the face of the tall man closely. There was something strangely familiar about it, especially the eyes, but when he stooped to pick up his bag and the fallen easel with a characteristic gesture, she was certain.

"Philip Drogan!" she exclaimed in a whisper. He nodded, putting his finger to his lips and motioning her to follow him into a room just down the hall from her own.

"I didn't think the brown hair and mustache would fool you for long," he said in his own midwestern tones once the door was closed. "But I think the disguise is quite adequate otherwise, don't you?"

"It's marvelous," Kyra said admiringly. "How did you learn to do the accent so well?"

"I spent some time in England on a case a few years back," he explained. "Did you know that I'm no longer with the New York Police Department?"

"Yes, I heard you're with Pinkerton now—pretty high up, too. Are you the detective they've sent?"

"Senator Howard demanded their best detective"—Philip laughed—"so they pulled me off another case and sent me packing on the first train out of New York City. I arrived while you were out riding and had a chat with Thurston. My cover will be that I'm a painter from London here to capture the essence of the American hunting scene after having done many English and Irish scenes."

"Was that your cover while on the case in England?" Kyra was quick to ask.

Philip grinned in appreciation and said, "I'd almost forgotten how fast your mind works, Kyra. Yes, only then I was an American Impressionist. It's a convincing cover for me, as I've dabbled in oils for some years in my spare time. I find it relaxing and a chance to empty my mind while working on a case—it's almost as good as a fishing trip, and more convenient."

"Yes, it would be," mused Kyra, giving him only half of her attention while she recalled the initial antagonism that had existed between her and the then Sergeant Drogan of the NYPD. He had been assigned to investigate the death of her Cousin George and had subsequently become involved in the telephone case. Their differences had gradually given way to mutual respect and admiration, and they had cooperated on several cases after that, before Kyra gave up detective work to raise her family.

Kyra breathed a sigh of relief at the thought of Drogan's help on this case—she had kept track of his career over the years and she could think of no one with whom she'd rather work. Eldridge Cooper was obviously going to be of no use at all. Aloud, she simply said, "I'm glad you're here, Philip. It will make everything much easier."

Drogan was putting his easel in a corner as she spoke, so his back was turned to her. He hoped she didn't notice how his hand trembled at her sigh and at the sound of her voice. He had never really gotten over Kyra, and her sigh meant more to him than she would ever know.

"I'm sure you'd have handled the whole thing brilliantly," he said cheerfully when he did turn around. "Even if it were a much more difficult case than it appears."

"It seems like a simple case to you?" Kyra asked. She had noticed how his hand trembled and wondered also at his extreme thinness and the peculiar glitter in his eye. Was he ill? Or had he been ill and become addicted to morphine or one of its many derivatives? She was all too familiar with the syndrome. She had seen it in her own Great-Aunt Lydia and again in Sarah Howard. But they were both old and had lived long, full lives—Philip Drogan was still young and had so much to give. Her heart went out to him, but her good breeding kept her from saying anything.

"It has to be either love or money," Drogan continued, unaware of her thoughts. "And there are only a certain number of suspects, all conveniently gathered together in one place. It's just a matter of time until someone makes a wrong move."

"Yes, Thurston was smart to keep them all here like that," Kyra agreed. "He's one of the few politicians whose intelligence I genuinely respect, and I've met a lot of them in the past few years."

"I'll bet you have," said Drogan, hungrily looking at her face. She had matured even more beautifully than he had expected. Was her husband worthy of her? It was really no business of his. But he still wondered. . . .

Kyra felt herself blushing under Philip's searching gaze. The silence grew too long and she groped for something to say, then realized with relief that if they were going to work together, she should tell him the events of the day, including her encounter with J. Eldridge Cooper, her own suspicions and deductions, and as much background as possible before it was time to dress for dinner.

CHAPTER 6

Ware Riot

ABOUT an hour later, Kyra emerged from Drogan's room and walked down the hall toward her own, wondering if Gerald would be there waiting for her. She wanted nothing more at the moment than to feel his arms around her. But she had only to open the door to the suite to know that she had just missed him. His individual scent was a faint trace in the air, like a ghost of the man himself. Kyra breathed in deeply, her nostrils quivering. She felt as if he were surrounding her, caressing her through the warm air, and she relaxed.

Then she saw the note he'd left on a table next to the door:

Dear Kyra,

Kepple telephoned to say that Lady Emilie's gone into labor and threatens to have a hard time. He's sent a boy to fetch the vet, who's at a farm nearby, but he wants me to come and assume responsibility. I couldn't stay away anyway, of course, and was prepared even to miss dinner, but Becky H. has offered to drive me over and back in

81

her automobile to save time. I shouldn't be too late, but please go down to dinner without me, if I'm not back.

Love,
Gerald

P.S. Thurston seems better—calmer—and plans to go in to dinner. He has more spunk than most men half his age! Take care of him if I'm not back.

Kyra held the note and trembled. The sensual pleasure of the moment before was shattered. Gerald had gone off with Becky Hollingshood. It didn't matter that he had gone for his favorite mare—Kyra felt unreasoningly abandoned and betrayed. She struggled to master her emotions, reminding herself of the scene in the woods that morning, of Gerald's tenderness and expressions of love. She had nothing to worry about. She couldn't ask for a better husband. But doubt gnawed inside her.

"I'm overly tired and tense," Kyra said aloud to herself in the empty room. She glanced at the small gold watch she wore on a chain around her neck. "There's still plenty of time for a bath," she added briskly. "That will make me feel better. . . ." She had taken one step toward the bathroom when she heard a tentative knock at her door.

She opened the door quietly, thinking that it might be someone who had waited for a private moment to approach her with information about Nathaniel's death. Instead, she found herself facing the homeliest young woman she'd ever seen, dressed in the Howards' standard upstairs maid's uniform. Kyra felt instantly sorry for the girl, who curtsied her lumpish body nervously.

"Ah's Alma. Ah's s'posed t' help th' ladies on this floor dress theirselves fuh dinner an' th' ball," she mumbled, looking down at her large feet, which she shuffled with excruciating embarrassment. Kyra had never seen her before, so she had apparently been hired for the weekend, to help out with the overflow of guests. Fortunately, there were not many women on this floor that would need help, as she didn't look capable of giving much. But Kyra always gave even the most unpromising servant or employee a fair try before making judgment.

"Could you find someone to press out my gown?" she asked in her kindest voice. "It got a bit wrinkled on the way over here."

"Oh, yes'm! Yes, o' course. Ah kin do it m'self. Ah's very good at ironin'. Ah'll have it done in a jiffy!" the maid replied excitedly, with several more curtsies and much wringing of the hands, which Kyra noticed were as large and as rawboned as the poor girl's feet. Kyra wondered if perhaps the girl were a bit retarded.

Kyra fetched the dress and handed it carefully to the girl, saying, "It only needs a bit of touching up, Alma."

"Ah'll have it back 'fore you know it!" Alma said as she curtsied a final time and turned to go.

"Wait a minute." Kyra stopped her. "Do you have a master key?"

"You mean th' key that fits all th' doors? Yes'm, th' head housekeeper gave me one fuh this floor."

"Good!" said Kyra. "I'm going to bathe now, so when you're finished with the dress, just let yourself in and lay it on the bed. Can you do that?"

"Yes'm!" was the reply, with another bobbing curtsy.

Kyra closed the door, smiling again. There was something irresistibly cheerful about Alma, in spite of her initial repulsiveness. Kyra was glad she'd given the girl a chance and even thought she might ask her to help with her hair later, since she had chosen to leave her own maid at home.

Kyra continued to smile as she walked into the bathroom, one of Hopsworth's most lavish. Thurston had refurbished the pre–Civil War mansion a few years earlier, with one of the improvements being indoor plumbing and completely modern bathrooms with the best available appointments. And in the main wing of the house he had taken special pains to make each bathroom distinctive.

The room Kyra entered was almost as large as the bedroom, but with polished Italian marble floors and slabs of the same marble covering the walls to shoulder height. On the far side of the room stood a thronelike porcelain commode with an ornately carved wooden flush box hanging on the wall behind it. Opposite the commode stood an imperial sink, carved in marble and supported by a fluted marble column. The faucets and soap dish were of finely wrought bronze, not quite as luxurious as the famous gold appointments of the railroad car outside, but nothing to sneeze at. The focal point of the room, however, was the enormous bathtub. The curved interior of the tub was of the finest porcelain, crafted in France, and the exterior was decorated with a hand-painted English pastoral scene that had clearly been the inspiration for a tiny replica on the commode's flush knob. The tub was supported by bronze lion's feet that were in themselves a work of art. The spigots and soap dish were bronze, matching the ones on the sink. Flanking the tub, like stalwart royal retainers, were two identical antique chiffoniers, set with mirrors and little shelves holding fresh towels, washcloths, and bottles of bathing salts and ointments to complete the sense of the room's luxury and opulence.

Kyra reached toward one of these shelves and took down a bottle of lavender-colored salts, which she opened and sniffed. They would do, although she preferred her own lemon-scented ones. Next she turned the spigots of the tub and poured a small amount of the salts under the steaming water, which gushed onto the porcelain. She left the water running as she unfastened her riding habit and stepped out of its cumbersome folds with relief. It took several more minutes to unlace her tall riding boots and pull them from her heat-swollen feet, thinking as she often had that English riding clothing must have been invented by someone with a truly sadistic turn of mind. Ordinarily, of course, her maid would have filled the tub and assisted her disrobing, but Alma clearly had no idea that was part of a maid's duties and would probably have been more of a hindrance than a help. Besides, as long as Gerald was not there, Kyra welcomed the chance to be alone, without the presence of a servant. It gave her a chance to think and relax.

And after this day, she certainly could use some relaxing. She felt the tension in her muscles as she finally lowered her body into the steaming water and lay back against the fine porcelain. She closed her eyes for a few minutes, willing her body to go limp in the soft, warm water, feeling the anxieties of the day flow out through her fingertips. She knew they would return in full force during dinner, but even a few moments of relief were rejuvenating. She wondered how the other guests were faring—she knew they were suffering from the tension more than she was, and it would get worse before it got better.

Whenever she'd had a chance to look around at the crowd during the day, Kyra had noticed people watching each other furtively, refusing to meet each other's eyes, suddenly dropping conversations in the middle and walking off with studied casualness. Ordinarily suave socialites were circling each other with all the wariness and suspicion of cavemen, each thinking the other could be the murderer. Perhaps, thought Kyra, modern man hadn't progressed very far beyond the primitives after all. She had experienced acute disappointment several times that afternoon when people she had always considered benevolent, good-hearted souls had sidled up to her like back-alley informants with bits of information or outright character assassinations designed to throw suspicion away from themselves and onto some other hunt member or neighbor. Nadine and Becky were the general favorites for such suspicion, although Oswald and Melvin received their share, and even Farmer Ingleson was not beyond accusation.

Kyra sighed and reached for the soap. There wasn't much she could do about human nature.

She had just finished lathering her body and had submerged her limbs under the warm water again when she heard the passkey in the door, followed by the rustle of silk and the squeak of Alma's ill-fitting shoes as she walked across the adjoining room to lay Kyra's dress on the bed. The maid then paused, and Kyra took advantage of the moment to call out, "Alma, could you come back in half an hour and help me with my hair?"

"Yes'm," came the muffled reply. Had Alma been crying, or was her mouth full of some sweet? Kyra didn't have long to wonder, as the maid's footsteps approached the door, which was almost directly behind her back. She began to turn to see what Alma wanted, when a towel was thrown over her face, stuffed roughly into her mouth, and wound around her whole head with an expert twist to keep it snugly in place. Before Kyra's relaxed body had time to react, strong hands grabbed her from behind, pinning her arms against her sides and dragging her out of the tub. Her assailant then squeezed her in a quick, forceful hug that knocked the wind out of her and left her gasping and choking into the towel as she was dragged across the room and thrown onto the bed, too weak from lack of air to resist. She was still unable to move as she heard her attacker rip up a sheet and use the pieces to tie her arms and legs to the bedposts. As she began to regain her breath and realized her position, she came close to fainting from sheer terror. Only her years of mental discipline kept her conscious as she felt a strangely soft hand touch her right breast and begin to move slowly downward, accompanied by harsh breathing.

Was this why Gerald had been called away? So that she could be raped and terrorized? The thought enraged Kyra, giving her new strength to fight against her bonds. She concentrated on making one gigantic lunge, hoping against hope that one of the delicately fluted posts she was tied to would snap. For a second, the strips of sheet held against her movement, then her right foot jerked free, accompanied by the crack of the bedpost breaking off. There was a thud of wood on skull and a surprised grunt as the swinging post hit her would-be rapist in the head.

At the same time, there was a knock on the door, and Philip Drogan's voice called out in his British accent, "I say! Mrs. McMasters, are you all right in there?" In the following moment of silence, Kyra felt, rather than heard, her attacker move away from the bed toward the window. She strained against her remaining bonds to no avail, managing only to send the broken piece of bedpost clattering to the floor.

That was enough for Drogan, who immediately began to ram the door with his body. It finally gave way and he came stumbling into the room well after a crash and tinkle of glass, followed by running footsteps on the grass outside, indicating to both that her attacker had escaped through the window.

"My God!" Drogan exclaimed before throwing an afghan from the foot of the bed over Kyra's nakedness. Then he gently removed the towel from her head. She had to close her eyes against the sudden brightness of the room as her mouth and nostrils greedily gulped in quantities of air. Drogan quickly untied her right hand.

"I'll untie the rest!" she panted. "Try to catch him!" But she knew it was impossible, that too much time had passed already.

Drogan disappeared through the window and Kyra was struggling with the knot on her left wrist when she was startled by a piercing scream from the doorway.

"Oh, *Mrs. McMasters*. Oh, my goodness! What's happened to you?!" screeched the familiar grating voice of Edna Harding. "Oh, help! Someone, please help!" she continued to scream hysterically, running a few paces into the room, then out into the hall again.

"If you would just shut your mouth and untie me, that's all the help I need at the moment," Kyra said harshly, hoping to shock the woman out of her hysterics.

It worked. Edna quieted down and walked meekly toward the bed, although she still sniveled from fear.

Her next words surprised Kyra. "The blood! All that blood! Shouldn't I call the doctor? Oh! I feel faint!"

Kyra followed the older woman's horrified stare to where the afghan was soaked in dark, sticky red. Had she been cut without knowing it? She reached out her free hand and brought it back covered with the red liquid. Her nostrils immediately flared at the smell of linseed oil and turpentine. At the same moment, she spotted a small ceramic pot of the type artists use to mix their oil paints. Next to it on the bedspread lay the pestle Drogan had apparently used to grind the dry color and to stir in the liquids. Kyra began to laugh with relief at the thought of how such a small amount of paint could look like such a large amount of blood.

"Aiih! She's gone mad!" exclaimed Edna, drawing back from the bed, where she'd been trying ineffectually to untie Kyra's left leg. "Stark, raving mad! It must be lack of blood!" She rushed out of the room, screeching, "Murder! Fire! Help!"

Kyra heard the door to Nadine's room open as Sobie looked out to see what the commotion was all about. "Sobie!" Kyra called out. "Sobie! It's me, Kyra. Please come help!" At the same time she wondered why there was no sound from the Dickeys' suite. Juliette was most certainly still under sedation, but Melvin should have been there dressing for dinner and heard Edna's cries for help. Had he come in earlier and already gone down, or was something wrong there, too?

"Why, Mrs. McMasters!" Sobie gasped when she saw Kyra.

"This isn't blood," Kyra reassured her. "It's paint. Quick now, use your little pocket scissors to cut these strips." She knew that all good maids carried a little pair of scissors, as well as needle and thread, in case emergency repairs were required on their mistresses' gowns.

As soon as she was free, Kyra flung a robe over her paint-stained body and ran across the hall to Juliette's room. The door was unlocked. Juliette lay in the bed, breathing, but just barely, while her maid snored in a nearby chair, a half-drunk cup of tea tipping precariously in her lap while the other tea things sat on a table next to her. Kyra pushed past her inert body and lifted Juliette's eyelid, then smelled her lips. She looked at the side table and saw several empty powder packets. Juliette had been overdosed, either purposefully or by accident, with the sedative Dr. Whitley had left.

Kyra grabbed the large woman's hands and pulled her into a sitting position, slapping her face to awaken her. She then jammed her fingers into Juliette's mouth to make her gag and spit up. It was imperative to get as much of the poison out of her system as possible. At the same time, she barked at Sobie, "Run to the kitchen and get a pot of the strongest coffee they have. Run!"

Sobie returned with the coffee just as Kyra was finally satisfied that Juliette's stomach was completely empty. Kyra again slapped the woman's cheeks until her eyelids flickered and she gave a groggy moan. Finally Kyra held a cup of coffee to Juliette's lips. "Drink this!" she ordered. "Drink it all down, then you must get up and walk around the room."

"Ooooo!" moaned Juliette, trying to lie down again. "I'm so sleepy!"

"You can't go to sleep!" Kyra commanded. "If you go to sleep, you'll die. You must wake up and walk! Come on now, up!" With Sobie's assistance on one side and Kyra's on the other, Juliette was soon on her feet and moving about the room.

"What's going on here?" Melvin's voice almost squeaked from the doorway. "Is Juliette all right?"

"No, she's not! And no thanks to you!" exclaimed Kyra. "Where have you been?"

"I—er . . . I—" the little man stammered, fluttering his hands in agitation. "Oh, this is all too much!"

"I agree, it's simply too much!" came Philip Drogan's voice, once more clothed in its British accent. "It's all like some bloody terrible American mystery story. I can't stand them in print, much less in real life! They're just too vulgar! Nothing like Sherlock Holmes, which is cerebral, don't you know.''

''Ooooo!'' moaned Juliette again, attempting to sit down but prevented by Sobie's and Kyra's strong grasp on her arms.

''I say!'' exclaimed Drogan, alias Paul Leonard Asquith III. ''What *is* wrong with her?''

''She's been given an overdose of sedative,'' Kyra answered. ''We must keep her moving until it wears off.'' Out of the corner of her eye, she could see that Edna had returned with a group of people, including Lord Randolph and Lady Pandora. They all stood in a circle outside the door, uncertain what to do in the face of this fresh emergency. For once, even Edna seemed to have nothing to say.

''Let me lend my assistance,'' offered the supposed artist diffidently. ''And perhaps her husband can take the other side.''

''Oh, yes, of course!'' Melvin exclaimed, jumping forward. ''I don't know what I'm thinking about!''

Melvin quickly replaced Sobie on Juliette's right, while Drogan replaced Kyra on the left. As he did so, he brushed slightly against Kyra. She felt him start and saw a blush move up his neck, but he quickly regained control of himself in true British stiff-upper-lip fashion.

As Kyra moved to examine the still sleeping maid, she heard Drogan say, ''This young lady's husband is a very brave man, if I dare say so. I found him chasing after the person who escaped through your window.''

''Really?'' said Kyra, her disbelief showing plainly in her surprise.

''Yes,'' Melvin answered somewhat primly and defensively. ''I had gone down to the train to see that our things were brought up to the house—they'd been forgotten in the general turmoil of our arrival, and I couldn't dress for dinner without them. I was just returning across the lawn when I saw this *person* leap from a window, right through the glass and all, and run toward the creek. Without thinking, I followed. I don't know *what* I would have done if I'd caught up, but when I got to the side of the creek behind the kennels there was no one in sight. Whoever it was had simply disappeared. Hid in the bushes, I suppose."

"This person you saw was wearing a maid's uniform?" Kyra asked.

"Yes," answered Melvin. "Black and white, just like the ones the rest of the staff use—but . . ."

"But it didn't look like a woman," Kyra completed for him.

"Yes, how did you know?" Melvin asked, amazed, then suddenly he added it all up. "It was your window, wasn't it? Are you all right? Were you hurt?" He blanched, and there was genuine concern in his voice. Perhaps he was really a decent person, underneath all of his irritating mannerisms.

"I'm all right," said Kyra, finishing her examination of Juliette's maid. "And this one will be fine, too. Her tea was drugged just enough to put her soundly to sleep for a while. But we need to find Alma."

"Who's Alma?" Melvin and Drogan asked in unison.

"The *real* maid," Kyra shot back. Then she turned to the little group that had gathered in the hallway by the door. "If two of you could take over walking Juliette, Melvin and Mr. . . . er . . . Asquith could go with me. And Edna, please go down and inform the staff that dinner is to be delayed an hour."

"Pandora and I will see to Juliette," volunteered Sir Randolph, British gallantry overpowering his usual inability to take decisive action.

"Oh, yes, the poor dear!" exclaimed his wife. "I feel so sorry for her! You don't think she'll . . . er . . . you know . . . all over my evening gown, do you? Or Randolph's dinner jacket? Should we perhaps cover ourselves with towels?"

When the Roseberrys were properly reassured and instructed in how to keep Juliette moving, Kyra and her two assistants left in search of Alma. They found her bound and gagged, wearing only her camisole and petticoat, on the floor of a little service room containing cleaning things, an ironing board, and a little charcoal brazier for heating an iron quickly.

They untied her and began to chafe her hands and feet to renew the circulation that had been cut off by the tight ropes. She sat up slowly, shaking her head as if to clear it. Kyra felt the left side and found the lump she'd expected.

"Did you see anything before he hit you?" she asked kindly.

"Yes'm!" came the answer as Alma's inherent cheerfulness began to reassert itself. "Theah's not much that sneaks up on Alma without bein' seen! An' this'un wuz th' ugliest thang Ah evuh seen. Even uglier'n me!" She said this last with a chuckle and added, "People think Ah don't knows how ugly Ah is, but that ain't somethin' that's easy t'scape. But this fellah . . ."

"Would you recognize him again?" asked Kyra.

" 'Course Ah would. Ah nevuh forgets nobody's face, an' *his* wuz one *nobody* would've forgot." Kyra smiled at Alma's clever playing with words—she was clearly much smarter than she appeared. It had probably saved her life and might save the lives of others yet.

"Could you describe him?" Kyra asked her.

Alma thought for a moment, then began to speak slowly with her eyes closed, as if she were looking at a picture in her mind. "He wuz thin, but *real* strong, an' he did'n' have no hair on his head, an' only *one* eyebrow that went all th' way 'cross ovuh his eyes, which were squinty little black thangs, even squintier'n mine." To illustrate her point, she opened her eyes and pulled at the edges, frowning at the same time so that her eyebrows came together. The effect was genuinely repulsive.

Alma closed her eyes again and continued. "He wuz wearin' a long gray coat o' some sort Ah nevuh seen before, 'cept th' colluh looked somethin' like th' one th' preacher wears, only it wuz gray like th' rest. An' he had baggy black pants like 'jamas and he had tiny little feet in *slippers* with pointy toes.'' Then she added as an afterthought, ''An' his skin wuz all yeller, like when Ah had the swamp sickness.''

Kyra looked at Drogan and could see that he was thinking the same thing she was, then he said in his best British accent, ''By Jove! I think the fellow's an Oriental! Have you ever seen a Chinaman before, my dear?'' This last was addressed to Alma, who shook her head.

''Theah wuz one on 'splay at th' fair last yeah, but Ah only had a penny left an' Ah went in t'see the snake lady instead.''

Kyra pulled the strand of gray wool from her pocket and showed it to Alma. ''Was this the color of his coat?'' she asked.

''Yes. That wuz it 'xactly,'' answered Alma, fingering the piece. ''An' that's what it felt like, too 'cuz Ah grabbed aholt of him when he wuz tryin' ta hit me.''

''Don't the Chinese wear silk, not wool?'' asked Melvin, who had been watching the scene silently up to this point.

''You're right,'' agreed Kyra, looking at the little piece of fiber with a puzzled expression. ''The Chinese don't like wool. They find it too harsh against their skin, so that if they use it at all it's as wadding inside quilted silk clothing.''

''Isn't it much more likely that what this young woman is describing is one of the convicts who escaped from the Virginia penitentiary last week? The newspapers said they were wearing gray woolen shirts and that one of them was just recovering from malaria, which would account for his yellow skin and pinched look, wouldn't it?'' Melvin suggested. ''He could have been hiding in the woods nearby and his appearance in the midst of the rest of this may be purely coincidental—he may have come in looking for food, or something to steal to sell for food.''

Kyra was unconvinced by Melvin's theory but could offer nothing better herself, so she said, ''Perhaps we should all retire to our quarters and prepare for dinner—whatever else happens, we must eat anyway."

"A topping suggestion!" agreed Drogan alias Asquith. "By the way, Mrs. McMasters, did you happen to find a pot of red paint in your room?"

"I most certainly did," she said, smiling as she remembered Edna's hysterics.

"I do hope it didn't spoil anything," Drogan continued as Melvin looked mystified, then suddenly irritated.

"This has been a day so full of the unexplained that I suppose a pot of paint shouldn't matter." The little man sighed. "But if you would be so kind as to explain what you're talking about, it would be one less thing on my mind." He said this with such heartfelt weariness that even Kyra felt sorry for him—perhaps he was a much nicer person than she'd given him credit for.

"Of course, my dear man!" exclaimed Drogan. "I would be ever so happy to clear up this one mystery, even if I am incapable of clearing up any of the others.

"I am an artist," he said as if he were talking to a petulant child, "a member of the British Royal Academy. I specialize in landscapes and hunting scenes and I came to paint tomorrow's hunt, by special permission of Senator Howard, who is an old friend of my family. When I arrived this afternoon, I was naturally shocked to learn what had happened to Nathaniel and I offered to leave immediately. The senator himself, however, insisted that I stay and requested that I do a memorial painting of the hunt that his son founded. Of course, I couldn't refuse. He even arranged for me to use one of the rooms on this floor, adjoining his own suite—which is how I became involved in all of this.

"I was making use of the time before dinner," he continued, "to prepare some paints for tomorrow. I had ground the raw pigments and needed to add the linseed oil and emulsifier, but the light in my room was not adequate to give true shades. So I went into the hall where the setting sun shone through the big window at the end. There I began to mix my pot of scarlet paint, which is *most* important when doing a hunt scene, don't you know."

"Yes, of course," agreed Melvin, still looking mystified.

"I had just started when I heard sounds of struggling from Mrs. McMasters's room. When my knock was greeted by further sounds of struggle, I simply forgot the pot of paint in my hand and barged through the door. I must have thrown the paint pot onto the bed with the afghan I tossed over Mrs. McMasters, who had been overpowered by the man you saw leap from her window."

"It sounds as if Kyra was very fortunate that you were given a shady room," Melvin suggested, clearly having understood the parts of the story Drogan delicately left unspoken. "And I'm very fortunate that you were both able to be so very helpful with my wife."

"Think nothing of it," Drogan said magnanimously. "I'm sure you would have done the same for anyone else yourself."

"I wouldn't have known what to do," Melvin said with uncharacteristic candor. In the same vein, he turned to Kyra and added, "Juliette and I do have our differences, as I'm sure you know, but I do care for her more than I can say, and I shall be eternally grateful to you for saving her." His eyes were misty, and he paused for a moment to regain control before saying, "If you will please make excuses for me at dinner, I believe I'll stay with her to make sure that nothing else happens."

"Of course," said Kyra. "I'm sure everyone will understand."

CHAPTER 7

Hold Hard

DINNER promised to be more tense and awkward than Kyra had expected. In spite of the hour's delay, Gerald had not returned in time to go in with everyone else, so Kyra was escorted to her place by a man who introduced himself as Poultney Bigelow from Oyster Bay, Long Island.

She was perplexed that none of the Daisy Hill Hunt Club members had volunteered to escort her and still more puzzled that they all seemed unwilling to even speak to her. During the brief gathering in the main parlors before dinner, where light aperitifs were served, she had noticed Edna Harding talking to one small group after another in undertones, glancing occasionally in Kyra's direction. Kyra had assumed that she was filling them in on what had happened upstairs, but that would have resulted in sympathy and concern, not ostracism. Whatever in the world could Edna have been saying?

During the first course, an excellent cold consommé, Kyra noticed that Randolph Roseberry and Tobias La-Farge excused themselves and left the table, a breach of good manners that caused a number of raised eyebrows. When they resumed their seats a few minutes later, they both glanced in her direction, quickly averting their eyes and pretending to eat when she returned their looks.

Not long afterward, Gerald entered the room and took his seat on the far side of the table. He glanced at her quizzically, then looked toward Roseberry and LaFarge and back at her. What was going on?

Kyra went through the rest of the dinner mechanically, barely tasting the expensive wines and eating little of the excellent fare—Thurston had one of the best French chefs in America. She was hardly aware of what she was saying to her dinner partner. The scene was like something in a nightmare: the long T-shaped table with its starched white linen covering, the antique silver and glittering crystal, the fine bone china with the Howard insignia embossed in gold, and the elaborate flower arrangements seemed larger, brighter, and more intense than in ordinary life, as did the men in their formal dinner jackets and the ladies in bare-shouldered evening gowns. Diamonds, pearls, emeralds, and other rare gems glittered at their necks, wrists, and fingers. It was a show of wealth and power such as is rarely gathered together in one room.

Conversation, which would normally have been animated and full of excitement about the races just concluded and the next day's hunt, was muted and restrained. Kyra attributed the dampened atmosphere to the day's tensions intensified by close quarters and the need to observe polite manners. In addition, Senator Howard sat glumly at the head of the table, saying little and staring off into space between courses, although he ate with considerable relish. He was noted for having an appetite that nothing spoiled and he was living up to that reputation.

Kyra noticed the portrait of Grandfather Howard at the end of the room and wondered what he would have thought of the current situation. He had hosted many a hunt dinner, some of which may not have been too different from this one in terms of tension and the undercurrent of suspicion and intrigue. He had been a kind of

Southern Scarlet Pimpernel. On the surface he'd appeared to be nothing but a rich playboy, interested only in his hounds and horses, not to mention pretty women. As far as anyone knew at the time, he'd whiled away his days in purely idle pastimes—he'd seemed to have no interest at all in the great political and social issues taking place around him. He'd even paid for a substitute to serve in his place in the Civil War, which was a perfectly legal practice in those days but not the gentlemanly thing to do.

In actuality, however, the orginal Nathaniel Howard had been one of the most active members of the underground railroad, assisting runaway slaves to escape to Canada, or at least to areas where they could easily get to Canada. In fact, he'd taken the term "railroad" quite literally and used the spur line that ran past Hopsworth to transport the escapees. He'd even had special cars constructed with false floors they could hide under, and rumor had it that Hopsworth manor itself had secret hiding places in the walls where the slaves would wait until they could be put on a train. Kyra wondered if any of those passageways or cubbyholes had ever been found.

Adrift in her own musings, Kyra had almost forgotten about Mr. Bigelow, who was seated at her right. He finally caught her attention by saying, "I've been looking forward to meeting you for some time, as one of my close friends and neighbors has spoken very highly of you on several occasions."

"Oh?" said Kyra, frowning slightly, trying to recall the people she knew from Oyster Bay. "Who might that be?"

"Theodore Roosevelt," he said with a grin, appreciating her surprise. "He has a house near us on Sagamore Hill, and when he's there, he and I often go for a ride in the mornings. It was on one of those rides that he first mentioned a charming senator's wife who used to be a lady detective and who hunts as well as a man."

"Clearly you can see that our honorable Mr. President has fallen prey to delusions." Kyra smiled, pleased nevertheless.

"May we all be deluded by so beautiful a woman!" was the gallant retort. Kyra smiled again, grateful to Mr. Bigelow for his gentlemanly kindness and sense of tact in a difficult situation.

Lady Pandora provided the dinner's other light moment when she turned to Philip Drogan, alias Paul Leonard Asquith III, and said brightly, "I hear that you paint?" to which he replied, "Yes." She asked solemnly, "What do you paint?" With equal seriousness and great courtesy, he answered, "Pictures." Satisfied, Lady Pandora returned to her plate of food. Kyra couldn't help but wonder if Pandora had thought perhaps Philip painted barns or houses.

Immediately after dessert, an enormous soufflé flambé, the ladies adjourned once more to the parlors while the gentlemen stayed at table for brandy and cigars. Kyra found herself again excluded by the Daisy Hill contingent, who stayed in a knot at one side of the room and whispered in low tones, occasionally glancing in her direction. Their behavior baffled her. What *could* be going through their minds? She tried one theory after another as she spent the requisite time chatting with some of the women from the other clubs about their horses and children—in that order. She had long ago observed that foxhunting ladies were generally more interested in their mounts than in their offspring. They certainly spent more time with the former than the latter, at least until the children were old enough to hunt, too. But, Kyra thought to herself, the children were probably better off in the care of their nannies and governesses, based on what she had seen of their empty-headed mothers. She had long wondered why men who were intelligent, well educated, and successful would marry women who had so little to offer. Hunt parties weren't the worst of it; she often felt lonely and out of place at social and political gatherings that she and Gerald attended in Washington, where she was expected to sit and talk only with the other wives. Most of them knew little about what their husbands did and cared even less. Their attitudes had astounded Kyra at first, but she had gradually gotten used to it. She could hold up her end of pleasantly meaningless conversations, although she could not resist occasionally throwing in a remark about some international event or controversial political issue. At such times the other ladies would lapse into surprised, almost hurt silence, or say something like, 'Oh, I leave all of that to my husband! He tells me not to worry my head about politics and I *always* do what he tells me!' Someone else would quip, 'Only when it suits what *you* want to do!' and everyone would laugh, the tension broken, and all would return to safe topics of conversation.

Kyra's position that evening was not too much different from usual. Most of the women she knew regarded her with some suspicion to begin with, because of her former career as a private detective and because she was known to take an active part in assisting and advising her senator husband. It was rumored that she had even accompanied him to some secret conferences with President Theodore Roosevelt. Whether that was true or not, the McMasterses were frequent visitors at the White House. Kyra had met and become friends with Edith Wharton at one of the Roosevelts' private family luncheons. "Teddy" had brought them together at one point, saying in an amused tone, "I always wanted you two strong-minded ladies to meet, as I knew you'd either hate each other instantly or become the best of friends—in either case, you'd be interesting to watch!"

Mrs. Wharton had quipped, "If you're not careful, Mr. President, I'll write you into one of my books and she'll involve you in one of her cases!"

Always the gallant, Roosevelt had responded, "In either event, I'd be honored."

Such episodes did nothing to improve Kyra's relations with her peers in Washington and Virginia. Tonight, however, one of the ladies unwittingly provided Kyra with a piece of information that could be the key to solving the mystery of Nathaniel's death—if it didn't prevent her from working on the case altogether.

While she was talking to a group of the Newcastle wives, one of them asked Kyra, "Is it true that your Huntsman's wife wished him dead in front of the whole hunt, just a few days before he was killed?"

"I wasn't aware of anything like that," Kyra responded with a pang of fear, remembering Edna's earlier comment, Eldridge P. Cooper's diatribe, and the fact that she had missed last Sunday's hunt at Hopsworth because of her sick children. What had happened? And why wasn't anyone telling her about it?

Just then Edna Harding spoke from behind her. "*Now* I see that you're getting close to the real crux of the matter!"

"What is this about Nadine wishing Nathaniel dead?" Kyra asked in her politest tone, refusing to be baited.

"*Well*, I suppose I might as well be the one to tell you, since I was right there," Edna pronounced in her most self-important tones.

"Yes, please do," Kyra said as demurely as she could manage.

"It was after the hunt," Edna explained. "Nathaniel was in the kennel, putting the hounds away, when there was a perfectly *ghastly* noise of hounds growling and fighting—it was a *horrible* fracas. Becky Hollingshood turned to Nadine and said, 'Doesn't it make you nervous to have your husband in the midst of all of that?' and Nadine retorted in the *nastiest* way, 'No, if he doesn't come out again, I'll inherit Hopsworth and all of his insurance money!' So now what do you think about your charming friend? Do you still maintain that she's innocent? Or perhaps you're covering up for *someone else* much closer to home, if you get my meaning. I saw you out riding last night."

Kyra certainly did get Edna's meaning. Edna had been the one spreading stories to Eldridge Cooper and the members of the Daisy Hill Hunt Club. Kyra had her to thank for that evening's cold reception. Could she continue on the case? she wondered. With such a burden of suspicion on her, she might just be a hindrance. She needed to talk the matter over with Gerald, and with Drogan, too, if possible.

After a suitable amount of time had elapsed, Kyra excused herself to go to the powder room. As she had expected, Gerald was waiting for her in the hall outside, having similarly excused himself from the men's gathering. "Are you all right?" were the first words out of his mouth as he reached to embrace her. "I ran into Lord Randolph and Tobias as I was coming in and they told me that you'd had a close call before dinner."

"Yes, I'm fine," Kyra assured him. "Did they say anything else?"

"A whole bunch of malarky that made no sense whatsoever!" Gerald said disgustedly. "I have less respect for their judgment every day."

"Well, that 'malarky,' as you call it, is causing me a great deal of difficulty right now—if it's what I think it is."

"That you . . ."

"Yes, that I'm one of the prime suspects." Kyra quickly explained Edna Harding's apparent role in arousing the sheriff's suspicions against her, concluding, "I don't know at this point if I can go on with the investigation. Have you seen Inspector Drogan?"

"Drogan? *He's* here?"

"Yes, I forgot you didn't know," said Kyra, running her hands wearily over her face. "Yes, he's here in disguise. In fact, you sat quite close to him at dinner—the British painter."

"I *thought* there was something familiar about him, but I couldn't quite put my finger on it!" exclaimed Gerald.

At that moment, Drogan himself came out of the dining room and walked toward the McMasterses. "By Jove, I hoped I'd find you two out here!" he said in his most jovial British accent. "Not a very private spot for a tête-à-tête, though!'' he added, taking a quick step and pulling open the parlor door, which had been standing ajar. Kyra felt a chill run up her spine. Had she simply failed to close the door all the way when she went out, or was someone listening? And if someone *was* listening, had she blown Drogan's cover?

"Oh! *Excuse* me, ladies!'' Drogan was saying. "I must have taken a wrong turn! These big houses *do* confuse one, don't you know? Not that I wouldn't *prefer* having tea with such *gorgeous* beauties to smoking smelly old cigars with the beasts!'' With that, he bowed gallantly and closed the door on the burst of feminine giggles he had caused.

"No one was listening, as far as I could tell," he said to the McMasterses as he turned around. "But why don't we adjourn to the library?"

"A very good idea!'' agreed Gerald. "And I'm delighted to see you again, Philip,'' he added, extending his hand.

No sooner were they ensconced in the library, with the door closed securely behind them, than Kyra burst into tears. Gerald held her against his chest and comforted her while Drogan looked on in embarrassed silence. Finally her tears began to subside, and Drogan proffered his pocket handkerchief.

"I-I'm s-s-sorry,'' she gasped as she dabbed at her eyes with the starched white cloth.

"Sorry!'' Drogan practically exploded. "You wouldn't be *human* if you didn't cry a bit after what you've been through today. Just the way those monsters were treating you during dinner would be enough to curdle a Hun's blood. And after what happened upstairs! Are those people you consider friends?'' He paced the floor as he spoke, unable to contain his indignation. "I thought friends were people who stuck by you in times of trouble—these people seem willing to believe any rumor, as long as it exonerates them. As far as I can tell, the whole lot of them have guilty consciences!''

"They probably do,'' said Gerald with a puzzled expression. "But I fail to see . . .''

"Oh, you missed one of the most disgusting debacles I've ever witnessed. In the drawing room, before dinner, word had gotten out that Kyra is under suspicion for having assisted Nadine in killing Nathaniel—and her supposed friends were practically falling over each other to get away. Not *one* of them bothered to check the story out with her, or even made so much as an attempt to be objective about it, to 'consider the source,' as the phrase goes."

"N-n-none of them are really close friends, though," Kyra offered. "We hunt together, but none of them really *knows* me."

"You don't need to defend them," Drogan answered, still irate. "They seem to be doing a pretty good job of it themselves. From what I hear, anyway, some of them have reason to be afraid they'd fall under suspicion."

"How's that?" Gerald wanted to know.

"Some of them were criticizing Nathaniel rather sharply of late. They considered him too dictatorial, felt he ran the hunt only the way *he* saw fit, regardless of what anyone else wanted. There was a move afoot to convince Nathaniel to give up control of the hunt, to change it from a private pack to a hunt run by the members. They even wanted to put in a new huntsman."

"No! I don't believe it," Kyra exclaimed in complete surprise. "Nathaniel loved those hounds! They were like children to him! No one could have hunted them as well as he did. And *everyone* liked Nathaniel."

"Not everyone," corrected Gerald sadly. "I *had* heard some of what Philip's talking about, but I didn't bother you with it. I know how you hate idle gossip and backbiting, and that's all I thought it was—people who could never achieve what Nathaniel's done on their own, people who buoy up their little egos by nitpicking and faultfinding. You thought highly of Nathaniel, Kyra, but that's partly because you're a competent person and naturally generous in your assessment of others. Nathaniel *did* have his faults, one of which was a tendency to do things the way *he* wanted. That rubbed some people the wrong way—but I don't see it as motive enough for *murder*." This last was directed at Drogan.

"Not just that," said the detective. "I suspect that at least *one* of the Daisy Hill Hunt Club members had a stronger incentive than the plans for changing the hunt's structure. For instance, your wife found some papers which indicate that there's a project to subdivide Hopsworth."

"Yes, I'd heard rumors to that effect, but I didn't take them seriously, " said Gerald. "The Howards seem to have enough money to do whatever they want. Why would they sell off the family estate? Especially when it's so conveniently located, less than half a day's ride, or only an hour by train or automobile from the White House?"

"Does Thurston have plans to retire soon?" Drogan wanted to know. "That could account for it."

"No, he's just started a new term," Gerald answered. "He's as involved in politics as he's ever—" Gerald's sentence was cut short as Kyra swayed and nearly fainted. Both men stepped forward to catch her, then eased her down on the sofa. Drogan pulled a little vial of smelling salts from his dinner jacket pocket, pulled out the stopper, and waved it under her nose until she gasped and coughed.

"It's a jolly good thing I've gotten in the habit of carrying salts for the wilting-flower society ladies I deal with," he kidded her in his Paul Leonard Asquith accent. "But I never expected to have to use them on *you!*"

"I'm just out of practice," she said as soon as she was able to talk. "I'm not used to dealing with murder and violence and suspicion anymore."

"No woman should ever have to deal with what you've dealt with today!" Drogan exclaimed.

"For that matter," contributed Gerald, "few men I know could go through what you've been through today without breaking down in some way or other."

"Most men would use a day like this as an excuse to

drink themselves into oblivion,'' interjected Drogan. ''By the way, doesn't the senator keep a bottle of Napoleon brandy in here somewhere?''

''Yes, would you like some?'' answered Gerald, surprised.

''I think Kyra should have a big snifter of it'' was the reply.

''Excellent idea,'' Gerald said, his eyes full of concern for his wife. He was wondering if she was pregnant again, but it wouldn't do to say anything in front of Drogan. Instead, he busied himself in a cabinet behind the desk, saying, ''Luckily, I know just where Thurston keeps his liquor.''

While Gerald poured out three drinks, Drogan moved two chairs next to the sofa. Kyra watched them both silently. Drogan's naturally blond hair was dyed mousy brown for the sake of his disguise, but he still had a blond's pinkish complexion. He provided a sharp contrast to Gerald's black hair and olive skin. In appearance, no two men could be more different, but in personality they were quite similar. Both had a driving need to do good in the world, which had led them into their respective professions. And both of them were in love with her. The thought ran through her suddenly like an electric shock. How could she have been so blind before? Of course. It would explain much of Drogan's behavior. She felt a sudden wave of pity for him—but she couldn't deny that she also felt pleased and flattered. She thought a lot of Philip, and if she hadn't already met Gerald when she'd come to know Drogan, who could tell what might have happened? Just then, Gerald handed her the brandy in its fragile, bubble-shaped glass and gave her a quizzical look.

''You must be feeling better,'' he said. ''You're smiling.''

''Yes,'' she answered, surprised again. ''Yes, I *am* feeling better.''

''Then let's make some plans for tonight,'' interjected

Drogan. "I have a feeling it's going to be long and eventful. And there's the hunt tomorrow, too."

"Do you plan to ride?" Kyra asked. "Or will you stand to one side in your smock and daub at your canvas?"

"I plan to do a bit of both," answered Drogan. "I shall be making oil sketches during the preliminary gathering and stirrup cup ceremony, then I shall whip off my smock, don my riding jacket, and be off with the hounds!"

"You sound genuinely enthusiastic about it," Kyra said. "I thought you'd not ridden much."

"Before I went to England on that case, I'd only sat astride a plow horse once or twice when I was a little boy," Drogan said. Kyra tried to picture him as a little boy and smiled again. Taking her smile as encouragement, he continued, "But my host in England was firmly of the opinion that I could never paint a hunt scene properly if I hadn't ridden out a few times and actually experienced the hunt. He gave me some quick pointers and mounted me on a horse which he assured me was the gentlest thing alive. It was. And I'd never had a more wonderful time in my life."

"I'll bet you were sore the next day!" Gerald laughed. Drogan's little story had broken the general tension.

"I couldn't even get out of bed," groaned Drogan. "My host had to send two footmen to pull me to my feet—then he put me back on a horse again! I thought he was a sadist for sure, but he assured me it was the only way to deal with saddle soreness. And he was right again. After a few days of hunting every day, I wasn't sore at all. And I was addicted to the sport. I can't afford to do it on a regular basis in New York, of course, but when Senator Howard called Pinkerton last night with a request for a detective at a hunt meet, I jumped at the chance—no pun intended."

"So *that's* how you wound up investigating Nathaniel's death," Gerald said. "And here I thought it was Kyra that brought you all the way down here."

"Hunt or no hunt, I would have come for Kyra,"

Philip said with just enough seriousness to cause Gerald to give him a quick, searching glance.

"But let's do get down to business," Drogan continued smoothly. "Kyra's filled me in on your activities today, and I assume you heard about what happened to her earlier this evening?"

"Yes, do you have any idea . . ."

"I have some conjectures, that's all at this point. But I think we can be pretty sure that your being called away was no coincidence."

"Yes, the mare was perfectly fine when I got there—no labor, no problems. Kepple was surprised to see me—absolutely denied having telephoned, though I would have *sworn* it was his voice."

"Then what kept you so long?" Kyra asked, wondering if something else had happened.

"The children heard Becky's automobile drive up and saw me through the nursery window. They were just ready to go to bed, and as soon as I knew that Lady Emilie was fine, I couldn't say no to tucking them in. They wanted a good-night story, so I told them all about how brave and dashing their mother was today. They send you hugs and kisses."

Kyra felt tears behind her eyelids again and swallowed hard. She noticed Drogan turn away for a moment, too, and clear his throat before turning back with a serious look. "Please excuse me," he said to Kyra, "I forgot you were now the mother of three young children—it's really not fair to have you expose yourself to such danger. You should go home immediately and watch after your little ones."

"And desert the case now?" Kyra retorted. "No, thank you. I'll finish what I've begun. My only concern was that the suspicion I'm under would hamper my investigation, but as you were talking I thought of a plan."

"We'll consider it," said Gerald. "But now that Philip's brought the matter up, I have to say I agree with him. What would happen to the children if you were killed?''

"I don't intend to be killed," answered Kyra firmly. "And I'll tell you about my plan in a minute. First, I need to get the night operator started on a long line call to New York—it always seems to take twice as long at night, for some reason." With that, she opened her reticule and took out the same little notepad she'd had in her riding habit pocket that morning. Then she rose from the sofa and gently picked up the telephone receiver from the instrument on Thurston's desk. She listened for a moment, to make sure no one else was on the line, then rang the operator. When she'd given the number and hung up again, she turned back to the two men and said, "I overheard Jerome Cushing call that number this morning, but this is the first chance I've had to check it out."

"Do you think *he's* involved in Nathaniel's death?" Gerald asked. "Why, he could afford to buy Hopsworth and everything on it about eight times over—why would *he* be involved?"

"I don't know," answered Kyra. "But we have to check out every possible lead, and he called this number under rather suspicious circumstances."

"She's right," Drogan interjected. "People become involved in murders for some very strange reasons—something that seems inconsequential to one person may be very important to another."

"Still, I wouldn't like to antagonize someone like Cushing without a pretty good reason," argued Gerald, his politician's instincts surfacing. Cushing had made some large contributions to Gerald's last campaign, with no strings attached. Supporters like that were hard to come by.

"I'm just checking out a number," Kyra reassured him, aware of his concern. "And while we're waiting for the operator to call back, let me tell you what I've been thinking."

Over the next few minutes Kyra outlined her plan to

the two men. They argued a bit and made several suggestions, but in the end they agreed that it was the best approach. They had just come to this conclusion when the telephone rang and Kyra quickly picked up the receiver.

"Hello? Yes, this is Mrs. McMasters. Yes, thank you, put it through, please." There was a short silence, then: "Extension four fifteen, please." A moment later: "Are you certain? That was four one five. How long has it been vacant? No, thank you very much." Kyra replaced the receiver with a perplexed air.

"What's wrong?" Gerald asked.

"That was the Ashley Park Hotel in New York—it may be pure coincidence, but that's one of the chain owned by Lord Randolph and Lady Pandora." She paused, then added, "According to the operator, the extension Cushing called this morning is located in a room that has been vacant for renovations all week."

"She was certain?" Drogan wanted to know.

"Absolutely. Four rooms on that floor were damaged by a fire two weeks ago and they've been vacant ever since."

"Could someone have just been using the telephone?" Gerald suggested.

"The operator says the telephones have been removed to prevent the workmen from using them. I suppose it's possible that I wrote down the wrong extension, but I doubt it."

"I doubt it, too," said Drogan. "And the big question is whether this implicates Lord Randolph and Lady Pandora. Are they involved with Cushing on some deal that would have resulted in Nathaniel's death, or is it coincidence that Cushing was calling someone staying at the Ashley Park?"

"It *is* possible," said Kyra excitedly, "that someone could have *tapped* into that line from another room—but the main operator would have to know to put a call through, and she didn't seem to."

"But wouldn't there have been a different operator during the day?" Gerald contributed.

"Of course! That's the answer!" Kyra exclaimed. "Now all we have to do is to find out who that was and question her."

"I can take care of that," offered Drogan, stepping to the desk and picking up the telephone. Within a few minutes he had put in his own long line call to an assistant in New York. "Isn't modern technology wonderful?" he said with a grin as they waited for the return call. "It's making it harder every day for criminals to get away with their schemes."

"Or easier," suggested Gerald. "Depending on your point of view. After all, they have access to the same technology, don't they?"

"You're absolutely right," Drogan agreed. "But I still think the good guys are at least a step ahead."

"Let's hope so, especially in the present case," retorted the young senator from New York. The expected call came through and Drogan gave his assistant the necessary instructions, including twenty-four-hour surveillance on the hotel and on room 415.

"I'll check back with you early tomorrow morning," he concluded, then hung up and turned to the Mc-Masterses. "Thurston said to spare no expense, and I think it's a worthwhile lead, don't you?"

"Yes, I think you're right to check it out thoroughly," conceded Gerald. "But you know, although I'd put nothing past Lord Randolph and his Lady, I still find it hard to believe that Cushing is involved in something shady. It's not just politics, either. The one time I met him, I liked him, and my instincts are not usually wrong on that score."

"Stranger things have happened," Drogan countered. "But isn't there a real old-fashioned hunt ball about to start somewhere around here? I've been hearing music for the last ten minutes, and my feet are itching—not to mention my neck in this collar."

"I didn't know you danced," said Kyra. "Weren't you a Baptist minister's son?"

"They're the worst kind." Drogan winked. "But I must admit, I took up dancing at about the same time I took up foxhunting. The two go together, don't you know," he added, resuming his British accent and bearing. "So, pip pip now! Let's be off!"

With that, the three of them rose and left the library together, crossing the grand old mansion toward the ballroom, unaware that their progress was being watched by more than one pair of eyes. They made quite a picture, the slim figure of the golden-haired woman flanked on either side by a tall, good-looking man.

CHAPTER 8

Bad Game

As Hopsworth's ballroom was located at the other end of the mansion, the easiest way for Philip Drogan and the McMasterses to walk there was along the paths of one of the formal gardens, which had been lit softly with Japanese lanterns for the occasion. Along the way, they could see other couples and small groups of their fellow diners strolling toward the brightly lit room, among them Edna Harding talking earnestly to Lord Randolph and Lady Pandora. Hadley Turbot walked next to them, pudgy and looking terribly uncomfortable in formal evening attire. Kyra hoped that the lesson Benny had given him that afternoon would ensure that Hadley behaved himself that night. She felt a bit sorry for the boy, tagging along after Edna without friends his own age, but he was so irritating that it was hard to feel too much pity for him.

A stream of carriages and automobiles moved slowly past the main entrance to the ballroom, depositing ladies in low-cut evening gowns and gentlemen in tuxedos. Through the open windows, the orchestra could be heard tuning up. Occasional trills of music floated out on the warm evening air rich with the scent of magnolia, wisteria, and lilacs.

"How could one human being possibly kill another in the midst of such beauty and serenity?" Drogan said, voicing what all three of them were feeling. As they entered the ballroom, a footman wearing the Hopsworth livery announced them formally to the assemblage and a few heads turned in their direction. Then the orchestra began to play again and there was a general stir as couples made their way out onto the floor for a waltz.

Hopsworth's ballroom was one of the most beautiful Kyra had ever seen—and after nearly seven years as a United States Senator's wife she had seen many ballrooms, both in the United States and abroad. It had been designed and decorated in the early 1870s for Thurston's young bride, Sarah, who had loved dancing more than anything in the world. In her enthusiasm, she had hired the architect who had designed the famous ballroom in Mrs. Astor's mansion at Fifth Avenue and Thirty-fourth Street in New York City. Sarah had attended her first ball there.

Like Mrs. Astor's, Sarah's ballroom sported a parquet floor that was kept waxed to mirrorlike perfection at all times, but there the similarity ended. Sarah had instructed that the walls literally be paneled with six-foot mirrors, each one held in place by elaborately carved mahogany woodwork, so that the dancers could see themselves whirling and twirling and the illusion of a much greater space was created. Above the mirrors, the walls were painted a silvery gray, merging into a sky blue on the ceiling, from which hung four enormous crystal chandeliers.

The only change Thurston had made in the ballroom when he'd renovated the mansion a few years earlier was to clean the walls and ceiling thoroughly and to install an electric generator to light the chandeliers. He was a fastidiously tidy man and had never liked the smoke and smudge created by gas jets. When Kyra had first seen the difference, she had immediately agreed with the wisdom of Thurston's decision: The specially crafted light bulbs, made to look like flames, illuminated the room with such clarity that for the first time she could appreciate the fine carving on the woodwork. The cleaning had also uncovered a beautifully executed ceiling painting that depicted Pegasus and Mercury winging their way to Olympus with a message for Zeus from the mortals below. Thurston had grimaced when Kyra admired the painting, saying, "I was a young senator serving my first term, and my dear Sarah intended the painting as an allegory of me carrying messages from my constituents to Washington—she was always an aristocrat at heart. But as I was an egalitarian, born and bred, this consarned ballroom of Sarah's caused me no end of grief."

Like Mrs. Astor's, Hopsworth's ballroom could comfortably hold four hundred people, and it had been rumored that the Howards were trying to start an exclusive "Virginia 400" club to rival the famous New York 400. Thurston, however, put the notion to rest for good. Hopsworth balls and parties included *all* of the Howards' friends—government clerks, office workers, and neighbors less fortunate than they as well as members of society. He was often heard to say, "The fact that I inherited a bit of money and a piece of land doesn't make me one whit better than any other man in this blessed country—or woman, either."

Thurston had insisted that the Daisy Hill Hunt Club's Ball conform to the tradition he began years before despite the disgruntlement of some members. He resisted their protests and proceeded to invite a number of nonhunting people from the neighborhood and from Washington.

One among these guests was Egerton Harding, another of Edna Harding's nephews, from her deceased husband's side of the family. Egerton was a fairly successful novelist and travel writer and had been one of the original members of the Daisy Hill Hunt Club. But he had lost most of his fortune through a stockbroker's mismanagement a year or so earlier. Far from being devastated, he had almost cheerfully sold his hunters

115

and whatever else he had of value to pay back some of his creditors, leaving on a speaking tour soon after to earn the rest. Edna, in particular, thought he was crazy.

"I've never heard of such a thing!" she had exclaimed. "Your bankruptcy was your broker's fault, not yours. Why should *you* pay back your creditors? Especially tradesmen and such. They just make up their losses by charging the next person higher prices."

"I bought things from those 'tradesmen,' as you call them, in good faith," Egerton had replied, "and I intend to live up to that faith."

Instead of admiring his honesty and standing by him, many of Egerton's "friends" began to leave him off their invitation lists and to whisper that they did so because of his fallen circumstances. Kyra considered such stories to be mindless blather and had shocked the other ladies by stoutly defending him. Now, when she saw Egerton across the room, she smiled warmly and acknowledged his bow with a nod.

At that moment, a servant came up to Gerald and said, "Mr. Oswald Harding would like to speak with you in the second anteroom, Senator."

Gerald met Kyra's eyes briefly, then turned to Drogan. "Would you mind keeping my wife company until I return? Oswald has been nervous and upset all day, and if I'm right, he's worked himself into a dither about taking over as Huntsman tomorrow—he's probably terrified, though he'd never admit it. But he'll do fine in the actual crunch, which is exactly what I'll tell him, don't you agree?"

This last question had been addressed to Kyra, who replied, "I'm sure he'll do fine. Tell him I said so. And tell him that Nadine was doing much better before dinner—I know he's concerned about her."

With that, Gerald was gone. Philip looked at her with almost a young boy's bashfulness and said, "Would you like to dance?" Kyra had hardly nodded her head before she found herself whirling around the dance floor in the detective's arms. She was frankly surprised at how good he was. Even Gerald didn't dance with such total mastery. Within a few seconds, Kyra felt her mind and body give way to the rhythm and movement of the music. For as long as the piece lasted, nothing else existed in the world but her body pressed against Philip's, the two of them moving in perfect unison. When the orchestra finally stopped, Kyra was flushed and shaking. She and Drogan stood for a moment, looking into each other's eyes. He regained control of his senses first, shook his head as if he were awakening from a dream, and escorted her to the side.

"I'll get you a cup of punch," he mumbled, then fled in the direction of the refreshment table.

Kyra was still watching his tall, almost painfully thin figure make its way though the crowd when she saw Pandora Roseberry standing a few feet away, chatting with Tobias LaFarge's wife, Justinia. Next to them stood three of the five LaFarge teenage daughters, giggling and poking each other with their fans as they watched the other two, who were out on the dance floor. Kyra smiled and walked toward this happy group, having temporarily forgotten earlier events. She was abruptly brought back to reality when Pandora gave her a chilling look and pointedly turned her back.

Kyra stopped on the spot, almost reeling from the impact of Pandora's hateful stare. Then she felt a hand on her shoulder. "Kyra!" a familiar voice said. "I'm so glad to see you!"

Kyra turned to face Egerton Harding, who embraced her enthusiastically, then whisked her out onto the dance floor. "I saw the look the sweet Lady gave you and I want you to know that I don't care what anyone says, or thinks," he announced emphatically. "*I* like you and I think you're the one person in this crazy hunt club *least* likely to commit murder. I could even picture Aunt Edna with a dagger in her hand before I could see you in that position! No, I think you're the victim of gossip generated by a bunch of empty-headed socialites without enough to keep them busy. They're jealous of you,

117

Kyra, and they're just venting their petty malice and frustrations."

"Thank you, Egerton," Kyra answered, feeling warmed by his friendship. She gave his hand a little squeeze. "I'm glad to see you back again. Was your speaking tour a success?"

"Absolutely, and I'm planning another for the fall. To Europe this time. I find I have a talent for speaking to groups—and there seems to be an insatiable appetite among the public to meet their authors. The average American is culturally starved and longs for something stimulating to think about—unlike *some* people we know who avoid thought and reflection as if they were poison. At any rate, I've found the whole thing enormously stimulating to my writing as well as to my own thought processes, which I must admit were beginning to stultify for lack of contact with thinking people—present company excepted, of course. But to make a long story short, I've begun a new novel, which I hope to finish this summer—and I owe it all to a crooked stockbroker!"

"That's wonderful." Kyra congratulated him. "I've always liked your fiction so much better than your travel writing and hoped you'd return to it someday. What is your new novel about?"

"That's a secret," he answered. Then a pained look crossed his face and he added, "As you know, I've always been a bit superstitious about letting people read my unfinished work—I always felt it would cause bad luck, but I thought that bad luck would simply be for the book, not—" He suddenly broke off, as if he had been talking in a dream, and added with forced cheerfulness, "But I'll see that you're the first to read the finished manuscript, if you like."

"Like! I'd love to!" Kyra answered, realizing suddenly how much she'd missed Egerton. He used to come to dinner frequently, and he was the one guest among the McMasterses' Washington acquaintance who loved to read and was as well versed as they were in history, literature, and the arts. They had lively discussions of the latest novels by Henry James and Mark Twain, not to mention Kyra's new friend, Edith Wharton, whom she had introduced to Egerton on one of Edith's trips to Washington.

"I see your husband looking for you over there," Egerton advised Kyra, "and that other fellow you were dancing with—I'd watch him, if I were you," he added teasingly.

"It was that obvious?" Kyra said, taken by surprise.

"Probably not to anyone who wasn't in love with you himself—but I should think that would cover at least half of the men in this room, if they were honest with themselves. Ah! Unrequited love!"

Kyra looked at him sharply, trying to determine how much of what he was saying was in jest, but he winked at her broadly and steered toward the spot where Gerald and Drogan were standing. On the way, however, he apparently saw something over her shoulder, for he tensed and his face grew hard. He said, "There *is* something I should tell you about, Kyra, but now's not the time. I need to check something out first. I'll try to catch you tomorrow before the hunt."

"Welcome back, Egerton," Gerald said heartily when he saw them. "We've missed you enormously, or perhaps it would be more accurate to say we've missed your incisive mind when it comes to analyzing the latest poem or story in *Scribner's*. Not to mention the books Kyra is continually buying—I would get away with reading only half as many, you know, if you were around to discuss them with her!"

"But then you'd miss half of the great literature of the new century," Egerton responded with a smile.

"Oh, no, I'd only miss the trash, because I'd take your recommendations on which ones were worth reading!"

"Touché!" Egerton laughed.

"And now," announced Gerald as the orchestra began a new piece, "I'm going to dance with my wife!" And he escorted her away from the others, onto the dance floor. Once there, however, he seemed preoccupied and tense, not at all his usual self. He danced as adroitly as ever, but Kyra could tell he wasn't really enjoying it.

"What did Oswald have to say?" she asked.

"I guessed right—he's worried about tomorrow. I tried to calm him down, but he *does* have real cause to be concerned."

"Why is that? Has something else gone wrong?"

"Michael is still missing, and he's the only professional Whipper-In Nathaniel had. Becky will be there, but she's still fairly new at it, and of course Oswald himself was Nathaniel's other whip. He's afraid he won't be able to control the hounds."

"And the result could be pandemonium, with injured horses and riders," Kyra finished for him. She had seen what could happen if a Huntsman's staff let the hounds get out of control and they ran riot. Even the most experienced, even-tempered horses sometimes caught the madness that infected the hounds at such times and ran amok, taking their helpless riders into bogs and over (or through) impossible fences. Not that it would happen as a matter of course, but Gerald was right: Oswald did have cause to worry.

"What did you suggest?" Kyra wanted to know.

"Well, I told him we still have Benny out searching for Michael, but even if he's found at this point, he's probably in no condition to be of much assistance tomorrow—he'll need to sleep off his drunk for several days."

"So what's the alternative?"

"I suggested that *you* ride as Whipper-In," Gerald said unexpectedly.

"Me!" Kyra exclaimed with disbelief, coming to a standstill. "I've never whipped before! Isn't there someone from one of the other hunts . . ."

"No one knows the terrain as well as you do. And no one is as well mounted—Diana can take you anywhere the hounds go, as fast as they choose to go, which can't be said of many horses. You also know how Nathaniel's hounds work, which is essential—you know which ones are likely to try to go off on their own and which ones can be reliably listened to. And you know their names.''

''Yes, but . . .''

''No buts about it, Kyra. You're the right person for the job. You may never have done it before, but with your trained mind and powers of observation, you know far more than many seasoned Whippers-In.''

''Gerald, I . . .'' Kyra began, then looked helplessly at him. Once his mind was made up about something, it was almost impossible to change. ''Let me think about it for a while,'' she finished lamely.

''Of course,'' he agreed. ''Take a while to get used to the idea.''

''Why don't *you* do it?'' she suddenly proposed.

''I need to ride with the visiting Masters,'' Gerald answered. ''There's been so much general upset this weekend, that I think the least I can do is to see that they have a pleasant chase. They'll want to stay ahead of the Field, as Tobias likes to take a more leisurely pace than they're used to.''

''Yes, he gets terribly red in the face every time we have a good run,'' agreed Kyra. ''I've been afraid several times that he was about to have an apoplectic fit.''

''So have a number of other people,'' Gerald commented. ''I don't think he'll be hunting for too many more years.''

They danced several more numbers and began to enjoy themselves in spite of everything that was on their minds. The orchestra was very good and the music had a hypnotic effect. When they finally took a break, Kyra and Gerald were ready to put on a good front and socialize a bit with some of the weekend's visitors, many of whom had gathered in the anteroom which housed the refreshment table.

''There's Jerome Cushing,'' Kyra said to Gerald as they walked toward the group. She inclined her head slightly to point out the shipping magnate, who was engrossed in conversation with a young man. They both had swarthy complexions and in the excitement of their conversation, they both rocked back and forth from heel to toe and gesticulated with their hands in a way that reminded Kyra of vendors she'd seen haggling with each other in Near Eastern bazaars.

"You're absolutely sure he's the one who made the call to New York?" Gerald asked.

"Yes, and that's the young man who seemed to be standing guard at the door."

"His son, I should think. Take away the gray hair and wrinkles, and Cushing would be his twin."

"You're right!" said Kyra. "Have you ever thought about taking up physiognomy?"

"Have you?" Gerald teased back. Neither of them thought much of this currently popular "science."

Before she could think of a reply, they heard Becky Hollingshood's voice from just inside the archway, out of sight behind a potted palm. "I do *wish* you wouldn't call me '*dear*,' " she said in her most disdainful tones. "*Anything* would be preferable to *dear*! It's *so* vulgar!"

Kyra had to suppress a smile as she heard Pandora Roseberry's flustered answer: "Yes . . . oh, yes, of course, dear. . . . Oh! I mean, yes, of course. . . ." She knew exactly how Becky felt. But in the next instant she felt sorry for Pandora, too, when she saw the little woman literally scuttle away from Becky, her sequined dress fluttering and her face wearing a truly stricken expression.

"That was cruel, Becky," Gerald chided. "You know Pandora can't help calling everyone 'dear.' It's just part of her character."

"It still irritates me no end!" Becky said disgustedly. "And this has been *such* a terrible day to begin with. Have you caught the murderer yet?" She addressed this last question to Kyra.

"I doubt I'll be the one to do any 'catching,' " Kyra responded.

"Well, what I *meant* was, do you have any idea who did it—any clues, or is it leads you call them?"

"We have some clues, of course," Kyra struggled to answer in her most patient voice. "But we don't have anything conclusive yet. Not enough to have someone apprehended."

" 'Apprehended.' What a nice, legal-sounding term," Becky said. "And who would do this apprehending?"

"Most probably the sheriffs."

"But you don't expect it will be tonight?"

"No."

"Then I'll sleep in peace, since I'm sure I'm one of the prime suspects. Thank you very much for the information. Please excuse me." And Becky walked back toward the party, where her friend Reggie promptly asked her to dance. Becky's tall frame towered over the little horse trainer by at least a head and he had to hold her at arm's length to keep from rubbing his nose on her bosom as he steered her around the floor. She hardly looked like the femme fatale she was reputed to be. In fact, Kyra suddenly remembered hearing that when Becky and Reggie had driven through Spain on her recent automobile trip across Europe, the locals had referred to the couple as "the big duck and the little cockerel." Ducks weren't murderers.

Or were they? Becky *was* known for her hot temper and vindictiveness when crossed. Could she and Nathaniel have had a quarrel and . . .

"I think she's had too much champagne punch," Gerald said, breaking in on Kyra's thoughts. "I can't imagine why she would act like that otherwise."

"I can," said Kyra evenly, trying not to let her dislike for Becky show too much.

"And so can I!" contributed Edna Harding's voice from just behind them. "She's basically a very vulgar person—and not to be trusted with *anyone's* husband. I assure you, if poor, dear Perseus were still alive, I wouldn't let him *near* that one!"

"What are you trying to say?" Kyra asked.

"Simply that if you want to get *yourself* off the hook, dear, you should concentrate on *her*. I want to assure you that *I* don't think *you're* guilty, not for a moment. I'm your friend, and behind you all the way. But there are *others* who feel quite differently—and naturally I can't do much about them. It's out of my hands, as they say!"

"Then why don't you shut your mouth about it," Gerald growled. "You're the one who's been spreading all of the rumors about Kyra—not to mention Nadine."

"Well! I never!" gasped Edna, looking at Gerald with scandalized astonishment. "I've tried my very best to help, and that's the gratitude I get! But I want you to know that they say things about you, too, Mr. Senator."

"*They* who?" exploded Gerald. "You mean *you*!"

"Well! I never!" Edna repeated, and bustled away.

"You seem to be having quite an effect on the ladies," commented Jerome Cushing, who had apparently been watching both conversations from his nearby station at the refreshment table. "Senator McMasters, I believe? And your lovely wife, Kyra?" He extended his hand to Gerald and kissed the back of Kyra's as he introduced himself and his son, Rodney.

"We met briefly in New York a couple of years ago," he explained, "and I must confess that one of the reasons I made the trip this weekend was to get to know you better—but I suppose I didn't pick the most opportune moment." His tone was apologetic as he looked in the direction of Edna's retreating back.

"Not at all." Gerald smiled, his usual good manners returning. "I shouldn't have lost my temper, but that woman is completely exasperating."

"Believe me, I wouldn't have been able to hold out half as long as you did!" Cushing said with empathy. "I could never abide busybodies, and she seems more aggravating than most."

"She is that," Gerald agreed. Then, changing the subject, he added, "You came down with the Newcastle Hunt?"

"Yes," Cushing responded with a smile. "I'm a relatively new member—this is my first year of hunting—but this sounded like such a wonderful expedition that I couldn't let it pass."

"You didn't participate in the races, then?"

"Oh, yes! I fell off twice, but I finished the course! I can't stand to just watch from the sidelines. That's why I took up hunting—I love the excitement. I'm especially looking forward to the hunt tomorrow—if there still is to be one?"

"Yes, that's the way Thurston wants it—though it won't be the same without Nathaniel."

"That's a sad business. A real tragedy," Cushing intoned, shaking his head. "I had never met the young man myself, but I was looking forward to doing some business with him this very weekend."

"Oh? What was that?" Kyra asked, trying to sound just politely interested.

"Apparently he owned a warehouse near my shipping yards in New York City," Cushing said. "It was convenient for a little project I have going, so I wanted to talk to him about buying or leasing it. Of course, my employees usually take care of such arrangements, but I thought that since I was coming here this weekend I'd talk to him myself. I like to keep my hand in once in a while, anyway—not get too far from the practical end of the business."

"Yes," agreed Gerald, "that's always wise. You're in the shipping business?"

"Just following in my father's footsteps—and his father's before him. We're a small family concern that tries to fill the gaps left by the East India Company and the other big guys," he said with an unconvincing simulation of modesty.

"You trade with the Orient, then?" Kyra asked.

"Yes, and a little with South America. Silks, coffee, cocoa, tea, pearls, that sort of thing."

"Isn't there quite a good market for opium, too?" Gerald asked.

"We don't touch it," Cushing answered a little too quickly. "The trade between India and China has always been a sticky problem, what with the Mandarins against it and all. We made a decision long ago not to get involved in the Chinese Opium Wars. And now the United States has put such high tariffs on the stuff that it doesn't pay to bring it here, either. There's a market for it, of course, but the profit margin is pretty slim."

"Yes, I suppose it would be," said Gerald.

"I'd rather make the ladies happy with silks and pearls," Cushing said with a smile for Kyra, "than pander to the big pharmaceutical companies."

"They're not your cup of tea?" Kyra punned. To herself, she wondered if he meant Melvin Dickey when he referred to "big pharmaceutical companies." She also remembered hearing that the resident "doctors" at the Roseberrys' health resorts were known to prescribe opiates all too frequently—could there be a connection between that and Cushing's earlier call?

"Exactly!" Cushing laughed. "And by the way, you're wearing a very fine silk yourself," he continued smoothly as he reached out and fingered the material of Kyra's dress. His touch was meant to be merely professional, but to Kyra it conveyed almost a sense of being violated. She used every ounce of self-control not to pull away from him.

"Reeled silk from the Yangtze-kiang River Valley, I'd say," he continued, apparently unaware of the revulsion he generated in Kyra.

"Perhaps it was made from a bolt that one of your ships brought over," Kyra managed to say, making small talk to hide her repugnance. She usually gave Gerald's intuitions a great deal of credit, but *this* time she was certain that his opinion had been swayed by Cushing's liberal contributions; her own reaction to the man was unremitting suspicion.

"Nothing would delight me more!" Cushing smiled back. "In fact, with your husband's permission, I'll send you silk enough for a new frock as soon as I'm back in New York."

"You're too kind," Kyra responded, "but please don't. I'd much rather just visit your shipping yard sometime. That's one thing I've always wanted to do, but the closest I've come is boarding a transatlantic steamer at the docks." She was thinking ahead, toward the possibility that the mystery of Nathaniel's death might not be solved that weekend. If so, she would want to investigate Cushing's designs on Nathaniel's warehouse.

"Your wish is my command," said Cushing with a flourishing bow as he presented Kyra with a small rectangle of pasteboard inscribed with the name, address, and telephone number of his business, Cushing & Sons, Int'l. She noticed that the offices were located quite close to the Ashley Park Hotel—a mere coincidence? she wondered.

"Please ring me on the telephone the next time you're in New York and I'll give you the grand tour," Cushing was saying.

Just then a buxom blond woman, young and a little homely, hesitantly joined the group. "This is my wife, Hilda," Cushing announced, beaming proudly and pulling her forward for introductions. "We were married just last month. Her father is also in the shipping business. That's how we met—Hilda was helping her father with the bookkeeping and now she helps me with mine!" He introduced each of them in turn and they chatted a few minutes longer. Hilda seemed shy and ill at ease with the group, but Cushing's son, who glowered at his young stepmother with evident dislike, apparently made her even more nervous. Kyra couldn't help but wonder: Why the tension? And why, with all his money, did Cushing have his new wife working in his office? Kyra could tell that Gerald was wondering the same things, and he didn't seem as positive toward Cushing as he had been earlier.

At that point, Cushing excused himself and escorted his wife onto the dance floor for a fast waltz. Kyra and

Gerald watched for a moment, rather amazed at the energy Cushing poured into the steps.

After a few minutes, Kyra said, "Do you think we'd be missed if we left right now?"

"Perhaps, but let's go anyway. Are you tired?"

"Exhausted. And we've got a big day tomorrow. But I'd also like to make a trip by the barn and check on Diana and Charger. They worked pretty hard today and I just want to make sure they're not tied up or anything."

"Yes, the 'or anything' is what worries me," Gerald said grimly. "Not that I think someone might actually tamper with our horses, but I'm going to check our girths and saddle billets *very* carefully tomorrow morning. In fact, I think I'll check every item of our tack for tampering."

"Yes, that was my concern," admitted Kyra. "After today, I'd believe just about anything." At that, they slipped away from the ballroom through a side door and walked back across the formal garden with its Japanese lanterns. The moon had come out, adding an eerie glow to the scene.

"I think there's enough light to see by," Gerald said. "Shall we just go on to the stables without stopping to look for a lantern?"

"Sure," said Kyra. "There'll be a lantern in the stables, anyway." They took a path that cut around behind the mansion and veered toward the stables. On the way, they could see the kennels, nestled in among the trees by the stream, far enough away from the dwelling so that the noise and odors of fifty hounds would not present major problems.

By day, the kennels were rather a cheerful place, with the hounds and puppies gamboling and playing in the runs, tails wagging and ears flopping. When a stranger approached, all would set to baying, a sound that was more melodic than frightening. Nathaniel's hounds were known for their musical tongues and high intelligence. But now, most of the hounds were inside asleep, and the low building with its armlike, protruding runs looked sinister, like a large spider squatting in the woods.

Gerald and Kyra stopped without thinking, fascinated by the kennel's altered look. As they stood watching, one of the older hounds, a large male, walked to the end of its run, sat down, and howled mournfully at the moon. The sound was painfully sad and Kyra imagined him mourning his dead master. Sensing her mood, Gerald put his arm comfortingly around Kyra's shoulders and pulled her against the warmth of his body.

An instant later, his embrace changed from comforting to passionate. He crushed Kyra's slim frame against his and kissed her uplifted mouth again and again, as his hands caressed her body through her thin silk dress. Her knees went weak, and had the evening been a little warmer, they would have sunk to the ground right there in the shadow of the trees. As it was, Gerald finally said in a voice hoarse with desire, "Let's check those horses quickly and get back to our room—I've got plans for you. . . ." Kyra knew from past experience that she was in for a night of lovemaking that would leave her feeling fresher in the morning than if she'd slept the night through. She nodded her head silently in the moonlight and they walked toward the barn.

In comparison to the kennels, the barn looked innocently safe in the moonlight. The white paint took on a glow that seemed to make the whole area lighter. Some of the horses were out in the white-fenced paddocks, grazing serenely. A foal gamboled around its mother, playing tag with its moon-made shadow. It let out a high-pitched whinny of joy, which its mother answered with a contented, guttural nicker. Kyra sighed in response—motherhood was a wonderful experience. Suddenly she felt a stabbing sense of loss. The peace and security of family life had been shattered by the events of the day. How could she have taken it for granted? Would she ever again feel the quiet animal contentment expressed in that mare's nicker?

She put aside her thoughts as Gerald opened the main

barn door and they stepped into the much deeper gloom within. A weak glow of light came from a dim lantern hung on a peg at the end of the row of stalls. Within a few moments, their eyes had adjusted and they could make out the large shapes of horses in stalls. Some of them stood with their noses almost rubbing the floor, sound asleep on their feet. Others ate hay from their mangers, their rhythmic chewing hypnotic in the barn's quiet. The silence was broken only by an occasional stomp of an equine foot or rustle of straw as one of the horses lay down with a groan and a *whoosh* of exhaled air.

Gerald took Kyra's hand in his own and they walked together toward the stalls that had been assigned to their horses. Kyra's mare nickered softly in the darkness and pushed her velvet nose through the bars for Kyra to stroke. Meanwhile, Gerald opened the lower half of the door to his horse's stall and ducked inside. Kyra was absentmindedly rubbing Diana's nose when she felt a dull thud at the back of her head, followed by a blinding flash of pain and light. Just before consciousness slid into numbing darkness, she realized that someone had struck her from behind with a cosh. Then everything went black.

When she woke up, she guessed that hours had passed. Her first sensation was of straw pricking against her neck. Diana's breath was hot against her cheek as the mare snuffled at her with a worried air. Her body was stiff with cold and from lying on the hard ground. She tried to move, but her hands and feet had been tied with what felt like two lead ropes, and she had been gagged with a rag that tasted of saddle soap and leather. But the knots were not too tight and in a matter of minutes she had succeeded in freeing her hands, removing the gag, and finally untying her feet.

She pulled herself slowly to a sitting position, leaning against the rough boards of the barn wall. Her head throbbed and she gingerly felt the tender spot at the base of her skull. Nothing seemed to be broken, anyway. She began rubbing her wrists and ankles to restore some of the circulation when she heard a low moan from the next stall. Gerald! She tried to stand but fell helplessly back to the straw. Her feet were numb blocks, unable to hold her weight. She crawled on her hands and knees to the stall door, then pulled herself upright inch by inch until she could reach out through the bars and unlatch the lower half of the door. As it swung open, she fell to her knees again and moved as fast as she could toward the next stall.

The first thing she saw was the dead horse. Its abdomen was already swelling and its legs were stiffening out to the sides. With her heart pounding, she looked farther into the gloom and saw a human form lying in a fetal position in one corner. "Gerald?" she whispered hoarsely. The form groaned again, leaving her no doubt as to who it was. She crawled toward him as fast as she could. The folds of her ball gown entangled maddeningly with the straw and her legs, causing her to fall several times, but she scrambled up each time and was at her husband's side in a matter of seconds.

Gerald had also been gagged, and his hands and feet were tied together with one rope, much more securely than hers had been. Kyra removed the gag first, then began to work on the knots with trembling fingers. Gerald groaned again and opened his eyes. She stopped working on the knots for a moment to embrace him, kissing his face repeatedly in her joy that he was alive and conscious. She attacked the knots with renewed vigor, finally throwing the rope to one side and rubbing Gerald's hands and feet, even though her own were still half-numb and tingling.

Gerald tried to sit up but fell back on the straw. In the faint light of the new day Kyra saw a bucket of water standing in the nearest corner, untouched by the dead horse. She felt in Gerald's pocket and found his handkerchief, which she dipped into the water and applied to the blue lump that was rising on his forehead. He groaned again, but this time he managed to sit up.

"Charger?" he asked.

When Kyra shook her head sadly, Gerald said, "He bit the man that was about to hit me from behind. You know how he was about any fast movements in his stall. He might have saved me, but there were two of them. While Charger was still shaking the first one, the second hit me, then whammed Charger just behind the ears with something that looked like a billy club. I saw it just as I passed out. Whoever killed him knew exactly where to place the blow. It was over so fast I hardly knew what was happening. I just remember seeing the horse go down, fairly certain that he was dead. I thought I was dead, too." He groaned again as he brought his hand to his head.

"I don't know why they *didn't* kill us," Kyra said. "We must have interrupted something, but why tie us up and leave us here?"

"It doesn't make any sense," said Gerald. "But I'm glad they didn't kill us, whoever they are. Now let's try to get back to the house before the stable boys and maids are up."

"You're right," Kyra said. "The fewer people who know about this, the better chance we have of catching the culprits."

Within a few minutes they were able to stand and walk by leaning against each other. They made their painful way back to the house as the first birds began to twitter, and in the distance one of Farmer Ingleson's roosters crowed a welcome to the new day. What would *this* day bring? Kyra wondered with a shudder.

CHAPTER 9

Ware Wire!

KYRA and Gerald had almost reached their room when Alma came sleepily down the hall from the opposite direction, still tying on her crisp white apron. "Oh! Oh, my Gawd!" she exclaimed when she saw them. "Did that horrible man come back?"

"We're not sure it was him," Kyra answered in a whisper. "But hush! Come in here so we won't wake anyone with our talking."

When they'd entered the McMasterses' suite and closed the door, Kyra continued, "I'm glad you're up so early. You can be a great help."

"Oh, my, yes, Ah'll do *anythin'* Ah kin t'help," Alma said with wide eyes.

"Good. Then keep quiet about this to other people. And I'll need some antiseptic for Mr. McMasters' head, a large pot of hot tea, and a nice breakfast for both of us—that should do more good than anything else at this point."

"Yes'm. Right away, ma'am," Alma said as she curtsied her way out of the room in her touchingly clumsy way.

As soon as she'd gone, Kyra ran a tub of hot water for Gerald, who was suffering more than she was. He submitted to the hot bath willingly and it seemed to help relieve his pain. He lay down on the bed afterward and immediately went to sleep. Kyra had just finished her own bath when Alma returned with a covered tray.

"Put the food over here, please," said Kyra, indicating a table in the sitting room.

"Ah made ev'rythang mahself," Alma said, beaming as she removed the cover and the room filled with tantalizing aromas. "Ah's one o' the bes' cooks Ah knows," she said with some pride. "Ev'n Mr. Howard's cook's ast me fo' sum o' mah rec'pes."

Kyra could well believe Alma as she filled plates for herself and Gerald, who had been aroused from his sleep by the smell of food. There was moist, hot cornbread, scrambled eggs with oysters and onions, fresh compote, slabs of fried ham, an assortment of sliced, fresh fruit smothered in clotted cream, and yams cooked with bananas and cherries. To go with this, Alma had chosen an English breakfast tea, which she had brewed to perfection.

"That's excellent tea," Kyra said as she let the first sip slide comfortingly down her throat. Alma beamed happily as she watched Kyra and Gerald finish most of the food she'd brought.

"After that feast," Gerald announced as he pushed his chair back from the table, "I think I'm even up to foxhunting today. Isn't it about time to start getting ready?"

"No, Gerald!" Kyra protested. "Not with that bump on your head! Besides, you don't have a horse."

A look of grieved and angry pain crossed Gerald's face at this reference to Charger, and he said grimly, "All the more reason to go— I'll borrow a horse from Thurston. Besides, aren't you planning to go?"

"Yes, but I wasn't hit as hard as you were," Kyra objected.

"No 'yes, buts' about it," Gerald said emphatically. "If you go, I go. Besides, I have a feeling that something is going to happen on the hunt today that we should be there to see. I think we'll find out the real reason why Nathaniel was killed—I dreamt something about it in the middle of the night."

"While you were out cold?" Kyra asked.

"Sort of," Gerald answered. "The dreams seemed incredibly real. It was as if I were right there, taking part in them."

"Like what?" Kyra asked, suddenly excited.

"For one thing, I thought I heard a train pull up close to the barn, very slowly and quietly. Then some men unloaded heavy objects, boxes or bales, from it. I could hear them grunting and shuffling under the weight, then the thuds as they put the objects down. They whispered among themselves some, but I couldn't hear what they were saying. Finally, the train pulled out again, just as quietly as it came."

"I don't think you were dreaming," Kyra said excitedly. "I heard the same thing, although I'd forgotten until you mentioned it."

"What do you think they were unloading?" Gerald said.

"I don't know," said Kyra. "And we don't have time to look now—we've got to get ready for the hunt."

Within a few minutes, Kyra had donned a fresh riding habit, this time in black, as well as her tall boots and a lady's top hat with veil, the standard costume for formal hunts. Gerald was also suitably attired in sparkling white riding breeches and shirt, black boots with brown tops, pink coat, and hunt cap. Although he winced as he put the hat on over his bruised forehead, he seemed completely recovered otherwise.

"We've still got some time before we need to join the others outside," Kyra said, looking at her pendant watch. "I want to check in on Nadine and Juliette."

"Yes, that's a good idea, and while you're doing that, I'll go talk to Thurston," Gerald answered. "All three of them should be over their initial shock by now and they might remember something that would help untangle this bewildering puzzle."

"My thought exactly," agreed Kyra. "Besides, after

what happened to us last night, I'd just like to see for myself that they're all alive and well."

When Kyra crossed the hall to Juliette's room she found that Melvin had apparently already gone out. The maid was nowhere in sight and Juliette was sitting in a chair by the window, pale but otherwise recovered from last night's ordeal. Nevertheless, Kyra had an overwhelming feeling that Juliette would never completely recover from the blow of Nathaniel's death. She had always depended on her older brother for a certain grounding in reality that she lacked, and Kyra now sensed that unless Juliette made a major personality change, she would probably drift aimlessly and despondently through the years to come if grief didn't kill her outright.

"Oh, Kyra," Juliette said when she finally looked up to see who her visitor was. "I'm glad you came. There's something I wanted to talk to you about."

"Yes?" said Kyra, her heart suddenly pounding. Perhaps Juliette held the key to the mystery.

"I want you and Gerald to be godparents to my child," Juliette said unexpectedly. "If I die, I want you to take him and raise him yourselves, don't leave him with Melvin. I'll put it in my will as soon as I get back to New York. And he's to be named Nathaniel Howard Dickey, after my brother. I'm sure he'll be a boy."

Kyra looked at Juliette for a moment in bewilderment, then moved her glance downward to the young woman's swollen waist. "Why, you must be five or six months along already, and I just thought you'd put on some weight!" she exclaimed. "But that's wonderful! You have something to live for—to raise a little boy just like your brother."

Juliette sighed and said, "Not with Melvin as the father—I haven't even told him I'm pregnant. I wasn't sure what I was going to do, but I know that no child would turn out decently if Melvin was raising him alone. That's why I want you and Gerald to be godparents— you can get my son away from Melvin. That way he'll have a chance, don't you see?" Her voice changed from a monotone to a desperate plea. "You will, won't you?"

"Of course we'll be godparents," Kyra reassured her. "We'd be very honored—but no more talk of dying for you. Whatever you might think about Melvin as a father, every child needs his own mother, including yours. And you've got the whole world to live in. You don't need to live in one particular place, with one particular person, you know. And there *is* such a thing as divorce, if it comes to that."

"Yes, I suppose you're right," Juliette said a little less listlessly. "I'll think about it."

"Good! And I want you to think about something else, too."

"What's that?" Juliette asked, but without much interest.

"I'm trying to find out who killed your brother," Kyra said without preamble. "I want you to think of anything you know that might help. Had he talked to you about any business deals or problems or enemies? Was he in financial trouble? Was he involved romantically with anyone? Anything you might know that could possibly lead to the guilty party. Do you understand?"

"Ye-e-s," Juliette said slowly. "I understand . . . but Nathaniel didn't talk to me much about business things. When he came to visit, we mostly talked about his hounds and horses. That's what I wanted to hear about, anyway. I've never cared much about business, you know."

"Did he talk to you at all about this?" Kyra asked as she pulled out the map of Hopsworth she'd found in Juliette's letter to Nadine.

"No, not really," Juliette said. "Melvin gave me that to forward to Nathaniel with my letter, but I didn't ask him about it. All I knew was that those plans were for a long time from now—maybe twenty or twenty-five years."

"How did you know that?"

"When I saw the map, I asked Melvin," Juliette answered.

"So that's what he told you?" Kyra asked.

"Yes, he had no reason to lie. He wasn't involved in the deal."

"Not that we know of so far," Kyra said seriously. "And by the way, how well does he know Jerome Cushing?"

"As well as he knows any of the first-year members of the Newcastle Hunt, I suppose," said Juliette.

"He didn't know him before then? Any business dealings with him?"

"Not that I know of. Well . . . perhaps. He might have come to one or two of our larger parties before then, but I'm not sure. I've always had such a poor memory for *both* names and faces—that exasperates Melvin no end. I just can't remember most people I meet, unless there's something very striking about them. And we meet so very many people in Melvin's business. When he isn't traveling, we're always having parties and dinners, and *going* to parties and dinners. I'm glad he travels as much as he does, or I'd never have any time to myself."

"I wasn't aware that he traveled that much."

"Yes, he's gone Monday through Friday, most weeks. He has to visit what he calls his 'branch offices,' which are actually just pharmacies. I've often wondered why he doesn't leave that to his traveling salesmen—he's got enough of them—but then I remember how peaceful it is when he's gone and I don't say anything."

"You really aren't happy with Melvin, are you?"

"No. But I've never felt it was a wife's place to complain. I wouldn't say anything now, either, but somehow I feel as if Melvin is *responsible* for Nathaniel's death. I have no proof, no reason for feeling that way—but I do. And if he *is* responsible, I want him to pay for it." She said this last grimly, with the first spark of animation Kyra had seen in her eyes. It was a look that chilled and frightened Kyra.

"You just rest and take care of that baby," Kyra said

reassuringly, trying not to let her real feelings show. "We'll find out who's to blame for Nathaniel's death."

"You'll let me know right away?"

"As soon as I know. Okay?"

"Okay." Juliette smiled feebly. Kyra embraced her for a moment, then left the room.

Sobie was in the hall waiting for her. "Alma told me you'd gone in to see Juliette," she explained, "but I didn't want to interrupt. How is she?"

"Much better this morning. How is Nadine?"

"That's what I wanted to tell you. She's come to her senses again. She doesn't seem to remember yesterday at all. She's been asking for you. In fact, she sent me to find you."

"Good. Let's go see her!"

The moment Kyra entered the room, Nadine rushed into her arms and burst into tears. She cried for some minutes without saying anything. When the tears began to subside, she said, "That horrible inspector's been here—and he's been saying the most terrible things. He can't possibly *do* anything, can he? He hasn't any *proof* of the things he says, does he?"

"Only circumstantial. Nothing he could act on, so far," Kyra answered. "Try not to worry about that too much. I'm sure we'll be able to find the real murderer quite soon." She spoke with more confidence than she felt, however, as she looked at Nadine's distraught face. Could Nadine possibly have sneaked out of her room and strung the wire along Ingleson's fence? She certainly knew how, and there were several hours when she could have slipped away unnoticed. But did she?

As if she'd read her thoughts, Nadine said, "I didn't do it, Kyra. I couldn't. No matter how angry I got with Nathaniel, I still loved him. Besides, there's something I haven't told anyone yet. Not even Nathaniel knew; I didn't have a chance before—" Her voice broke and she fought to regain control. Kyra sensed immediately what was coming but could hardly believe the coincidence.

"I'm going to have a baby," Nadine finally managed.

"Nathaniel's baby," she added, her eyes filling with tears. "Why would I kill the father of my child? We had been having some problems, but when Dr. Whitley told me on Friday, I knew it would make everything all right. Nathaniel's wanted a child for so long. I was going to tell him Friday night, after dinner when we were alone, and I thought we could announce it to everyone else at the ball this weekend. But then he didn't come back. . . . Oh, Kyra! I can't believe he's dead! I keep thinking he's going to walk in any minute and I can tell him about the baby. . . ." With that, she burst into tears again, sobbing inconsolably. Kyra led her to the bed and Sobie mixed one of Dr. Whitley's powders in a glass of water, which they persuaded Nadine to drink. In a short while, her tears subsided, although she still heaved great sighs.

"Listen, Nadine," Kyra said to her sternly. "I have to go now, but I want to tell you something important first."

"Yes, what is it?"

"Juliette is pregnant, too. And she's feeling just as badly about Nathaniel as you are. I want you to go and comfort her. Tell her about your baby and encourage her about her own. She needs your strength, Nadine. You can help her. Do you understand?"

"Yes, of course. I'll do what I can," Nadine responded with a little more control. Kyra had learned long ago that a bereaved person could sometimes be persuaded to help someone else when they couldn't or wouldn't help themselves—and in the process they invariably *did* help themselves. She was just considering going back to Juliette with the same request when there came a knock at the door, which Sobie answered.

"Is Mrs. McMastahs heah?" It was Benny Mulchanney's voice.

"I'll just be a minute," Kyra answered from behind Sobie. "Please wait for me in the hall and I'll be right out." She took her leave of Nadine as quickly as she could and joined Benny a few minutes later.

"Sen'tor McMastahs said Ah would fin' y'all heah,"

Benny explained. "We done looked in all the bars and cain't fin' ol' Michael anywheres. He jus' seems t'have disahpeared off'n th' face o' th' earth. The sen'tor thinks he's asleep unner a bush somewheres."

"And what do *you* think, Benny?" Kyra asked. Benny sometimes had a sixth sense about such things.

"Ah thinks he's hidin' somewheres aroun' here, that's what Ah thinks," Benny retorted stoutly. "Ah foun' out that he wuz real mad at Nathan'l and he prob'ly thinks he'll catch th' blame fo' what happened."

"Who told you he was mad at Nathaniel?" Kyra wanted to know.

"One o' th' grooms. They'd been drinkin' sum brandy an' he said he wuz real mad, that he wuz jus' as good a Huntsman as Nathan'l, and then he jus' took off. An' he hasn't been seed since. But that's not why Ah cum up. The sen'tor said to tell y'all that Os'ald wud like y'all to whip, iffen y'all cain." Benny was using his broadest Southern accent, which was almost always a sign that he was either upset about something or trying to relay some message to her.

"Oh, I see I've forgotten my riding gloves," Kyra said. "Why don't you walk back to my room with me to look for them." As soon as they were safely inside the room, away from any eavesdroppers, Kyra said, "What's happening, Benny?"

He grinned at her correct reading of his accent, and said, "Ah jus' don' think you shud go on that hunt today. An' Ah certainly don' think you shud *whip*! It jus' don' seem safe. Not with all that's been happ'nin'."

"But you don't have any specific reason?" Kyra asked sharply.

"No ma'am, Ah jus' gots a feelin', that's all," Benny said, looking down and shuffling his feet like an abashed little boy. Kyra couldn't resist tousling his curly red hair and giving him an encouraging pat on the shoulder.

"I'll be all right, Benny. Don't worry about me. But I'd appreciate it if you'd go search under all those bushes. We really need to find Michael—and I've never known you to fail before." As Kyra spoke, Benny hung his head and shuffled his feet some more, in apparent shame.

"Ah don' think Ah's gonna fine him," he finally mumbled to Kyra's astonishment. "Don'tcha have anythin' else Ah kin do?"

"No, I want you to *find* him, without any more excuses!" Kyra answered somewhat harshly, then immediately regretted being so hard on Benny. How could she possibly doubt that he'd tried everything there was to try? If Benny couldn't find Michael, he probably wasn't anywhere to be found.

"I'm sorry," Kyra apologized, putting her hand on Benny's shoulder. "I didn't get much sleep last night, so I'm a little short-tempered. Forget about Michael for now—I have something else for you to work on."

Benny's eyes lit up and he said, "Sho' 'nuff! Whatever y'all wants."

Kyra took pencil and paper and drew a quick diagram of the carriage wheel tracks she'd seen in the dust by the booby-trapped jump. One of the wheels had been repaired recently and the mark it left was distinctive. "Take this to each of the local blacksmiths and ask them if they've repaired a wheel in the last week or so that would leave a track like this. Find out who owns the carriage and where they live."

"Sho' 'nuff!" Benny repeated, looking much more cheerful. "Ah'll have it fo' y'all by the time you're back from th' hunt!"

"Which reminds me," Kyra said, "I've got to get down there—and you've got to get my horse ready."

Just then, Kyra glanced out of the window and her eye was caught by a movement on the grass below. With a start she realized she was seeing Becky Hollingshood walking quickly away from the French doors of the ground floor room just beneath the one she was in. Something in her walk indicated that she was upset and was trying to get away as quickly as possible without actually running. Who could Becky have been visiting? And why?

Kyra wished she had time to check out the room, but she was almost late as it was.

Benny had followed her glance and said, "Y'all want me to keep an eye on that one, too? Looks 'spicious t' me."

"No, she'll be on the hunt and I doubt there's much trouble she can get into there. You just find that carriage, okay?"

"Okay," Benny said in a slightly subdued tone. He clearly felt that he'd been assigned a piece of busywork as a result of his failure to find Michael.

"You really do love detecting, don't you, Benny?" Kyra said, turning to her young assistant once more. A little encouragement would have to go a long way today, she thought.

"Yes'm!" was the quick response. "Ah jus' don' like th' idea of y'all bein' in danger, what with th' little'uns an' all."

"Don't worry, Benny. I'll be all right," said Kyra with greater confidence than she felt. There were some very risky things about whipping under the best of circumstances. She began to pull on her riding gloves as they walked, to hide her agitation. She also wondered how Gerald had fared with Thurston and how he would react to the news she bore from Juliette and Nadine.

American hunt breakfasts were traditionally sumptuous affairs, especially on race meet weekends, with each hunt vying to outdo the other. The first thing Kyra saw as she walked out of Hopsworth's front door were the long tables on the lawn, covered with white linen and set with the most elaborate hunt breakfast she had ever seen. Thurston's cooks must have been working all night. An enormous ham, cooked with pineapple sauce (a Hopsworth specialty) dominated the center of the main table, with a carver standing ready to serve slabs of juicy meat to the hungry foxhunters. The rest of the table was covered with side dishes, including four different types of eggs, biscuits, sweet rolls, cornbread, green beans with almonds, baked beans, lima beans with bacon, fried chicken, and braces of wild duck, pheasant, and partridge cooked in buttered sherry sauce (another Hopsworth specialty), not to mention bowls and pitchers of assorted condiments, gravies, and sauces. A second table was required for desserts, which included a huge cut-crystal bowl of English trifle, six different types of cake, a large pan of gingerbread with whipped cream, an assortment of pies, including cherry, berry, apple, and squash, and another cut-crystal bowl filled with every fruit imaginable, including fresh mangoes and papayas Thurston had imported especially from South America. In the center of the third table was a silver bowl the size of a small bathtub, filled with a cold rum punch. Waiters were also pouring glasses of sherry, and two large silver urns provided steaming cups of coffee and tea for those who did not choose to imbibe alcohol so early in the morning.

Most of the Daisy Hill Hunt Club members were already gathered on the lawn with plates of food in their hands, chatting among themselves and with the members of the visiting clubs. They were eating and drinking with a gusto that always astonished Kyra. She had often wondered how they could consume so much and then immediately mount up. Of course, she and Gerald had eaten a good breakfast themselves, but they had allowed more than an hour for it to digest before they needed to get on their horses. She knew from past experience that some of the Daisy Hill members would continue to stuff themselves with the rich fare until the very minute they stepped into the stirrup. And it never seemed to bother any of them in the least. Edna Harding, for example, had already finished off a plate of ham with all the trimmings and was just starting on a dessert plate heaped with trifle, berry pie, and two kinds of cake. Her cheeks bulged as she followed a forkful of cake with a bite of pie, managing all the while to carry on an animated conversation with several people at once. She waved her fork in the air as she described a series of jumps during a previous hunt.

It was obvious that Edna, at least, seemed to feel less tension today. In fact, Kyra noticed, the whole group was less tense, and she felt a momentary flare of anger: they were already forgetting about Nathaniel's death, going on with their lives as usual, enjoying themselves while he lay stretched out on the billiards table in the basement. Could their shock and grief of yesterday have been only concern that they were under suspicion? And now that suspicion had shifted away from them, onto her, was their strongest emotion relief? Kyra felt almost nauseated looking at them.

She wondered what Thurston felt, or how Nathaniel would have felt if he had known how these people would react to his death. She remembered how hard Nathaniel had worked to create the Daisy Hill Hunt, and she became even angrier. She had asked Nathaniel once why he had started the Hunt and he had answered, "I enjoy hunting hounds, of course, but I guess the real reason is that I wanted to bring to people something they would enjoy, something that would give them some of the same feeling of exhilaration I feel during a good chase." Kyra had wondered at the time if those other people were worth it. Now she knew the answer.

But being angry was not going to do any good, so Kyra looked around for Gerald. Off to one side, in front of the stable, grooms and stable boys were frantically busy getting their employers' horses brushed and tacked up for the hunt. The horses were stomping and snorting impatiently, ready for the chase. They were all seasoned hunters and they knew the excitement that lay ahead.

Off to the other side, on a little rise where he had a full view of the scene, Philip Drogan, in the guise of Paul Leonard Asquith III, was seated on a little camp stool in front of his easel. He wore a painter's smock over his hunting clothes and was busily sketching the scene in front of him on a large canvas. He smiled and beckoned to Kyra when he saw her looking in his direction. She had moved only a few steps, however, when she was stopped by Edna Harding's shrill voice.

"Oh, Mrs. McMasters, that's simply terrible news about your husband's horse! Such a nice-looking stallion, too! Do you think he just hit his head while he was rolling in his stall?" This morning Edna grated worse than ever on Kyra's nerves, but she was determined to be civil to the woman.

"Yes, probably," Kyra answered as evenly as she could. "One never knows what will happen next with horses."

"Or people, either, for that matter," suggested Edna, for once saying something that was almost profound.

"Or people, either," Kyra agreed. Edna's next remark was cut short by the arrival of Hadley Turbot, who thrust his chubby body between them, exclaiming, "Aunty Edna! Aunty Edna! I've got to talk to you right now! In private," he added, looking suspiciously at Kyra, who immediately wondered if Edna's nephew had loosed another of his menagerie on the grounds.

As soon as Edna had disappeared inside with Hadley, Kyra walked up the little rise toward Philip Drogan, thinking on the way that she should fill him in on the events in the stable, if Gerald hadn't already. Gerald himself was nowhere in sight, and Kyra wondered if he was still with Thurston or if he had gone down to the stable to arrange for Charger's burial. It was traditional to butcher the carcass of a deceased hunt horse and feed it to the hounds, but exceptions were made if the horse's owner was particularly attached to the animal or, naturally, if the horse had died of some disease that could possibly be communicated to the hounds through the meat, such as rabies or distemper. Kyra felt sure that Gerald would not want to feed Charger to the hounds.

"Good morning!" Philip Drogan said cheerfully, interrupting Kyra's morbid thoughts. "Isn't it a perfectly gorgeous day for a hunt!"

"Yes, it certainly is," Kyra answered in the same light tones, aware for the first time that a small group of the Newcastle hunters, including Melvin Dickey and

Jerome Cushing, were just approaching the easel from the opposite side of the rise.

"If you came to inspect the painting, Mrs. McMasters, you're in for a treat," Melvin said in the same social tone. "Isn't she, Jerome?"

"Most certainly," agreed the shipping magnate, "although I'm no judge of art."

Kyra obligingly walked around to the other side of the easel and experienced a moment of genuine astonishment when she saw the oil sketch: It was excellent. With quick strokes of light and dark, mixed with vibrant reds and greens, Drogan had captured the essential quality, the *feeling* of the hunt breakfast with an accuracy that was truly breathtaking. Kyra had no idea that Drogan was so talented. She had thought of his painting as a pastime or hobby that had come in handy for his disguise. She glanced from the canvas to the scene below and back again several times before she vouchsafed a comment.

When she finally spoke, she addressed her remarks to Cushing, rather than Drogan. She suddenly felt shy about talking to the detective, as if he had become an entirely different person. "You may not know much about art, but you're definitely right to like *this* painting," she said to Cushing, with her very real admiration showing in every word. "My mother was a talented artist, with many artistic friends, so I've seen a lot of paintings, but I've never seen one I've liked better. And what's most impressive is that Mr. Asquith has done such a difficult subject so well in such a short time." She paused for a moment, then added, for the sake of Drogan's disguise, "Our British visitor certainly deserves to be a member of the Royal Academy, if he's not already."

"I was wondering why none of us have ever heard of such a talented artist," Melvin said, with a hint of suspicion in his voice. "Since you specialize in hunting scenes, I should think we'd at least have heard your name before," he said to Drogan.

"Ah!" Drogan sighed. "If fame were only that easy to

come by, my dear man! Then I should have no worries in the world—but unfortunately not everyone shares Mrs. McMasters' very flattering opinion of my talents, and those who do admire my small efforts are not always in a position to publicize their views to the public at large.''

''Perhaps we can do something about that,'' volunteered Cushing. ''If you have other paintings of this quality, perhaps a couple dozen, we might be able to arrange an exhibition in New York. We can call it 'An American Debut for a British Artist,' or something along those lines. I'm not up on the art scene, but it seems like that ought to draw crowds.''

''That's one thing I like about you Americans,'' Drogan responded with a hearty smile. ''You're so willing to jump right in and *do* something where an Englishman would hesitate and vacillate until the proper moment was entirely past, don't you know?''

''It's settled, then? We'll do an exhibit?'' said Cushing.

''If you still want to when you've seen more of my work,'' Drogan answered with the same broad smile, relishing his double entendre. But Kyra could tell that under his amusement, he was pleased that Cushing liked his painting so well—and even more pleased that she did.

''If we're going to get something to eat before it's time to mount up, we should leave the artist to his work,'' Melvin suggested. Turning to Kyra, he added, ''Would you care to join us, Mrs. McMasters?''

''Oh, no, thank you,'' she said quickly. ''I've eaten already and I thought I'd stretch my legs a bit. So please don't let me keep you.''

''We took our walk before breakfast,'' Melvin answered. ''I recommend a stroll through the woods in that direction,'' he added, pointing back the way they had just come. ''Lovely spring flowers. I thought of picking some for Juliette, but I was afraid they'd wilt before I could get them up to her. Perhaps she'll feel well enough by this evening to walk that far herself. And by the way, thank you both again for all of your help with her last night—she seems much better this morning."

"Yes, I stopped in and saw her myself before I came down," said Kyra. "But don't underestimate the effect Nathaniel's death has had on her—they were very close, and I think it will take her a while to adjust."

"Of course," agreed Melvin, "but then again it might be the best thing for her in the long run. *I* always maintained that they were *too* close—not that anyone ever listened to me. Perhaps now she'll be more willing to pay attention to her lawfully wedded husband. But that's enough on that topic for now. We really *must* go get some breakfast."

The kind feelings Kyra had experienced toward Melvin the night before evaporated as she watched his retreating back. In his own way, he was as abrasive as Edna Harding. And like her, he did not seem to have the least awareness of the effect he had on people. Or perhaps it was only on some people, as they both seemed quite popular in their own ways and even seemed to get on quite well together, once she thought about it. Perhaps like *did* attract like.

"He's one I wouldn't turn my back on in a dark room," Drogan said warily. "I wouldn't be surprised if he didn't poison his own wife."

"I agree," sighed Kyra. "He had the perfect opportunity, didn't he? All he had to do was to make sure the maid's tea was drugged and then . . ."

"Exactly." Drogan nodded, adding another dab of paint to his canvas. "I found the maid who'd brought the tea up yesterday afternoon—she'd set Juliette's tray on the hall table while she took one in for Mrs. Howard. And when she came out the tray was gone. She knocked on the Dickeys' door and found the maid already pouring herself a cup of tea. Unfortunately, she didn't ask who brought it in, she just assumed that the maid had heard her in the hall and had done it herself."

"But Melvin could easily have done it, which would have given him the opportunity to slip a sleeping powder into the pot. Then, when the woman had dozed off, he could have come in and dosed Juliette, who was already sedated, with an additional lethal amount, unseen by the sleeping maid," Kyra finished for him.

"And thereby hangs the tale," said Drogan.

"By the maid, you mean. We must find her and question her immediately," Kyra said with agitation. "We must find out who brought that tray in before . . ."

"Yes, before another attempt is made on Juliette's life. I agree," said Drogan calmly. "But Melvin gave the maid notice last night, as soon as she woke up. Quite a natural reaction on the part of a distraught husband, don't you think? To fire the careless maid who's overdosed her mistress? At any rate, she packed up and left last night on a train that went by between one and two in the morning. One of the grooms flagged it down for her. It went to Charlottesville, then joined up with the transcontinental for San Francisco. There's no way to tell if she got off in Charlottesville, transferred to another train, or went on to the west. The groom who flagged the train for her said that she was very distraught, that Melvin had apparently given her a severe dressing down and had proclaimed that she would never get another job on the East Coast."

"So she may have decided to go west—if she had the money. But we should be able to find out if a ticket was sold to a young woman in Charlottesville this morning. The station there isn't very large and they would certainly have a record of such a transaction. The ticket agent would probably be able to identify her," said Kyra excitedly. "I'll go send a wire to them right now."

"I've wired already," Drogan said quietly, "but I doubt we'll get an answer in time to do much good today. And we certainly won't be able to get hold of the young woman herself in time to get the information we need—she'll be good to have in court, that's all. In the meantime, we have a desperate murderer on our hands and I'm not completely convinced that it's Melvin—or at least not Melvin alone."

"Why is that?"

"What's happened so far is too bizarre, as if a crazy person had—" But before Drogan could complete his sentence, Hadley Turbot came panting up the hill toward them, pumping his fat legs in what was clearly meant to be a run. "Mrs. McMasters! Aunt-Edna-and-Senator-Howard-want-you-to-come! Mr.-Howard-said-the-artist-fellow-is-to-come-too-and-do-you-know-where-Mr. McMasters-is?" His words tumbled out so fast between his gasps for air that they could hardly understand him, but his pale face was genuinely distraught and even the whites of his eyes showed grotesquely.

"What's wrong?" Kyra asked, placing a hand kindly on the child's shoulder—he *was* after all just a child, and obviously very frightened. "Take a couple of deep breaths, Hadley," she said soothingly, "and then tell me as calmly as you can what's happened. Okay?"

Hadley nodded and followed her instructions, then said more slowly, "I went to play a joke on my Cousin Egerton this morning, but I couldn't wake him up and he looked real queer. So I got my Aunt Edna to come look, and . . . and . . . he's *dead*!"

CHAPTER 10

Gone Away!

EGERTON Harding was still in bed, looking as if he were asleep, except for the telltale purplish-gray tinge to his skin. Senator Howard and Edna Harding were there when Kyra and the two others walked in. They stood together at the foot of the bed—silent, deflated, and sadly bewildered, the senator especially so. Kyra thought she knew exactly how they were feeling: It was all too much. So many terrible things had happened in the last day and a half that Egerton's death left them just numb. The grief would come later, she thought sadly.

Respecting their silence, Kyra said nothing and proceeded to examine the body. It was already cold. He must have died sometime during the night, presumably in his sleep. His skin and mouth smelled slightly of liquor, as would be natural after the ball, but there was no trace of any other odor that might have indicated poison or sleeping powder. He was not wearing a nightshirt and only a sheet covered his trim and athletic body. There was no sign of a blow to his head or any other violence, just a small mark on his ankle that looked to be a slightly scratched mosquito bite. But something about it bothered her, and she kept returning to it in her mind as she looked at the rest of the room.

Nothing had been disturbed, as far as Kyra could see. Egerton's tuxedo from the night before was hung neatly on the valet rack. There were no other clothes in the closet, which puzzled her at first, until she remembered that Egerton had come in from Washington just for the evening. But why then did he stay? And how did he get this room? Hadn't all of the rooms been filled?

As if he'd read her thoughts, Senator Howard volunteered, "I told Egerton to stay last night. I was out for a midnight walk when I saw him leave the ball. I invited him in for a drink and we talked until two or three in the morning. It was too late then for him to drive all the way back to Washington, so I rang Corrie, my housekeeper, who was still up, to see that our guests were well taken care of after the ball, bless her dear soul. I asked if there was any place to put Egerton, or even just a sheet he could use on the couch in my library. She said that the gentleman who was to have used this room had not come at the last minute, so I told her to put him there."

"Who was that gentleman?" Kyra asked. Perhaps Egerton had been killed by mistake. Perhaps this other man was the one who should have been dead, but wasn't.

"I don't recollect, but I'm sure Corrie has a list. I'll ring for her."

"Good," said Kyra, who continued her search while they waited for Corrie. This room did not have its own bathroom, but sported an old-fashioned washstand in one corner instead. Egerton had apparently washed his hands and face before going to bed, as the basin contained a small amount of soapy water and a rumpled towel lay next to it. On the bureau next to the washstand, however, lay the leather portfolio case Egerton always carried with him—on the chance that he would get an idea he wanted to write down immediately. Kyra opened the case and leafed through the contents, mostly bills, vouchers, and blank sheets. Tucked into the back, however, was something that sent chills up and down her spine: several pages of manuscript, presumably from his new novel, describing the catapulting fall of a horse and rider snared by a wired fence. The original description had been changed in several places to make it more accurate, indicating to Kyra that Egerton had consulted with someone about the technical details. Who? And when? And was that the person he had to "check something out" with before talking further with her? Or perhaps he had discussed the pages with Nathaniel and someone else had been there at the time. Oswald? Nadine? Michael? The senator himself? She itched to show the pages to Drogan but knew she couldn't in front of Edna, so she refolded the pages and made a show of putting them back into the portfolio, while she actually slipped them into the copious front pocket of her riding habit.

"Nothing much of interest there," she said as she put the portfolio back on the bureau. "Had Egerton come to visit here any time in the last fortnight?"

"Not that I know of," Thurston replied. "Of course, I was in Washington most of that time—he could have come to see Nathaniel or Nadine during the day and I wouldn't necessarily have known about it. I was pretty busy and not paying much attention to anything but the Senate. Why?"

"Just wondering," Kyra answered absently as she finished looking over the room. She noticed Drogan looking sharply at her, aware that she'd found something.

Other than the portfolio, there seemed to be no clues in the room. No dirty footprints on the carpet, no cigar ashes, no sign of a forced entry. In fact, if someone had wanted to get in, they could have walked right in through the French doors, which Egerton had undoubtedly left open to the warm evening. That would explain the mosquito bite on his ankle.

Something nagged at the edge of Kyra's brain. She walked to the doors and looked out. It was the same view as from . . . of course! *This* was the room she had seen Becky Hollingshood leaving so furtively a short while ago! Could *Becky* have murdered Egerton? And if so, how? And when? Egerton had been dead for several hours and Becky had left only recently. Surely she would not have stayed around that long. Or risked returning at such a late hour. But if she had simply found the body, why wouldn't she have told anyone? Was she afraid she'd be blamed?

The thoughts whirled in Kyra's mind as she walked back toward the main door where Drogan and Hadley Turbot were standing quietly, almost carefully, just inside the room. She felt a flash of empathy for Drogan, who, disguised, had to stand by passively and forgo a complete examination of the room. But he couldn't risk blowing his cover in front of the biggest gossip in the Daisy Hill Hunt.

Nevertheless, Kyra felt sure that Inspector Drogan had managed to examine the body and the room from where he stood. His thoroughness and exactitude of observation had made him famous among detectives. She hoped that before too long they'd get some time alone to compare notes.

As if he'd read Kyra's thoughts once again, Thurston said, "I asked Hadley to bring Mr. Asquith in the hope that he might consent to draw death portraits of both my son and this gentleman. I would like to have a likeness of both of them to remind me of how precious life is."

"Most certainly, Senator, I would be honored," Philip immediately responded. "Would you like me to start right away?"

"After the hunt will be soon enough," Thurston said. "I think that we should not say anything to anyone about Egerton's death. The plans should proceed as scheduled, which means that the four of you should be going out to mount up in a few minutes." He gave Edna a particularly severe look and added, "Do you understand what I'm asking?"

"Yes, Senator," Edna answered with an uncharacteristic blush. "*I* can hold my tongue as well as anyone—if people only *knew* the secrets I've kept!"

"That's just the point," Thurston said acidly. "Not to let anyone *know* this secret." Edna looked properly rebuked but was saved further embarrassment by Corrie's knock on the door.

"We need to have a look at your guest list, Corrie," Thurston said as the middle-aged, large-bosomed woman entered. In response to her shocked gasp when she saw Egerton's body, he added, "And I've just been telling these people that we do not want *anyone* to know about this until after the hunt—even the sheriffs. Is that clear?"

"Yes, sir!" she said. "Was he . . ."

"We don't know yet. He may have died naturally in his sleep. We'll probably need medical help to determine that. But do you have the list with you?"

"Yes, oh, yes!" was the flustered answer as she searched through a small bundle of papers in her apron pocket. "I've been carrying it with me, so I know who's in which room, what with all of these strangers. Yes, here it is." She held it out toward Thurston, who took it from her and ran his finger quickly down the straggling, ink-blotted column of names. Kyra recognized Nadine's large, awkward handwriting and realized that her friend had probably written the list out for Corrie in preparation for the weekend. It was probably one of the last things she'd used her desk for before it had become a repository for Anthony's head. She suddenly wondered if Drogan were right, if the murderer *was* insane—severing a hound's head like that was *not* the action of a rational person.

"George Christianson," Thurston read, "from the Essex Hunt in New Jersey. Hmmm! The only one from there, too. Nathaniel never mentioned that any of the Essex hunters were coming. Perhaps I'll give a jingle to my friend Senator Wilson from New Jersey and see if he knows this fellow. Wilson used to hunt with the Essex, but he gave it up back in 1901 for health reasons—said it took him two days to recover from half a day's hunting." He was mumbling a bit and rambling on in a way that indicated to Kyra that he was probably about to collapse into another of his fits of grief over Nathaniel. All things considered, he was holding together very well.

Just then Hadley gave forth an effeminate screech and leaped onto the nearest chair. He pointed wordlessly toward the bottom of the washstand, his face dead white and his hand shaking with fear.

The others looked to where he was pointing in time to see a small flicker of motion. Kyra's first impression was of a mouse, but then she realized that what she'd just seen was the tail of a very small snake. It disappeared under the bottom curtain of the stand. Was this another of Hadley's little tricks? Kyra looked sharply at the boy.

Seeing her glance, Hadley whined defensively, "It's not mine. I didn't put it in here. I came to play a joke on Egerton, but that isn't *my* snake! I don't keep snakes. I only brought that darned skunk and a little fox I was going to get one of the grooms to let loose for the hunt. But Aunt Edna took both of them away. Honest!" Kyra believed him, not because of what he said, but because he looked genuinely terrified as the snake poked its head out from under the ruffle again.

"Eeech!" exclaimed Corrie with horror and disgust. "It's one of them adders! We found a nest of them just outside this room last week. Caught them all, we thought, but one must have escaped." She paused, then looked from the washstand to the bed and back again as a new thought dawned on her. "You don't think it *bit* him, do you? They *are* poisonous, and he'd been drinking, so the poison would work faster—get to his heart real quick."

While Corrie was still talking, Kyra had thrown the sheet back to look at Egerton's ankle again. Corrie leaned over and looked, too. "That's it," she said. "That's what one of them bites looks like. I've seen them before on the men that have gone fishing in the streams around here. There's a lot of them adders and you can't hardly feel it when they bite you. This fellow probably didn't even know. Probably just went to sleep, from the looks of him, and never woke up."

"Well, that mystery seems to be solved!" said Drogan with his British accent. "Clearly, the adder must have escaped being caught by hiding under the washstand. When Egerton washed his face last night, his foot disturbed the snake, which bit him. He'd probably had one or two too many drinks and didn't realize he'd been bitten."

"Yes! That must have been *exactly* what happened!" contributed Edna. "And it's just a coincidence that it happened this weekend along with . . . everything else," she finished lamely with a concerned look in Thurston's direction.

Kyra was not at all convinced, but she let the moment pass without comment. She was, however, puzzled by Drogan's apparent eagerness to explain away Egerton's death. But of course he hadn't seen the manuscript pages she'd just read or heard Egerton's parting comment at the edge of the dance floor. What had Egerton wanted to tell her? Who did he intend to check it out with first? What did he intend to check out? And why was it important to tell her before the hunt? Until she'd read the manuscript pages, the events in the stable had caused her to forget that Egerton had said he would contact her this morning.

Aloud Kyra said, "We'd best be getting back outside, then. I suppose we can just close off the room, snake and all, until later? Is that what you'd like to do?" She directed her questions to Thurston.

"Yes, uh . . . oh, yes! That's what I'd like to do. I need to get back to my library, now, if you don't mind. Corrie, will you lock up?" Distracted, he turned to leave. His face looked pained again, and Kyra was glad when the door opened and a gust of wind carried Dr. Whitley's voice to them. The good doctor would be able to soothe Thurston and see that he was all right until she and Gerald returned.

Edna yanked Hadley rather roughly from his perch on the chair and the four of them walked outside and around the corner toward the front lawn. At the last moment, Kyra looked back at the room and Corrie motioned for her to return. She let the others go ahead and stepped back to the housekeeper, who extracted an envelope from her apron pocket.

"This was delivered a few minutes ago," the woman said. "I didn't know who to give it to, and the senator seemed too upset just now to ask. Since it said 'Inspector,' I thought you might know who it would go to—you bein' a detective, and all."

The envelope was addressed to "Inspector Philip Drogan, c/o Hopsworth Manor." Kyra nodded, put it into her pocket together with the manuscript pages, and said, "Thank you, Corrie, I'll see that he gets it." She then hurried to rejoin the others as Corrie locked the French doors behind her.

She was just in time to see the Field Master, Tobias LaFarge, give a signal for the grooms to bring the saddled and bridled horses over to their owners. The first to see the approaching horses gave the word: "Time to mount up!" There was a general flurry of last bites and drinks before the foxhunters set their plates and glasses aside, adjusted their hats, pulled on their gloves, and mounted. In their haste, a few forgot to make sure that their saddle girths were tightened properly and wound up resettling their saddles with embarrassed looks. But within minutes, most of the field members were already on their horses, pacing around the grassy area, waiting for the slower ones to mount up. In addition to the grooms, a number of spectators had gathered to see the hunters off. Kyra noticed in particular several well-dressed young women who were clicking away with portable Kodaks. These still rather cumbersome black boxes were new on the market and the latest rage among the affluent avant-garde. Kyra had been amazed at the high quality of some of the Kodak pictures, and she wondered how these particular ones would turn out. She would have liked to have a few.

As soon as Benny saw Kyra, he brought her mare over to her; he was followed by Edna's grooms and the groom Thurston had assigned to assist Drogan. Kyra noticed that another of Thurston's grooms was adjusting

Lady Pandora's girth, and she fleetingly wondered where the Roseberrys' ever-efficient Indian groom was.

"They've given me a very fine horse," Drogan said by way of conversation, stroking the neck of the animal he'd been presented with.

"They have only fine horses here," Edna said haughtily. "Not like some places where any old hack is considered fit for hunting. Why, Nathaniel even used Truly Fine as a hunter."

"Truly Fine?" Drogan asked.

"Hopsworth's best stallion," Kyra answered. "The horse Nathaniel was riding when he was killed."

"Oh, really? I didn't know that. How simply awful," he said in his most supercilious voice. "Was the horse killed, too?" Since these were all things Drogan knew very well, Kyra figured he was still trying to put up a front for Edna, so she played along.

"Would that make a great deal of difference?" she said with irritation in her voice. "Thurston's only son is dead—do you think he gives a fig about the horse?" With that, she took a leg up from Benny and flounced onto her horse with an excellent simulation of disgust.

"Your husband said t' tell y'all he went ahead t' th' kennels t' help Os'ald pick th' hounds for today," Benny said as Kyra adjusted herself in the sidesaddle. "He said he wanted t' help Os'ald 'cuz he seemed real edgy."

"Good!" she said. "I was hoping he'd do that. Oswald will probably need all the help he can get today." They were now mounted and ready to join the others as they paced around the lawns, gently warming up their horses. As if the breakfast had not been enough, waiters were walking between the horses, balancing crystal champagne glasses on silver platters, serving the traditional champagne stirrup cups to the riders. Although she never drank in the morning, and not much at any other time, Kyra took one of the bubbly drinks and downed it quickly. The liquor spread warmly in her stomach, helping her to relax and forget about what they'd just seen in the house. She noticed that Drogan also took a glass, but

Edna abstained and slapped Hadley's hand away when he reached for one. "Little boys don't drink that!" she exclaimed.

"I'm *not* a little boy anymore, Aunt Edna," Hadley wheedled. "Can't I have some, just this once?"

"I said no and that's it!" Edna pronounced.

"Damn!" muttered Hadley, kicking his pony so viciously that it squealed and jumped. He then wheeled it around and took off for the other side of the lawn.

"Well, I never!" gasped Edna. "Children these days! The *language* they learn! I just don't know where they get it!" With that she spurred her own horse after Hadley.

But she did not have time to catch up with him before a short series of notes were heard from Oswald's hunt horn. The substitute Huntsman approached from the direction of the kennels with the Daisy Hill Hunt's pack of hounds in tow. Becky Hollingshood and Gerald, unfurled hunt whips in hand, rode before and after the pack, respectively. The hounds were so well trained that this light containment was all that was needed to keep the pack under control and following at the Huntsman's heels. It was a tribute to Nathaniel's training that even with the sudden substitution of Huntsman, the pack maintained proper formation. Kyra remembered Nathaniel often saying that a well-treated hound had implicit trust in human beings and would do everything in its power to please them. Here was living proof.

Kyra had always enjoyed the sight of a pack of hounds, fresh from kennels and eager to be off, their eyes bright, senses alert, and bodies fairly trembling with excitement. The hounds Nathaniel had bred were also very beautiful examples of the American foxhound. Like their English ancestors, their short hair was tricolored, black, white, and a rich chocolaty brown, with tails (called "sterns" in foxhunting lingo) that curved slightly upward, strong athletic bodies, and wide intelligent heads with long silky ears and soft brown eyes. But because of the greater distances and rougher country they had to traverse, American foxhounds were bred to be larger and sturdier. They had longer legs, bigger feet, and greater stamina than their English counterparts.

For the most part, however, American foxhunting was not so very different from what the English practiced. Kyra had once seen an old English engraving of a hunting scene, the image of which always came to her on hunting weekends. The hunt had never seemed quite real to her, but then that was part of its charm: although foxhunting had originated as a method of ridding farmland of "vermin," including rats and badgers as well as foxes, it had gradually become an ornamental sport. It was a fantasy, an escape from everyday life into another world and another time—and that was enough as far as most of its devotees were concerned.

But Nathaniel's death had brought a very real and very ugly reality into the matter. Kyra glanced from Oswald, now stopped with the hounds in a milling bunch around him, to the other hunters who were gathering around the Field Master. Which one or ones of them were responsible for Nathaniel's death? Would she and Drogan be able to find out before the end of the day, when the company would disperse? And would there be any more deaths before the day was over?

With these thoughts in mind, Kyra urged her horse forward toward Gerald on the far side of the pack, with the intention of taking over his position as Whipper-In. As she reined up next to him, he smiled and handed her a small metal object, saying in a low voice, "If you run into any major problems, blow this and I'll find you." Kyra glanced at the object in her hand: It was a whistle. She nodded and put it in her pocket. Without another word, Gerald turned and rode back toward Tobias LaFarge, who as Field Master was making some announcements and introducing the guests from other hunt clubs.

Kyra had always thought that Tobias sat a horse a bit like depictions of the insane Roman emperor Caligula. He somehow always looked as if he were swaggering (even on horseback), and his face always wore the shadow of an idiotic leer. He was notorious for his ability to consume liquor, and although Kyra had never kept count, she suspected that some of Tobias's instability in the saddle was caused by too many stirrup cups, not to mention punch and sherry. He was also noted for his vicious streak when crossed, and watching him now, Kyra wondered if Nathaniel's death might have been the result of his having crossed Tobias in some way. She doubted that Tobias would have any more compunction about killing a person than he would about squashing a bug that got in his way.

Or a snake. Kyra's mind leaped from Tobias to the snake in Egerton's room. Tobias kept snakes as a hobby. He collected them from all over the world. He had boas, pythons, cobras, and every other kind imaginable, but he was especially noted for his extensive collection of native American snakes, including every species and subspecies known to science. He would naturally have been the person Corrie called to catch and dispose of the adders—he regularly performed such services for his friends and neighbors and sometimes found a rare subspecies that way. Kyra could have hit herself for not having thought of it sooner. Even if Tobias had not kept any of the adders that day, he certainly had some in his collection and could easily have let one loose in Egerton's room. Even supposing that were true, one important question remained: For whom was the snake intended and why? Was it meant to kill Egerton or the unknown man from New Jersey? And why not use a more certain method? The snake could easily have hidden away and not bitten anyone. Or the room's occupant could have seen the snake first and given an alarm or simply killed it. What would be the piece or pieces that would bring the whole puzzle into focus?

She glanced back toward the mansion and saw Thurston standing at the top of the front steps with Dr. Whitley, watching the hunt's departure as he had done so many times when Nathaniel was alive. Thurston had hunted when he was younger, and he still rode each day, but he now found riding to hounds too strenuous and exhausting. He liked to see others enjoying the sport, however, and sometimes followed along the roads in a carriage. Kyra had assumed he wouldn't be doing that today, but then she saw Thurston's carriage, pulled by a matching pair of grays, draw up to the steps. Apparently he intended to do everything as closely as possible to the way it would have been done if Nathaniel had been there.

Tobias concluded his remarks with a short prayer for Nathaniel, during which all of the men took off their hunt caps and top hats and everyone bowed their heads. Kyra found that she could not bow hers as Tobias sanctimoniously intoned some lines he had cribbed from the Episcopalian *Book of Common Prayer*. She was not a religious person, but the thought of Tobias uttering a prayer for Nathaniel seemed sacrilegious. Philip Drogan had not bowed his head, either, in spite of his early religious training, and he caught her eye with a meaningful glance at Tobias. Philip didn't know some of the things about Tobias that she did, but he had managed to come to the same conclusion as Kyra.

When Tobias finished his prayer, he lifted his head and without a pause exclaimed, "Let's hunt!" To his obvious bafflement, the assemblage did not let forth their usual cheer at this proclamation but remained reverently silent, hats still doffed and heads bowed for several moments longer in memory of their departed Huntsman.

Oswald was the first to raise his head and replace the reinforced cap worn by Huntsmen, Masters and Whippers-In. He then began to move slowly toward a white-railed fence that surrounded the pasture next to Hopsworth's lawns. Becky and Kyra kept the hounds well behind him so that they would not be in the way of his horse when he jumped the five-foot fence.

After Oswald's horse made the jump easily, the hounds swarmed through the rails to catch up with him as he trotted off toward a meadow where one of the grooms had reported seeing a fox earlier that morning. Hopefully the scent would still be fresh enough for the hounds to pick up. As soon as the area near the fence was clear of hounds, Becky and Kyra jumped it. Becky, as first Whipper-In, then circled around in front of Oswald to keep any overeager hounds from passing him, while Kyra stayed a short distance behind and urged a few slow hounds up with the pack. Tobias and the Field followed at a short distance behind.

When they reached the meadow, Oswald pulled up and said, "Kyra, you stay here with me and hold the hounds for a few minutes while Becky goes to the other side of that covert." He pointed to a small grove of willows that bordered the meadow. "When the fox was sighted, he was headed in that direction."

The hounds were eager and hard to hold, but Becky galloped quickly around the covert and soon signaled that she was in position. Oswald then gave the peculiar yipping cry and hand motion that told the hounds to cast for a scent. They needed no further urging, and within moments they had fanned out over the meadow and were zigzagging through the grass with their heads to the ground and sterns held stiffly behind. Old Bella, the strike hound, was as usual the first one to feather, or wave, her stern as an indication that she had scented something of interest. Several of the younger hounds quickly gathered around her, casting now in small circles to try to pick up the scent. Suddenly Bella gave tongue and was quickly honored by Sargent, Singer, and Meriweather, their combined voices making a strangely pleasant music that always gave Kyra a thrill of excitement. They were running on the scent now and the rest of the pack had converged behind them, adding their voices to the medley.

The covert was larger than it looked and the hounds disappeared into it for some minutes, followed by Oswald. Kyra stayed on the near side to send back any hounds that strayed, and the Field went pounding past, circling toward the spot where Becky had been stationed in the likely hope that the hounds would emerge on that side. Kyra hoped that Tobias would not lead them over the fox's path, as he had done all too frequently in the past, obliterating the scent completely, much to Nathaniel's disgruntlement. The Huntsman would then have to re-collect his hounds, take them over the defiled area, and recast them where he thought the scent would likely be. And it wasn't always there. The Daisy Hill Hunt had lost several good runs that way during the past season and Kyra had sometimes wondered why Nathaniel didn't appoint a new Field Master. But now she supposed it really didn't matter.

Kyra was musing about this when her mare suddenly pricked her ears forward and snorted. A moment later she saw a flicker in the brush just ahead of where her horse was standing and found herself looking straight into the eyes of the largest dog fox she had ever seen. He gazed at her for a few moments, then walked sedately out of the shade into the bright sunlight of the meadow, where he picked up a lope. His thick red fur rippled slightly as he moved. He was a fine specimen and had obviously outwitted Nathaniel's pack many times. He was probably, in fact, the fox known to the Daisy Hill Hunt as "Old Harvey," who often led them a merry chase and always went to ground, usually in one of several inaccessible spots at the bottom of a ravine about ten miles from Hopsworth. He had been frequently spotted from a distance, but this was the first time anyone had seen him from such close quarters.

Kyra was about to call out "Tally ho!" to let the hounds and the other hunters know that the fox was on this side of the covert, when she realized that the hounds' cry had suddenly changed. It had grown louder, more strident, and accompanying it was the sound of Oswald's horn playing "Gone Away!" to urge the hounds forward even faster. But they were going in the opposite direction! Could they be running heel? Kyra listened for a few moments before concluding that the hounds had picked up a different scent, and a very strong one at that. They were at full cry! Even from so far away, the sound was exciting. But Kyra was still puzzled. She glanced back at Old Harvey, who had heard the hounds, too, and was sitting on top of a nearby knoll with a look on his face that Kyra could only interpret as smug. "You old devil, you," she said softly. "At least they haven't gotten you like they got Nathaniel!" Then she turned her horse and cantered around the covert in the direction of the hounds, glancing back once to see Old Harvey still sitting on the knoll.

Kyra knew just where she could cut across a pasture and intersect the path the hounds seemed to be taking, but she was still puzzled by the sound of their cry. It was too loud and they were moving too fast. It sounded like . . . The thought struck her with an almost physical thud. The hounds were following a drag! Could Oswald have ordered a drag laid to ensure at least one good run that day? If he had, he was even more desperate and unsure of himself than Kyra had realized, because such a practice was frowned upon.

Then another possibility dawned on her. Someone could have laid the scent without Oswald's knowledge, someone who would know that Oswald was inexperienced enough to think it was a live trail. But why? Could it be leading toward another trap, another wired fence, or even worse? Kyra whipped her horse into its fastest gallop, clearing fences and bushes as if they were mere hillocks in an agonizing rush to intersect the hounds before they led the hunters into . . . into what?

CHAPTER 11

Doubling Back

THE first person Kyra saw was Becky Hollingshood at the side of the Killdare Ravine. This rugged gash in the landscape had been named for its sheer sides, which were almost impossible for a horse to negotiate. For more than a century local wags had dared each other to race to the bottom, resulting in a few deaths every couple of years. The hounds were baying and yelping somewhere far below, hidden from sight by heavy foliage.

"They've either treed something, or it's gone to ground," Becky panted, still out of breath from the hard ride. "Oswald wants you and me to try to find some way down here. He went around to the other side, to see if there's a better way there."

"Where's the Field?" Kyra demanded through her own fast breathing.

"They followed him."

"We've got to catch them! There's something terribly wrong!" Kyra had already turned her horse in the direction Becky had indicated and was moving again.

"*What's* wrong?" Becky wanted to know, bringing her horse alongside Kyra's. Kyra looked at her, thinking fast. Could she trust her? She might need help, but was

168

Becky the person to ask? She made a split second decision which she hoped was the right one.

"Someone's set a drag," she explained hastily as she kicked her horse into a gallop again. "The fox the hounds were on originally went the other way. Someone *wants* to get everyone at the bottom of that ravine."

"Why?" Becky yelled over the rushing wind as she galloped beside Kyra.

"I don't know! Perhaps they've set dynamite and intend to blow everyone to bits!"

"Oh, my God!" was all Becky could manage as she kicked her horse into a faster gallop to keep up with Kyra.

Just then Kyra caught a glimpse of a horse clearing a fence into a copse of firs at the far side of the rocky pasture that bordered the ravine. It had a bobbed tail like most of the hunt horses, but it was going in the wrong direction. She saw it for only an instant before it disappeared into the dense undergrowth, so she couldn't identify it for sure or tell who was riding it. But her detective's instinct told her to follow it. It could easily be carrying whoever had set the drag. She glanced over at Becky, who was looking straight ahead and had apparently not seen anything. Kyra made another split second decision.

"Becky, *you* warn the others, I've got to go do something else—I can't explain right now. Just *don't* let Oswald and the others go down into that ravine!"

"All right!" Becky shouted back as Kyra turned her horse across the pasture toward the copse.

In her urgency to catch up with the mystery horse, Kyra galloped at full speed toward the fence, without stopping to consider the danger of badger holes or rocks that could easily trip her horse and send her sprawling. Fortunately, Kyra's mare was an experienced hunter, who looked out for holes and watched where she put her feet. Kyra could usually give her a free rein in the hunt field, no matter how fast the chase, and Diana would pick the safest path to follow. Today was no exception and she carried Kyra safely to the fence, which she cleared easily.

There was only one trail through the woods on the other side, which Kyra sped along, ducking overhanging branches and dodging trunks where the path made several sharp turns. Beneath her in the soft forest mulch, she could see fresh hoofprints, but she could hear nothing in the distance. She supposed the other horse had already come to the opposite edge of the woods and she only hoped that she would be able to follow the tracks as easily there, where the soil would be harder.

She had forgotten that a country road traversed the woods until the moment the trail opened out onto it. She pulled up abruptly and looked in both directions. Nothing. Then she looked at the ground. Carriage tracks. The same carriage tracks she'd seen the day before at the rigged jump—the same telltale series of nail heads on the imprint made by the right rear wheel gave it away. Kyra was glad she'd instructed Benny to check with all the local blacksmiths—but she wished she'd had him do it yesterday. He would undoubtedly have the information for her when she got back from the hunt, but that did her little good at the moment.

The carriage had waited at the edge of the road for some time. There were several piles of manure and numerous hoofprints in front of a sapling to which the horses had apparently been tied, as well as a scattering of oats that probably fell from nose bags given to the horses to keep them quiet. One of the horses, Kyra noted, was missing a front shoe, whereas it hadn't been yesterday. That probably indicated some hard usage between then and now. Why?

Kyra turned to the left and followed the carriage tracks and the prints of three horses—two pulling the carriage and one following behind. This puzzled Kyra, as the road was easily wide enough for a mounted rider to stay alongside the carriage. Of course, that assumed the rider had met the carriage and they were going somewhere together. Another alternative was that the rider was following some distance behind the carriage or just happened to be going in the same direction. Yet another was that the rider had dismounted and was riding *inside* the carriage, with the horse tied behind.

Kyra's mare was breathing hard, so she let her ease into a trot, certain that they would soon catch up to the slower-moving carriage anyway. Besides, she needed a bit of time to collect her thoughts. What would she say, or do, when she *did* catch up to the carriage? Who was the most likely person to have laid a drag? Why? She was running through these questions when she saw Thurston's carriage approaching from the direction the other carriage had gone—they must have passed each other.

"Hello!" Thurston said, leaning out of the carriage window as Kyra reined in next to it. "If you're chasing after the runaway, it's been safely caught and I've just given instructions for it to be taken back to Hopsworth. How's the unfortunate rider?"

"The horse was *riderless*?" Kyra was dumbfounded. She had been certain there was a rider on that horse when it had cleared the fence into the woods. And she hadn't found a downed rider anywhere along the trail. Besides, why would a riderless horse run *away* from the rest of the horses? It just didn't make sense. "Are you certain?" she asked Thurston.

"It was tied behind a carriage, muddy and limping badly. Looked like it had taken a nasty fall somewhere. I sent it back, as it was too lame to do its rider any good now, anyway. I figured we'd pick her up in the carriage."

"*Her?* The horse was wearing a *sidesaddle*?" Kyra was even more dumbfounded. Could a *woman* have possibly laid that drag? The only possibilities Kyra could think of were Nadine Howard and Becky Hollingshood. But Nadine was in bed and Becky had been busy whipping at precisely the time when the drag would have had to be laid. Scent didn't last very long, and the trail the hounds had hit was fresh and strong. Was it possible that Nadine had gotten out of bed and . . . No! Nadine *couldn't* be guilty. Kyra tried to shut the possibility out of her mind, but what other explanation was there? "Did you recognize the horse?" she finally managed to ask.

"I can't say that I did," Thurston said with a tired sigh. He ran his hand over his face and added, "I used to have a great eye for a horse—if ever I saw one, I would always recognize it again. But lately there's just been too much else to think about."

"That's perfectly understandable," Kyra answered, thinking how she would feel if one of her children had been killed. And how much worse would Thurston feel if Nadine were guilty? Was it possible that Thurston didn't recognize Nadine's new horse? She'd only had it a few weeks and the old man might not even have seen it, as he'd been even more busy than Gerald finishing up the last Senate sessions before the spring break. He'd been staying nights in his apartment in Washington for most of that time.

These thoughts went through her mind in a flash when she remembered that the horse she'd seen go over the fence was the same color—a dark bay—as Nadine's new horse. Of course that was a common color . . . No! It couldn't have been Nadine's horse. Unless someone else were using it. *That* was possible. But who? It was wearing a sidesaddle, which meant the rider was a woman. But what woman? . . . Kyra's mind reeled. Then, out of nowhere, she remembered a dictum from a Sherlock Holmes story: When something seems impossible, look for the obvious explanation. Some good that did! That was easy enough to spout in a fictional story, but when you were faced with a real murder it was a different matter. Kyra felt an uncharacteristic wave of anger and resentment. Mystery writers made it look so easy!

It was only with a great exertion of willpower that Kyra returned to her former train of thought and asked, "Could the horse's rider have been in the carriage?"

Thurston looked confused for a moment, then said, "You know, I didn't think to look! They said they'd caught the horse running loose, and I didn't think to question them.''

"Who *did* you see in the carriage?''

"The driver and just one other man who stuck his head out the window to talk to me. There could easily have been someone else inside.''

"You didn't know the man?''

"No. He was a stranger in these parts, as far as I know. Said his name was Jones and he'd come out from Washington to look for early mushrooms, but hadn't found any. Was just about to start back when this horse comes bursting through the woods as if a thousand devils were chasing it. But when it saw his carriage horses it stopped dead, so he was able to catch it and tie it to the back of his carriage.''

Kyra thought about this for a moment. The story accounted for the carriage's long wait at the side of the road and for the pattern of hoofprints she'd been following. But the coincidence of the mended wheel still bothered her. "You're absolutely sure you didn't see anyone else with him?'' she asked again.

"No. Just his driver. The surliest-looking old man you ever saw—and one of the ugliest, to judge by what I saw of him, which wasn't much.''

"Was his skin yellowish and was he wearing a gray coat or sweater?'' Kyra asked urgently.

"Yes . . . and a shapeless sort of gray hat that practically covered his face,'' Thurston answered. "Why?''

"He may be the man who attacked me yesterday evening and the one who dug a hole for my horse to trip in during the steeplechase.''

"And I let them go!'' Thurston exclaimed. "I let them right past me! Driver—turn the carriage around! They can't have gotten too far.''

"Wait!'' Kyra said, and explained her suspicions about a drag and how she had left Becky Hollingshood to warn the others. "That horse,'' she concluded, "may not be muddy from a fall at all, but from sliding down the side of Killdare Ravine, not to mention climbing out again. It may not even be lame, but simply overtired—it was going hard and fast when I saw it."

It was the senator's turn to be dumbfounded. "You think someone may be trying to kill *everyone* in the hunt?" he said incredulously. "*Why*, in the good Lord's name?"

"I don't know!" Kyra said with exasperation. "Why would anyone want to kill Nathaniel in the first place?"

"But someone did," Thurston reminded her grimly. "And I intend to find out who! Right now, I'll catch up to that carriage. My driver and I can take care of them just fine—*you* go back to that ravine and make sure no one else gets hurt. That's an order!" he added when he saw Kyra's look of protest.

There was nothing to do but follow Thurston's command and hope for the best. He probably *was* still a match for just about any man. Besides, Kyra was concerned about the hunters. Becky alone might not be able to convince them to give up their hunt. Foxhunters were notoriously single-minded and stubborn when they were onto game. They would go over, under, and through obstacles that would daunt any man in his right mind. One of the most exhilarating things about a fast chase was the sense of omnipotence it created, the sense of "I can do anything, I'm invulnerable." Kyra was certain that during the height of the chase none of the hunters would ever consider themselves to be in any danger. That was precisely what would put them in the most vulnerable position for any kind of trap or attack.

As Thurston's driver turned the carriage around to pursue the strangers, Kyra urged Diana back onto the path through the woods toward Killdare Ravine. Fortunately, the short time Kyra had spent talking to Thurston had been enough for the hardy mare to gain her second wind. She galloped back along the path with as much energy as if she were fresh from the barn, and she took the fence at the edge almost effortlessly.

What Kyra saw when she got to the ravine would have made her laugh if the situation hadn't been so potentially dangerous. Apparently still thinking that the hounds were following "Old Harvey," Oswald had managed somehow to follow them down into the deepest part of the ravine before discovering his mistake. Even in the midst of her concerns, Kyra couldn't help wondering what his face had looked like when, instead of a fox treed or gone to ground, he'd found hounds milling around the dead end of a scent line. At the moment, however, he was completely hidden by undergrowth and beyond the reach of human voice. Kyra could hear him moving farther and farther away, occasionally blowing his horn to collect the hounds, which had scattered at the bottom.

Meanwhile, Tobias and a small contingent of hardy riders, referred to among foxhunters as "thrusters," had attempted to follow Oswald. The first few had gotten through and were no doubt with him, but the steep trail on the side of the ravine had since collapsed, leaving half a dozen riders stranded on the side of the precipice, unable to move forward and unable to turn around on the narrow trail. The last one of these had managed to dismount and was trying to back his horse up the trail to a wider spot where it could turn around. But several others were ladies in sidesaddles, who were unable to dismount on the steep slope without assistance, so they could not attempt the same maneuver. In the meantime, their horses had grown nervous at the strange delay and were dancing impatiently on the narrow trail, creating the danger of further cave-ins or just plain stepping over the edge. The ladies, in turn, had grown more nervous themselves. A couple of them had put their arms around their horses' necks and hidden their faces in the manes to keep from looking down over the steep drop-off.

The rest of the Field watched from the top of the ridge, shouting down instructions and advice. A couple of the men had even gotten off their horses and were walking down the trail to try to help. Once there, Kyra figured that they would have to pry the frightened ladies from their mounts and carry them up the hill on their backs, leaving the horses and male riders to fend for themselves.

Becky was among the group at the top and rode over when she saw Kyra. "They were just like this when I got here," she said, shrugging her shoulders and shaking her head. "They're so involved in what they're doing that they don't care whether they were following a drag or a will-o'-the-wisp. One of the Newcastle hunters even commented that under the circumstances he thought it was enterprising of Oswald to have had a drag laid, though he would have chosen a slightly easier ending place."

"Well, nothing too terrible seems to have happened," Kyra commented. "Perhaps someone *did* just lay a drag to ensure sport today." She felt relieved, but oddly disappointed, too. Would they just get everyone, including the hounds, out of the ravine and go back to Hopsworth without making any further progress toward discovering who had murdered Nathaniel? Kyra had somehow been expecting a grand climax, some kind of a catharsis that would reveal everything, solve everything, tie everything up in a neat package. Instead, she was confronted with a plain and simple mess.

Then she remembered the riderless horse. "Becky," she said, "did anyone come off their horse during the run?"

"Not that I know of," Becky responded. "Of course, I was up front during the first part of the run, and then I waited for you and came up from behind. I didn't see any downed riders then, and no one has mentioned anything since we've been here. Why?"

Before Kyra could answer, Gerald came riding toward them. "Quite a mess, isn't it?" he said, expressing exactly what Kyra had been thinking a moment earlier.

"Yes." Kyra sighed with resignation at the thought of the work ahead of them. It would probably take hours to collect the hounds and extricate the stranded horses and riders from the trail. And almost infinite tact and patience would be required to keep such a strong-minded group of people happily working together until the last rider was out of the ravine. Foxhunting protocol decreed that when faced with such a situation, no one could leave the scene until everyone was safe.

Kyra repeated her question about a downed rider to Gerald, who knew nothing of it either. With a start, Kyra remembered that she hadn't had a chance to tell Gerald about Egerton.

"I need to talk to Gerald for a moment in private," she said to Becky, who nodded and rode back toward the other hunters.

"No!" Gerald expostulated when Kyra had broken the news. "Not Egerton! Why would *anyone* want to kill *him*?"

"That's what I said about Nathaniel," Kyra reminded her husband gently. She then told him about the manuscript pages and about seeing Becky leave Egerton's room.

"Damned if I know what's going on!" swore Gerald, who almost never used profanity. His eyes flashed with anger and frustration against the senselessness of it all. His borrowed horse reacted to his rider's surge of emotion and moved restlessly. Gerald responded by walking the horse in a circle around Kyra. He was the kind of man who needed to *do* something when faced with a problem.

"I suppose all we can do at the moment is to try to get things rolling here as fast as possible," he said so characteristically that Kyra had to smile. "And we can worry about unraveling this mare's nest when we get back to Hopsworth."

As he spoke, Kyra studied the group of riders at the edge of the ravine, as if seeing them for the first time. "How many people rode out this morning?" she suddenly asked Gerald.

"About fifty," he answered. "Give or take one or two."

"And how many are down there with Oswald?"

"No more than half a dozen."

"Do you know who they were?"

"Mostly Newcastle hunters—those guys are *real* thrusters. They were right up in front all the way. I would probably have been down there with them if I'd been on my own horse. I had to slow down a bit to save this one—he's not used to working quite so hard." As he spoke, he patted the horse, which had calmed down.

"Gerald," Kyra said softly, but in a tone that made her husband glance quickly at her, knowing that something had just clicked. "I don't see more than thirty riders over there," she continued. "Where are the rest?"

"You're right," said Gerald, after quickly counting for himself. "Allowing for the ones at the bottom and stuck on the side, there are still eight or ten riders missing. And our run didn't take us through any really rough terrain or difficult fences where riders would have gotten lost or come off."

"Let's figure out who's missing," Kyra suggested.

"First of all," Gerald said, "I don't see either of the Roseberrys." The words were hardly spoken, however, when Lord Randolph and Lady Pandora came walking out of a nearby copse, leading their mounts.

"Perhaps the others are cooling out their horses, too," suggested Gerald. "Perhaps we should ride over to the group and each take our own count. Let's meet back here in a few minutes."

"Yes," Kyra agreed, "that's a good idea." And without another word, she moved her horse toward the other riders, who were so intent on the scene below that they hardly acknowledged her arrival. The one exception was Hadley Turbot, who had dismounted and was sitting on a rock a short distance from the group, picking his teeth with a pocketknife while his pony grazed nearby. After an appraising look at the rest of the group, Kyra slipped off her own horse and walked over to Hadley.

"Your pony's going to step on her reins if you let her do that," Kyra warned.

"I don't care," Hadley said truculently. "Hunt's over, anyway, and it was a pretty lousy one, if you ask me."

"I didn't ask, but why do you say so?" Kyra responded.

" 'Cause there was only one lousy run," Hadley pouted. "And no fox at the end, either, to get torn to bits. *That's* what I came to see!"

"Oh, I see," said Kyra, thinking that was typical of Hadley. For herself, she always secretly rooted for the fox to get away, and she suspected that most other foxhunters did, too. After all, it ensured better and better sport in the following weeks as the fox learned the limits of the hounds and began to play with them. Kyra had seen this happen several times and had confirmed her observations with veteran foxhunters: foxes were fun to hunt in large part because *they* joined into the spirit of things and made a game of it themselves, often outwitting both hounds and men. It was almost always an old or sick fox, or one that had made a grave error in judgment, that was caught by the hounds. Her thoughts were interrupted by a voice from behind.

"I should think the young man would enjoy the type of hunting they do in Australia," said Jerome Cushing, who had appeared from nowhere, leading his horse. "I couldn't help but overhear what you said," he added, smiling at Hadley, who scowled back.

"You're a lot like my son was at your age," continued Cushing, unabashed by the boy's dour look. "They love blood and thunder," he added for Kyra's benefit. "I could never figure it out myself, but they seem to get real pleasure out of watching things get torn apart. I think this young man would like an Australian hunt."

"Why?" challenged Hadley, still scowling but unable to contain his curiosity.

"Do you know what they hunt in Australia?" Cushing asked.

"How would I know that?" Hadley countered scornfully. "I've never been there. No one ever takes me on their darned trips."

"I thought you might have read about it in a book," answered Cushing, still talking evenly and cheerfully.

"But then I suppose you aren't the type who reads much. You strike me as the type who likes action."

"Yeah, action. I like action," said Hadley, warming up a bit at this accurate and nonjudgmental appraisal of his character. "What do they hunt in Australia?" he added with a hint of positive interest.

"Kangaroos," Cushing answered. "They course them with horses and a pack of English foxhounds, complete with fox terriers to dig them out if they go to ground."

"What's so exciting about chasing a bunch of kangaroos?" Hadley wanted to know, lapsing again into his frown. "They're weird-looking."

"They may be weird-looking," granted Cushing, "but they sure can run. And turn! They can turn at right angles going full speed! But what you'd like would be chasing the female kangaroos, the ones with babies in their pouches."

"Why is that?" asked Hadley, looking interested again.

"Because they jettison their babies as they go along. First one does it, then another, as they get tired. They just toss them out, and of course . . ."

"The hounds rip them to pieces!" Hadley finished for him with relish. "Really? Do they *really* do that? I *would* like to go to Australia! That sounds even better than foxhunting." He had visibly cheered up, even to the extent of getting up off the rock and yanking his pony's head toward him in preparation for mounting up again.

For her part, Kyra felt sick to her stomach, not only at Hadley's bloodthirsty attitude, but at Cushing for catering to it. No wonder his own son seemed like such a lout. She had turned to go when Cushing said, "I hope I haven't offended you, Mrs. McMasters."

"As a matter of fact," retorted Kyra candidly, "you have."

"I'm sorry to hear that," Cushing said with genuine regret. "Actually, I was just getting to the best part of the story, which was when one of the female kangaroos decided to go back for her baby, got confused, and picked up a fox terrier instead. She ran with it in her arms for miles and finally put it down unhurt, to the great relief of its owners.''

Kyra stared at Cushing, unable to respond to this latest attack on her sensibilities, almost physical in impact. Somewhere in the background she was dimly aware of Hadley saying, "I liked the first part of your story best." Then she saw Gerald returning to their meeting place and remembered why she had stopped to talk to Hadley.

"Where's your Aunt Edna?" she managed to ask.

"She had trouble with that old nag of hers over one of the first fences, so she went looking for a gate," Hadley said sneeringly.

"You didn't wait for her?" Kyra asked, knowing the answer.

"And miss the run?" Hadley responded incredulously, just as Kyra had expected. "Besides, that Malcolm fellow had trouble with his horse, too, so he's with her."

"Malcolm?" Kyra questioned, not remembering the name from the guest list. "What does he look like?"

"You know him," Hadley said impatiently. "The little guy, the one who's married to old man Howard's daughter—Dicey, or something like that."

"You mean Melvin Dickey?" Kyra said as she suddenly realized whom Hadley meant.

"Yeah, I guess so. At any rate, this little guy on a big fat horse went with her, so I figured she'd be all right."

"But they haven't gotten here yet?" Kyra asked. Could it have been Edna's horse she was following? It was roughly the same color, but it was such a distinctively large, raw-boned animal that she was almost certain she would have recognized it.

"Maybe they stopped to have tea," Hadley suggested insolently. Kyra had had just about enough of him.

"Perhaps you'd be kind enough to take care of this child in the absence of his aunt," Kyra said to Jerome Cushing with complete malice aforethought.

"I'm not a child!" Hadley protested.

"The Daisy Hill Hunt has a rule that no *child* under eighteen years of age can ride alone on a hunt without adult supervision," Kyra explained to Cushing, ignoring Hadley's continued protests. "And since you seem to get along so well with the young man, I thought perhaps you wouldn't mind . . ."

"No, not at all," Cushing assured her. "I'd be happy to."

"Thank you," Kyra said, wondering if she detected a note of irritation in Cushing's voice. "Now if you'd excuse me, I see my husband beckoning to me. By the way," she added as an afterthought, "where is *your* son today?"

"Oh, he's not much of a rider. Too busy with business to take the time—you know how young men are. They don't appreciate the opportunities they have until they're too old to enjoy them. He just came along for the festivities this weekend because he had some business in Washington on Monday. He's no doubt working on his briefs."

"I see," said Kyra. "Then if you'd excuse me."

"Of course," responded Cushing, sweeping his top hat off and bowing with exaggerated gallantry.

Kyra joined Gerald a moment later a short distance away. "What did you come up with?" she asked.

"There *were* a few people in the woods, and as far as I can tell, the only one who's actually missing is Melvin Dickey—no one seems to know where he is, but they're sure he wasn't with the thrusters. By the way, your friend Philip was way up in front—no one could figure out if he was a genuine thruster or if his horse was running away with him."

"Melvin's with Edna Harding," Kyra said, watching Gerald's reaction.

"Edna! By Jove, I guess I didn't see *her*, either. How could I have overlooked her absence!"

"Probably because you like her so well," Kyra suggested with an ironic lift to her eyebrows. "At any rate, Hadley says she had some trouble with her horse at a fence, as did Melvin, and the two of them went together in search of a gate."

"Odd they haven't shown up yet."

"They may have just gone back," Kyra suggested. "I don't see that anyone would have had any reason to do away with them in particular—but then I would have said the same thing about both Nathaniel and Egerton."

"So you want to go back to Hopsworth," Gerald said, correctly reading Kyra's mind.

"Yes, I'm concerned about Thurston, too," she added, briefly explaining about the episode in the woods. "I want to make sure he got back all right and find out who was in that carriage—not to mention whose horse that was."

"You're right, of course," said Gerald. "I'll ask Lord Randolph to take over and I'll come with you—I should never have let you out of my sight this morning. I worried the whole time."

"And I thought you were the one who was riding into a trap!" Kyra expostulated. "I just can't figure out why someone would go to all the bother of laying a drag into such an absolutely impossible place. . . ." Then a new thought struck her, the obvious solution, the thing she *should* have thought of before.

"Gerald!" she exclaimed. "Do you suppose the drag was set to keep us *away* from Hopsworth as long as possible?" As she spoke, she led Diana next to a stump and remounted.

"But why?" Gerald asked. "Why would someone want to keep us all away?"

"I don't know," she answered, "but it's the only logical explanation. I think we should get back there as fast as possible to find out what's going on."

A few minutes later, Senator and Mrs. Gerald McMasters were galloping across country, over fences, and through streams, taking the quickest route back to Hopsworth. Some distance behind, a single figure followed, keeping to the shadows and staying well out of sight.

CHAPTER 12

The Fox Catches
the Hounds

HOPSWORTH was in pandemonium. Black smoke seethed from the library windows and flames were already scorching a path up the outside wall. A petroleum-powered pump run by two manservants hosed a thin stream of water into the window with little effect. The other servants had formed a bucket brigade from the creek to assist the pump's efforts. Even Nadine and Juliette had been roused from their beds and were in line hefting buckets. The lawn was strewn with precious works of art and antiques that had been removed before the conflagration became too much of a danger for servants to run in and out. Now, it looked as if the whole central portion of the house might go up any minute—the fate of the semidetached wings would depend on the whim of the wind.

"Where's Senator Howard?" Gerald yelled over the roar of the flames to Corrie, who seemed to have taken charge.

"Isn't he with the hunt?" Corrie replied. "I haven't seen him since he went out in his carriage after all of you this morning."

"We went cross-country and lost him—he'll probably be back soon," Kyra quickly explained, not wanting to worry Corrie unduly. "How did the fire start?" she added.

"No one knows," Corrie answered. "We just all of a sudden saw smoke and the whole room was on fire. The senator may have dropped a cigar on the sofa, as it seemed to be burning the most. He was always so careful about his cigars, but with all that he's been through this week he may have become forgetful."

"Yes, that's possible," Kyra agreed, although Corrie's story made her suspect that the fire had been set purposefully. A smoldering cigar would not have caused the room to go up that quickly. More likely the sofa and surrounding area had been doused with kerosene and set on fire. But why? Did the senator have documents in the library that someone wanted to destroy? Certainly, he would have kept anything important in his Washington office. Or would he? He was noted for working at home, during the night. Her mind made a giant leap and suddenly she wondered aloud, "Could Nathaniel's death actually have had something to do with his father's work?"

At that moment a horseless fire engine arrived. The crew jumped down and quickly assembled a pump while the captain shouted to the crowd, "Three more horse-drawn engines are behind us—but keep that bucket brigade going until they get here!" His words encouraged everyone, and the buckets were passed with renewed vigor.

Kyra and Gerald were about to join the brigade when a sudden thought struck Kyra. "I want to check around back!" she yelled to Gerald over the general uproar. He nodded, immediately understanding her reasoning—there was a chance that the fire had been set to draw attention away from something else.

They urged their mounts around the mansion as fast as was humane. The horses had galloped hard on the way back to Hopsworth and were sweaty and tired. Kyra and Gerald weren't much better off themselves, especially after the night they'd spent. Their minds were working more slowly than usual and the unexpected silence behind the house had an almost physical impact on them. They stood looking at each other blankly for a moment until they realized that now was the perfect opportunity to investigate the strange sounds they had heard in the barn the night before. They turned in that direction and the tired horses moved a bit faster, hoping for some water and a good feed of grain.

Kyra was the first to notice the train. It had pulled in on the parallel spur line on the far side of the Newcastle Hunt Club's train, so that it was almost completely hidden from view. The noise of its arrival had no doubt been covered up by the commotion of the fire. A group of men were busily loading boxes. The boxes appeared as if from nowhere, until Kyra realized that they were being shoved aboveground from under the horses' wash rack next to the barn. The slotted wooden cover that allowed the water to flow into a drain was now gone, revealing a gaping tunnel underneath. But where did the tunnel go to? What were the men loading into the train? And why?

The men were so preoccupied with their work that Kyra and Gerald watched for some time before they were noticed. Then Melvin Dickey appeared in the doorway of the train, stared at them quietly for a moment with an almost aggrieved look, and said to the two largest workmen, "Bring them here, but don't hurt the lady!"

The workmen quickly grabbed the bridles of Kyra's and Gerald's horses and motioned for them to dismount. Seeing no alternative, they complied and one of the men hustled them unceremoniously, though not roughly, into the first of several passenger cars on the short train. The other man led their horses into the barn. Kyra and Gerald were too tired to resist and Kyra's exhausted mind could think only of her horse. When she saw Melvin inside the train, she blurted out, "Please see that they cool Diana out properly and don't give her too much water!"

Melvin turned to one of the men and gave him orders

in rapid syllables Kyra did not understand. Then he said to her, "Your horse will be well taken care of. Kemal was once in charge of the Shah's stable and knows everything there is to know about horses."

"You must have been speaking Persian, then," Gerald said. "I didn't know you spoke a foreign language."

"I've found it necessary to learn several in the course of my business ventures, since I always suspected that the translators were, let us say, taking a share of the profits to which they weren't entitled." Melvin smiled. "Fortunately, I also found I have a facility for learning languages."

Suddenly Kyra's mind cleared, her exhaustion gone. Persian! Istanbul! The Turkish opium trade. Melvin was in the pharmaceutical supply business and the new tariffs on opium must have made a big difference to him. He must be smuggling it into the country! But what did that have to do with Nathaniel and the Daisy Hill Hunt? Were the boxes full of opium? Why were they under the Hopsworth barn? And how did they get there?

Aloud, she said, "You had someone set the drag to keep everyone away from here long enough to load the train—and the fire was set to keep the servants busy for the same reason?"

"I see you're catching on," Melvin sighed. "I was afraid that would happen eventually. But I was hoping it would take you a bit longer—even a few minutes would have been long enough. We need to be getting underway quite quickly, so why don't you have a seat and I'll explain everything to you when we are moving. Your intelligence does you credit. I won't insult you by tying you up—I understand you had a taste of that last night."

"If you call being hit over the head and trussed like a hog being tied up, then yes, we did," Gerald countered with some heat. "I don't know about Kyra, but my head still feels like putty where your thugs hit me."

"They *hit* you? And *Kyra*, too?" Melvin uttered with disbelief. "I was told that they simply tied and blindfolded you to keep you out of the way, nothing more.

And by the way," he added, turning to Kyra, "I want to assure you that I had *absolutely nothing* to do with what happened in your room before dinner last night. I'm convinced that it was a freak occurrence."

"Was your wife's poisoning a freak occurrence, too?" Kyra asked sarcastically. "And the dead hound's head in Nadine's desk?"

Melvin took a deep breath and closed his eyes. "I know you won't believe me now, but I suspect that Juliette's poisoning was a suicide attempt. She's tried the same thing several times recently, and I live in constant fear that she'll try it again. If I'd known that all of those packets were in the room, I would have removed them. But what's this about a hound's head in Nadine's desk?"

"You tell me about it," Kyra countered.

"I know nothing about it. Could it have been a practical joke?" Something in the absurdity of this suggestion made Kyra believe that Melvin really hadn't known about the head.

"No," she answered simply. "It was no practical joke."

"Then I really don't know—" At this point Melvin saw something outside the window that apparently required his attention. "I've got to leave you for a while," he said, "but I'll have Abdul stay to make some tea for you and I'll tell him you're not to leave. All right?" With that, he spoke to a massive turbaned figure in the same short syllables he had used a few minutes earlier for Kemal and left the car without another word to the McMasterses.

The smiling Turk served them cups of very strong black tea and little cakes, which they accepted gratefully, in spite of their captivity. Kyra could feel the tea reviving her tired body and she could tell from Gerald's expression that it was having the same rejuvenating effect on him.

Finally, Gerald whispered to Kyra, "Did you notice the clubs this fellow and Kemal are wearing in their belts?'' Kyra nodded silently. She had indeed noticed the solid oak sticks, about two feet long and two inches in diameter, that the two men had tucked into their cummerbunds. They were apparently bodyguards of some sort.

"I think they're the ones who attacked us in the barn last night," Gerald continued.

"Then it must have been Kemal who killed Charger!" Kyra exclaimed. "And he's taking care of Diana!"

"He won't hurt her without cause," soothed Gerald. "Besides, that's the least of our worries at the moment."

"You're right, of course," agreed Kyra. "What *are* we going to do?"

"I don't know about you, but I'm interested in finding out what Melvin has to say," Gerald commented. "I always wondered where he got his millions."

"Yes, I did, too, but I'd rather find out some other way," Kyra responded. "I don't think he'd have a bit of compunction about throwing us off this train while it was going full speed."

"No, that would be too risky for him. I'm sure he'll try something more subtle, maybe an 'accident' like Nathaniel's."

Conversation became impossible for the next few minutes as the brakes screeched and the engine, which was quite close, huffed and puffed. The cars were backing off the siding and onto the main line. Where was the train going to go? And how long would it take to get there? Kyra suddenly thought of her children at home. Perhaps Philip Drogan was right after all—a mother of young children had no business getting involved in something like this. And where was Drogan, anyway? She supposed he didn't know enough about hunting to realize they had been on a drag. He was probably back with the other foxhunters at Killdare Ravine. Some help he'd proven to be.

As if in answer to her thoughts, Melvin came in at that moment leading Philip Drogan, whose hands were tied behind his back and whose mouth bore evidence of a recent gag. "I thought you might appreciate some company until I'm free to talk with you," Melvin explained to them with a smile as he untied Drogan's hands. "This one showed up a short while before you, so I was forced to keep him out of the way while we finished loading. But I'm sure he won't do anything to endanger his ladylove, will he?" With a chuckle at his own humor, Melvin left the car again.

Gerald gave Drogan a quick, sharp look, then grinned. It pleased him when men he respected found Kyra attractive—his reaction was a kind of reverse jealousy. He knew she would never betray him, and he was proud of her charm. When she thought about it, she realized that she felt the same way about him.

"So you figured out what the drag was for, too?" Gerald said heartily to Drogan. "We weren't sure you realized it was a drag."

"I wasn't, until I got to the ravine. The hounds were milling around in a spot where no hounds would have lost a scent if there *was* one. So I figured it must have been a drag. It was a short step from there to becoming a hound myself and following the trail left by the drag layer's horse up the other side of the ravine. It was a difficult climb, but Senator Howard had provided me with an exemplary mount."

"We thought he'd run away with you," Kyra interjected. "We heard you were way up in front with the thrusters."

"Yes." Drogan grinned. "That's the first time I've ever been able to do that. It was wonderful! I don't think I've ever done anything quite as exciting before in my life! I was only sorry not to have viewed the fox, but then there wasn't one, was there?"

"No, there wasn't one," Kyra repeated. "Unless you count Melvin."

"He has always rather reminded me of a fox!" rejoined Gerald, smiling at Kyra's analogy. "Except in this case, the fox has caught the hunters. Do either of you have any suggestions as to how we're going to get off this train?''

"I have no intention of getting off," Drogan explained. "Unless we can capture it first. It's loaded with high-quality Turkish opium, which I intend to confiscate in the name of the U.S. Government Customs Office. I've been working on this case a long time, and I'm not going to give it up now."

Kyra and Gerald looked at him blankly for a moment. "That's why you're so thin and—" Kyra began, and Drogan interrupted:

"Yes, I've been working undercover and had to starve myself to look like an addict—you didn't think . . ."

"Yes, I did," Kyra said with relief, "but aren't you with Pinkerton . . . and didn't Thurston . . ."

Drogan answered patiently, with a smile made brighter by Kyra's very real concern for him, "Yes, I'm with Pinkerton, but we've been working in conjunction with the U.S. Customs Office for some time to try to stop the smuggling. When Senator Howard requested a special effort be made on opium, I was put on the case because of my contacts with the New York City underworld. They called me off the case I was working on there and told me to come here because Nathaniel Howard had been killed. Right away I suspected some connection, but I didn't expect to find the cache stored at Hopsworth, right under the senator's nose."

"Yes," agreed Gerald. "That did take a certain amount of gall, if not downright arrogance."

"What is the connection to Nathaniel's death?" Kyra asked, picking up on the other part of Drogan's comment.

"I'm not sure," Drogan answered. "Perhaps he had discovered the cache—but why then wouldn't he have said something about it to his father? My only guess is that he didn't know what he knew, and was killed before he could figure it out. I suspect that something similar happened to your friend Egerton."

"And is about to happen to us," Kyra couldn't help but add. "Unless we make some plan of escape." She wished she could show him the manuscript pages she'd found in Egerton's room, but it was too risky.

"Do you speak English?" Drogan said to Abdul, who had just handed him a cup of tea, "Speakee Inglee?"

The Turk smiled and nodded and said, "Ein biesien. A leetle bit," holding up two fingers about an inch apart.

"Good!" Drogan exclaimed with a wide smile. Speaking very slowly, he said, "I-would-like-some-milk-for-my-tea," accompanied by the proper gestures.

"Ah! Yes!" Abdul said with a grin after a moment's puzzled frown. "Milk! I get."

As soon as his back was turned, Drogan leaned toward the McMasterses and whispered, "Kyra, we can get you off when the train slows down at the junction with the major railroad. If it stops altogether . . ."

"I'm not leaving Gerald," Kyra said emphatically. She was not aware, even a second before she said it, that she would react this way. But suddenly she realized that even her children were not as important to her as this man she loved so much—she couldn't leave him to face possible death alone.

"I'm asking you to go for help!" Drogan added, still in a whisper. "They won't shoot at you. Melvin has turned out to be very superstitious about hurting a woman—I heard him bawling out one of his two Turks for hitting you over the head, and he's told his men in no uncertain terms that you are *not* to be harmed, no matter what."

"So you think they won't go after me," Kyra said with disbelief.

"Oh, no, he'll send men after you all right, but they won't shoot. That gives you an advantage over either of us—and I'm sure you know all of the tricks for shaking a tail. Just get yourself to the nearest police station and get them to intercept this train. Okay?"

Kyra smiled a bit at Drogan's use of detective lingo but didn't answer, as Abdul was returning with a jar of milk. The plan seemed plausible to her, but she had another idea. . . . She thought about it while they drank their tea in silence and decided to try. There was no way to tell Gerald and Inspector Drogan about it now—so she'd just have to play it by ear. As clichéd as it was, the phrase reminded her of the musical career she had given up so many years ago. About the only thing she sang now was lullabies. The thought of lullabies gave her yet another idea. . . .

"Now what am I going to do with you three?" Melvin said with mock earnestness as he walked back into the car.

"Why don't you try telling us what's going on?" Gerald suggested somewhat testily.

"Temper, temper, now," Melvin chided. Then he changed his tone a bit. "I must say, however, that I'm sorry you were hurt last night—and I'm particularly sorry about your stallion, McMasters. That was inexcusable on the part of my men." Then he turned to Kyra. "It was even more inexcusable that they hurt you, and I want you to know that they will be soundly reprimanded. You have my assurance that you will not be hurt again. In fact, none of you should worry about that—I just need to keep you here with me for a few more hours, then you can go home to your families."

"You're running opium into the South," Kyra said evenly. "The new tariffs have spurred the Coast Guard and customs officials to tighten their controls on the southern ports, so that it's easier to bring it in from the New York Customs Office, where you undoubtedly have paid connections. You brought a load in on a special train last night—but where did the rest of what we saw come from?"

"Yes." Melvin smiled. "I admire your perceptiveness. It isn't often that I deal with a woman as intelligent as you are and I keep underestimating your powers. I won't make the same mistake again, however."

"What do you mean?" Gerald asked, sounding alarmed.

"Don't worry," soothed Melvin. "I said I wouldn't harm her, and I won't. I was just referring to the fact that this little escapade will earn me enough money to retire to South America, where I can live like a king and raise my son like a prince."

Kyra gave a start of alarm in spite of herself. Seeing her movement, Melvin added, "Oh, yes, I've known for quite some time that Juliette is—ahem—expecting, as the ladies say. She didn't have to tell me. She forgets how very transparent she is, has always been to me. She could never tell me the slightest falsehood without my knowing—how could she expect to hide something like that?"

"Why haven't you said something to her?" Kyra asked.

"Her state of mind has been so fragile," Melvin explained. "As I said earlier, that little incident last evening wasn't the first time she's tried to commit suicide."

"Why should we believe you?" Kyra exclaimed. "She didn't say anything to me this morning about suicide."

"She wouldn't. She doesn't know you well enough. But as I say, she can't lie to me. I had the whole story from her last night, except for one thing that didn't make sense."

"What's that?" Kyra asked.

"Juliette claims she woke up and found Miss Peterson, her maid, who was actually her guard, asleep in a chair, cup of tea in hand, just as we found her later. She made use of the opportunity to find the packets Dr. Whitley had left and overdose herself. That part I find entirely consistent. But my problem comes here: You say the tea was drugged, but both Juliette and the maid deny having put anything in it. Since they were the only ones in the room, one of them has to have been lying."

"And Juliette can't lie to you, so it must have been Miss Peterson," Kyra finished for him. "But why would she drug her own tea?"

"That's what doesn't make sense, unless we assume she had been regularly imbibing Juliette's various remedies for the narcotics in them. Maybe this time she underestimated the effects of the powder, or her hand slipped and she put too much into the tea. At any rate, I sent her packing for fear that there would be another such incident."

"But if what you're saying is true, won't leaving Juliette alone just make it easier for her to find some other way to kill herself?"

"No. She always seems to wait a while between attempts," Melvin answered with incredible calm. "I'll get her a new caretaker as soon as I've made this delivery—once we're on our way to South America."

"But why did you unload at Hopsworth?" Gerald wanted to know. "I assume that was what was happening last night."

"Yes, that was the last of several shipments. We're not only importing opium for smoking, you know. That's really a very limited market. The big money is in supplying the Negroes with cocaine from South America and the Pacific Islands, as well as various opiate preparations suitable for tinctures and hypodermic injections such as morphine. If we avoid paying the tariffs, the profits are really quite high—high enough to tempt an ordinarily conservative businessman like myself."

"And who else?" Kyra demanded. "You said 'we' a moment ago."

"Did I?" Melvin answered innocently. "If I did, it's in the sense of the royal we, as this is my own venture, pure and simple—a natural extension of my pharmaceutical business, but one that will give me a chance to retire twenty years early. I couldn't turn down that kind of an opportunity." Something in the way he said this, however, made Kyra suspicious that he was *not* alone in the venture, that he was covering up for someone.

"Does Juliette have any idea what you're doing?" she asked.

"Absolutely not. I never bother her with the details of my business and she's never shown the slightest interest," Melvin answered emphatically.

"But could she have found out what you were doing and told Nathaniel about it? I assume he found out and that's why you killed him." Kyra was gratified to see Melvin give a genuine start.

"I don't deny that Nathaniel was getting a bit difficult and I suspected that he'd found out at least something about what I was doing, but I didn't kill him. That's not my style. His death was as great a surprise to me as to Juliette—I've been trying to figure out for myself who might be responsible," he concluded. But again, something in the way he spoke made Kyra doubt that he was telling the complete truth. What was wrong?

Suddenly, the kaleidoscope of questions and possible answers that had been whirling around in her head came to a stop and the fragments formed themselves into a coherent picture. Was it the right picture? The only way to find out was to get back to Hopsworth.

Kyra turned away from the others and vomited the tea she'd just drunk onto the floor of the train car. It wasn't hard, as the motion of the train had made her slightly nauseated—it had given her the idea in the first place. She knew that if she vomited, she would look alarmingly pale afterward—pale enough to require resting for a while. The only bunks in the car were toward the front, separated by a door from the parlor where they were currently seated. It could work.

The three men reacted just as she had expected. They stood in unison, alarmed looks on their faces, and Gerald was at her side instantaneously. "Open the window!" he ordered. "Give her some air." Drogan complied immediately, while Melvin offered Kyra his clean handkerchief with unlikely solicitude.

"Would you feel better lying down?" he asked, just as she'd hoped he would.

"Yes, I think so," she answered weakly, whereupon Gerald lifted her in his arms while Melvin scurried ahead to open the door to the bunk area and pull aside the bed curtains. When Gerald had deposited Kyra on the bed, Melvin hovered anxiously in the background, worrying his handkerchief into knots. "Do you think this is an aftereffect from the blow on the head?" he finally asked.

"It could well be," Gerald growled. "See how her eyes are dilated? That's one sign of possible concussion."

"Oh, my, what should we do?" wailed Melvin, wringing his hands.

"Get her some ice, to start with," Gerald barked. "Then she'll need to see a doctor."

"Abdul!" Melvin barked in turn. "Bring ice! Much ice!" Switching to Persian, he spoke rapidly and Abdul literally ran to the icebox at the other end of the car, returning a few minutes later with a quantity of shaved ice in his bare hands.

When the ice had been wrapped in a towel and applied to Kyra's head, Gerald asked once again about a doctor. The little man looked pained but shook his head. "We can't stop the train right now to take on a doctor, as we wouldn't make our connection. We have a very precise schedule to follow and if we don't, it could ruin months of planning and preparation."

"What's more important, your schedule or a human life?" Gerald flashed.

Melvin's expression changed abruptly from his previous hand-wringing agitation to ruthless hardness—the hardness of a New York street boy who would brook no argument. Seeing his look, Kyra wondered how far a woman could test his protectiveness toward the "weaker sex" before she would be struck down. Every system of beliefs had its limits, and she was willing to wager that Melvin's limit could be summarized as something like, "No woman stands between me and my money." She could understand Juliette's desperation and suicide attempts—living with the two Melvins would be terrifying.

"I understand your concern over your wife, but she's not that bad," Melvin said to Gerald with thinly veiled irritation. "At worst, she has a bit of concussion and the doctor would do nothing more than we've done already. We'll check on her every hour or so, but what she really needs is rest. Don't you agree, Mrs. McMasters?"

"Yes," she managed weakly. "I just need some rest. You go back and sit with Inspector Drogan, dear. I'll be fine here." As she spoke, she squeezed his hand in a way that meant. "Do exactly as I say." They had agreed on this code long ago and she hoped he remembered it.

"All right," her husband said with reluctance. "I'll do as you say, but I'll be checking on you in an hour." His unspoken words were, "Don't do anything dangerous." She knew he had gotten her message.

"Okay." She sighed and closed her eyes as if with intense weariness.

On his way out, Melvin closed the door to the narrow hallway all but a crack, just as she'd hoped he would. The one good thing about men like Melvin was that they always underestimated the women they supposedly idolized.

As soon as she heard the men resume their seats in the parlor, Kyra reached into her pocket for the telegram addressed to Drogan. There had been no chance to give it to him, and she decided to read it herself. She tore open the envelope and quickly scanned: "Phone call to Chief M.D. for Ashley Park Health Resorts STOP Nathaniel Howard investigating NY Customs Office STOP Possible connection to opium imports STOP." She had to get the train back to Hopsworth!

Kyra looked around the tiny space for something to put in the bed in her place. A rolled-up blanket and a pillow arranged under the coverlet simulated her body, but the head was a problem until Kyra realized that she still wore her hat. She quickly removed it and placed it at the top of the form. Beige pigskin gloves went where her golden-chestnut chignon had lain moments before. In the gloom, it looked amazingly like her. Hopefully it would give her the time she needed.

And hopefully no major changes had been made in the area's railroad lines in the last few years—and none in the way a locomotive operated. During her childhood travels with her father, she had memorized the location of every railway line in the United States—something she had found useful to keep up as long as she was working as a detective, but which she had let slip in the past few years. She had been allowed to sit in the locomotive with the engineer on many occasions. Once, while traveling with Gerald and a party of senators and their wives, she'd run a locomotive. One of the senators had sponsored a bill that would have barred women from operating automobiles and other large vehicles. Another of the senators was a former president of the railroad they were traveling on and he had disagreed vehemently, claiming that mechanical vehicles were far easier to control than a buggy and pair of horses. To illustrate his point, he'd offered to teach any woman there to drive the locomotive pulling their train. Kyra had immediately volunteered. At the next station, she had taken over for the very worried engineer. With the senator's instruction she had run the train for over an hour, bringing it safely into the final station. Even the senator had been surprised at how quickly she'd learned, until she'd explained her childhood preoccupation with trains. At the moment she was grateful for both that childhood preoccupation and his instruction—she only hoped it would be enough for what she had in mind.

After making sure that the door to the rest of the car was still open only a crack, Kyra slipped out of the bunk area and edged her way along one side of the short hallway toward the next car. Thank goodness, the door was not locked. She slipped through, hoping that by so doing she'd not created a noticeable breeze in the parlor. She found herself on a narrow platform between cars.

The next car was the coal car. It was the old-fashioned type equipped with a series of hand- and footholds along the side. To get to the engine Kyra would have to inch along the side, using the holds, or crawl over the top of the car, which was open and full of coal.

Unless Melvin had thought to post a guard with the engineer, his only companion would be a young boy whose job it was to shovel coal into the burners to keep up the proper head of steam. Kyra was counting on her sudden arrival to surprise both of them. Fortunately, she had slipped a small handgun into the bustle of her riding habit that morning and Melvin had not thought to search her—in fact, he hadn't searched any of them, which gave her hope that Gerald and Philip had guns or other weapons secreted about their persons, too.

Before anything else, however, she had to get to the engine. She grabbed the first handhold and swung herself toward the first foothold—they had been designed with six-foot men in mind, she concluded as she stretched toward the next pair. Fortunately, her riding habit and boots gave her more mobility than she would have had in a conventional dress. She had negotiated herself halfway to the engine before she saw the tunnel ahead.

She hadn't thought about tunnels when she'd set out along the side of the train. She knew that some of the older ones left only inches to spare and she hoped fervently that this was a new one as she flattened herself against the car. Even if there had been time to climb on top, the clearance there might be less. A moment later, everything went dark and cold. She felt the side of the tunnel brush against her bustle and she pulled her stomach a fraction closer to the car. The roar of the engine inside the tunnel was deafening and the smoke made breathing almost impossible. Kyra held her breath as long as she could, hoping the tunnel would be short. Her lungs felt about to burst when the train shot out into blinding daylight.

Kyra clung in place for a few moments, gasping the fresh country air in great gulps. The scent of bluegrass and lilacs was suddenly precious. When she had recovered her breath, she continued toward the engine.

Less than a minute later, she jumped onto the platform at the rear of the engine, pulled the gun out of her bustle, and stepped inside. She was right about the surprise her sudden arrival would cause. The engineer's mouth dropped open in consternation and the boy dropped his shovel, scattering coal all over the floor. She motioned for him to pick up the shovel—she didn't want any sudden loss of propulsion to give away her presence in the engine. When the boy had finished stoking the fire, she handed him the stock tie from her riding habit. Speech was impossible in the din, but when she motioned for the engineer to turn around with his hands behind his back, the boy understood he was to tie him for her, which he did in short order, glancing nervously at her gun. Kyra checked the knot quickly, then motioned for the engineer to sit on a narrow bench near the interior coal bin and gave the boy her belt to tie his feet to the leg of the bench.

As soon as the engineer was secured, Kyra stepped to his usual place and took her bearings. Thankfully, they had not gone too far. They had been bearing west from Hopsworth and had not yet turned onto the main southern route—it was still possible to turn south on a minor route Kyra knew about and circle back to the Hopsworth spur line. She just hoped the route was still operating.

Keeping an eye on the coal boy and motioning from time to time for him to add another shovelful to the fire, Kyra watched for the switch over. When she saw it ahead, she began to brake and slow down to a crawl, so that she could reach out of the window and throw the switch, changing the rails to shuttle her off onto the other line. This was her most vulnerable time, but she knew Melvin was expecting a southerly turn shortly and hoped he wouldn't notice that they'd turned back in the direction they had come from. She also hoped there was no train going in the opposite direction on this line—she'd have to keep a sharp eye out.

The turn went smoothly enough, and after switching the main tracks back to their original position, Kyra let the train resume normal speed and gave a sigh of relief. She had another twenty minutes at least before Gerald and Melvin would check her bunk. It would take a good forty-five minutes to get back to Hopsworth, even without any problems. Once there, they would have help in controlling Melvin and his cohorts.

But just as Melvin had underestimated her, she had underestimated him. He was a man of precision. He knew to the minute when they should have arrived at the southerly turn and a quick glance outside told him this was not the place. Another quick glance told him that Kyra was not in her bunk, and his hand went for the brake cord.

Melvin's hand was caught, half an inch away from its object, by Inspector Drogan's large, hard grasp. An instant later, he was lying on the bunk, gasping for air, while the detective tied him securely with strips of sheet he had ripped like paper from the bedding. Through the door, Melvin could see that Gerald was holding Abdul at gunpoint and he knew that his other men were probably engaged in a card game in one of the other cars. Melvin saw that there was no point in yelling for help. He lay on the bunk and swore at his stupidity for not tying his captives—*they* were not making the same mistake! What he couldn't believe, though, was that that *woman* was running the engine. But there was no other explanation for her absence and the train's sudden departure from its assigned route—he supposed she was taking it back to Hopsworth. He smiled at the thought. Perhaps all was not lost yet. . . .

CHAPTER 13

At Bay

WHEN Kyra pulled into the Hopsworth siding, she was at first relieved to see J. Eldridge Cooper and his men at the little platform. But when Cooper heaved his enormous body into the engine, brandishing his gun in her face, she knew something had gone terribly wrong.

"You are under arrest for hijacking this train, young woman!" he shouted. "Untie that man!" he said to the boy. "We've got to get this train back on schedule!"

Cooper was taken totally by surprise by the quick upper thrust with which Kyra knocked his gun out of his hand. She was in turn surprised when the coal boy followed suit by hitting Cooper on the head with his shovel. The inspector sank to the floor without even a groan.

"Thank you," Kyra said to the boy as she quickly fastened Cooper's hands with his own handcuffs.

"That's all right, ma'am," he answered. "I just don't want you to think I had anythin' to do with these fellows and their cargo of damnation. I didn't know nuthin' about it until the last minute, and when I tried to beg off, they said I'd do it or else. I don't know who you are, but I've been hoping you're better'n *they* are, and I saw this guy with them before, so I knew *he* wasn't to be trusted."

"You knew what the cargo was, then?" Kyra said.

"Yeah, I heard some of the men talking about the split they were going to get—running this stuff is dangerous business. That's one reason I didn't want to have anythin' to do with it. I want to have a good, clean record so that I can work up to engineer someday. That's my ambition," he concluded with a proud smile.

"That's a fine ambition," Kyra said. "And I'll see that your name is kept clear in this business—what is your name?"

"Andy Moore, ma'am, and thank you," he said with a grin. "And by the way, ma'am, you did a fine job runnin' this ol' baby. She's not too easy to handle sometimes." The words were hardly out of his mouth when there was a barrage of shots from the other side of the platform and a bullet pinged against the metal window frame just inches from Kyra's head. Cooper's men were firing on them.

Kyra and the boy ducked below window level and looked at each other in consternation. Just then Cooper, who had regained consciousness, bellowed out, "Come on, men! There's only two—" He stopped abruptly when Kyra jammed the muzzle of her gun against his fat side. He could see in her face that she would shoot if he said one more word, and he blanched.

Together they listened to shots being returned from inside the train, as well as sounds of shouting and pounding. As the minutes passed, Cooper visibly gained confidence. Finally he said to Kyra, "Your friends can't hold out much longer. There's only two of them against all of my men and Mr. Dickey's as well."

"How do you know there's only two?" Kyra asked.

"Mr. Dickey left Kemal behind to take care of your horses and to bring me up-to-date on what had happened. When we got a telegram a short time later asking why the train was late making its connection, we figured out the rest."

"So you're working with Melvin?" Kyra asked.

"He couldn't have done what he's done without my

assistance," J. Eldridge Cooper said with a smug smile that was a parody of the coal boy's proud smile of a short time before.

"And no doubt Melvin's paid you handsomely," Kyra commented dryly.

"I wouldn't have done it any other way." Cooper smiled. "No self-respecting man can exist on what the state of Virginia pays its sheriffs—we all have to supplement where we can, and I just happen to have a greater talent for making money than some."

"Or less compunction about where it comes from," suggested Kyra. "Do you know what's in this train?"

"Oh, I have a pretty good idea. Nothing's actually been said, but it has to be pretty valuable to require the special handling it's been getting. Smuggled in past customs, I understand," he added meaningfully. Kyra noticed that for all his bluff ignorance, Cooper was smart enough not to actually say what the cargo was.

There was a lull in the shooting, so Kyra raised herself up far enough to peek out of the window. Cooper's men, five in all, had taken cover behind various boxes and packing crates on the other side of the loading platform. Behind the men, the lawns stretched up a gradual hill toward the house. The hound kennels, barely visible among the trees, were behind the house farther down the hill to the right. Though the fire at the mansion had subsided by this time, the horseless fire engine was still on the front lawn, and Kyra could see a small group of people huddled behind it, out of the way of the gunfire.

As Kyra watched, Oswald, on his horse and surrounded by the pack of hounds, appeared at the crest of the hill. Becky was still riding whip and a second later the rest of the Field appeared. Kyra could see one of the figures behind the fire engine gesticulating wildly, but she could not hear what was said. Oswald and the others behind him stopped to listen—everyone, that is, except Hadley Turbot. Unseen by the rest, who were dividing their attention between the small crowd at the fire engine and the charred front of the mansion, the boy darted away on his pony. He circled behind the fire engine and dismounted at a small gardener's shed behind one of several gazebos that graced the lawns. A second later, a small red form shot out of the little building, running straight for the hounds. Then it apparently saw its danger and abruptly changed course, but not before Old Bella had gotten a good whiff.

The well-trained old hound looked to Oswald for direction at precisely the moment he moved his hand in answering the people behind the fire engine. Oswald's motion was close enough to a casting signal for Bella. She put her nose to the ground, stern feathering, and a second later opened on the fox.

In the short time it took Bella and the other hounds to give tongue and set off in hot pursuit, the fox had headed straight down the hill toward the loading platform. It stopped for a second at the sight of Cooper's men, then appeared to decide that they were less of a danger than the hounds. It ran between two of them and right over a third, onto the platform, while two others lunged to catch it but missed. Once on the platform, it paused again, seeing its route blocked by the train, and looked around for some place to go to ground. The closest thing to a cave or a culvert was the door to one of the boxcars, which stood slightly ajar. The fox dove for this cover as the first hounds reached the bottom of the hill.

The forty hounds, bearing down on Cooper's men with their mouths open in full cry, looked and sounded ferocious. One of the men began to take aim on the lead hound with his gun, but another yelled, "That ain't gonna have no effect on them—they're bound on a kill! Drop your guns an' run for your lives!" In a panic, the men threw down their guns and ran toward the barn. But before they reached the door, Senator Howard appeared in his carriage, blocking their way. Seeing this, and knowing that foxhounds would never attack a human, Kyra jumped down from the engine and ran toward the milling, terrified group. She was glad to see

Gerald and Philip emerge from the passenger car and move in behind the men as well.

Assisted by the senator, they had all five of the men tied in short order, then turned back to the hounds, who had pawed the sliding door open wide enough to get into the boxcar, in spite of Oswald's attempts to call them off. They had clearly had enough of following a different master. Even Becky's attempts to whip them off had been ignored. They pushed their way through the widening crack with a wild, bloodthirsty howl, certain of their prey. Suddenly the door slammed open and Melvin's group of guards flung themselves out of the boxcar with their hands in the air, begging for mercy. Kyra and her cohorts soon had them tied as well, while in the background the hounds searched frantically among Melvin's precious boxes of drugs for the fox.

The Field, which had automatically followed the hounds down to the platform, sat on their horses and watched in bewildered silence. On the side of the hill, Hadley Turbot was doubled up with laughter, and his pony had wandered off again, eating grass and stepping on its reins.

After taking this all in, Kyra turned to Thurston's carriage and spoke into the darkened interior: "Nathaniel, why don't you call your hounds off? And then I'll tell you who's responsible for your murder."

When Nathaniel stepped out of the carriage and climbed onto the platform with Kyra, the whole Field started. Only Lady Pandora put words to their reaction, however, blurting out, "Oh, dear, we thought you were *dead*!" Meanwhile, Tobias LaFarge once more turned rosy red, his mouth opening and closing like a fish gasping for air. Several others looked quickly from side to side, as if contemplating escape, but thought better of it. Kyra, however, had noticed their looks and smiled sadly to herself: they were just the ones she had expected.

Looking a bit bewildered, Philip Drogan said, "But whose body is in the billiards room?"

"Nathaniel, why don't you explain about the body on

the billiards table," Kyra suggested. "It's Michael, isn't it?" she added.

"Yes," Nathaniel answered grimly. "It was Michael who died in my place, the victim of a trap intended for me. I'll explain how that happened in a moment, but I want you to know first that my father and I decided to investigate his death just as though it had been me that was killed."

"So you put your hat and clothes on the body, whose face was already mangled beyond recognition, then you hid in the secret passageways at Hopsworth. Meanwhile, your father spread the rumor that Michael was off on a drunk," Kyra suggested.

"Yes, exactly," agreed Nathaniel. "Only my father didn't even have to start the rumor, because Michael *had* been drinking, which is actually the reason he was killed in my place."

"How was that?" Kyra wanted to know.

"Well, late Friday afternoon, I had just mounted Truly Fine and was heading out to have a go over the course I had in mind for the Wild Goose Chase. But then my father rode up on his horse and said that as he was heading out for a ride himself, he'd noticed that some of the gates to the kennel runs appeared to be open and the hounds out. So we rode over there together and found Michael sound asleep in the feed room with the horse he used occasionally standing nearby, still saddled and bridled. He'd apparently ridden into town, gotten drunk, then come home and started to give the hounds their usual morning feeding, even though it was probably already afternoon by that time. In his drunken stupor, he'd opened some of the runs, then realized he didn't have any feed with him. So he went back to the feed room and promptly fell asleep where we found him."

"So you woke him up?" Kyra queried.

"Yes. He'd pretty much slept off the liquor, but of course both my father and I were quite angry. We gave him his notice to leave as soon as we could find a replacement. He was a good kennelman and even a fine horseman when he was sober, but we couldn't trust him in a crunch not to go off on a spree."

"And then what happened?" Kyra asked.

"Clearly, the missing hounds had to be found," Nathaniel continued, "so I gave up my plans to check out the course. The only problem was that I didn't want to take Truly Fine through a lot of brush just before race day, and I didn't have time to go back to the barn and have another horse saddled before dark."

"So I suggested that he ride Michael's old horse, Maria," interrupted Thurston. "She was all saddled and had had several hours to rest herself while Michael snored—and from the looks of it, she'd even helped herself to some of the oats we cook into gruel for the hounds. I thought it would do her good to work them off.

"So we sent Michael back to the barn with Truly Fine and we set off in search of the missing hounds. When we were about half a mile away, I realized that I must have dropped the tentative map I'd made of the steeplechase course. But I figured it would probably still be on the feed room floor when we got back, so I wasn't too concerned.

"What we didn't realize," Thurston continued, "was that Michael had picked up the map, thinking perhaps that it was a check or something else of value. When he saw what it was, he must have decided to ride the course himself. He was always trying to show that he was just as good a horseman as Nathaniel—and we'd left him with the perfect chance to prove it by riding Nathaniel's own horse over the steeplechase course."

"So Michael took off on Truly Fine while you were out looking for the missing hounds?" Kyra asked.

"Yes," answered Nathaniel. "And by chance our search took us near part of the course, and we found Truly Fine standing over Michael. He was already dead— must have been killed instantly. When we saw the wired fence and realized that it was a trap meant for me, we decided to let everyone think it *was* me that had been killed until we could find out who was behind it. And I think that was the right decision, because if my suspicions are right, we've turned up quite a different crew—quite different," he added with a sigh.

"So you exchanged your clothes and hat and even riding crops, and then? . . ." Kyra prodded.

"Uh—oh—yes," Nathaniel said as he returned to his train of thought. "I rode off into the brush and hid until dark, when I returned to Hopsworth and took up temporary residence inside Hopsworth's special wall passages, like the Negroes my great-grandfather had helped to escape from slavery."

"Meanwhile, I took the hounds we'd found back to their kennel, then returned to the barn as if I'd had an entirely ordinary ride," interjected Thurston. "I waited until Truly Fine limped in well after dark to set up an alarm about Nathaniel being missing."

"And when you 'found' Michael, everyone in the search party accepted his body as Nathaniel's, and since it was dark, no one noticed the footprints and other marks you and Nathaniel had made while changing the clothes and so forth," Kyra added.

"No one noticed a thing," agreed Thurston. "And I was quite sure any clues we left would have been obliterated by the search party, but apparently you noticed something."

"Yes, neither your own nor your horses' prints had been entirely destroyed when we visited the site the next day, but I couldn't make any sense over the extra prints until Benny began to act strangely today."

"Benny? How was that?" Thurston wanted to know. The whole assemblage looked toward the redheaded young man, who had driven a carriage in behind Thurston's and was just climbing down from the driver's seat.

"I had asked Benny to find Michael," Kyra explained. "Based on past experience, I had every expectation that he would have returned with the man by last night. Benny is very good at such searches—I've never known him to fail before. But this morning he gave me a strange story about how he couldn't find Michael. That didn't make sense. I've never known Benny to give up on a search until he'd found what he was looking for. But there he was asking me to give him something else to do. I had other things on my mind at the time, so I didn't immediately put two and two together.''

"But when you did," Drogan broke in excitedly, "you realized that Benny *had* found Michael, but didn't want to tell you."

"Yes, exactly." Kyra smiled. "And the only reason for that would be if he was covering up for someone, and the only person that could possibly be was Nathaniel himself. From there it was a short step to remembering the physical similarities between Nathaniel and Michael, then the rest fell into place."

"Y'all ain't mad at me?" Benny asked with a grin as he opened the carriage door and motioned for its three occupants to get out.

"No, Benny," said Kyra, "I'm not mad at you, but if you had told me what you knew, I would have figured out the rest much quicker. I take it that's the carriage with the mended wheel?"

"Sho' 'nuff," Benny replied. "Ah wuz jest returnin' from a very innerestin' conversation with th' blacksmith who fixed it last week fuh our friend Os'ald Hahdin', when what do you know, *theah* it wuz, big as life, right in th' middle o' th' road! Sen'tor Howard wuz holdin' these three at gunpoint, an' natchely Ah offuhed t' help tie 'em up an' drive 'em back fuh him. Duz anyone reconize any of 'em?"

As Benny spoke, two men and one woman in a formal riding habit stepped down from the carriage, somewhat clumsily because their hands were tied behind their backs. The first was an extremely ugly Chinaman in a gray woolen coat, whom Kyra was certain must have been her assailant of the evening before and the person who dug the hole by the jump; the next was Jerome Cushing.

Kyra quickly surmised that when Senator Howard had met them unexpectedly on the road, Jerome had been able to pass himself off as a mushroom hunter because the senator had not met him the previous day—and they had sat at opposite ends of the table at dinner. But what was the relationship between him and the Chinaman? They had apparently gone out to meet the third occupant after she had set the drag. But who was she?

When the strange woman followed the men out of the carriage, Kyra stepped forward and lifted the heavy veils that shrouded her face—revealing Lord Randolph Roseberry's Indian groom.

"Of course!" exclaimed Kyra. "The one person who could have set the drag. Now everything makes sense."

"Demmed women!" exploded Lord Randolph unexpectedly. "I *knew* I shouldn't have listened to a bunch of demmed women." He subsided quickly to low-toned sputterings, and attention was drawn away from him by a sudden commotion generated by Oswald Harding.

Kyra had noticed that Oswald had blanched when Benny had driven the carriage up to the group; then, when Benny had identified it as Oswald's, the temporary Huntsman had shook so hard that he'd dropped his hunting horn with a clatter. Now he jerked his horse around and kicked the poor tired animal into some semblance of a gallop over the hill the way he'd just come. His face wore a haggard expression and his eyes gleamed crazily.

"Wan' me t' go ketch 'im?" Benny offered.

"I suppose so." Kyra sighed wearily. "Here, take this," she added, picking up one of Cooper's men's guns and tossing it to Benny. "But don't shoot unless you have to."

"Yes'm," answered Benny cheerfully, expressing his irrepressibly good humor with a wink as he sprinted to where Hadley Turbot had just rejoined the group, leading his pony. "This heah pony's th' freshest hoss aroun', an' we'll ketch that crazy man in no time flat!" Benny announced. With that, he unceremoniously took the reins from Edna's surprised nephew, catapulted into the saddle, and galloped off over the hill after Oswald.

While this was going on, Nathaniel had picked up the hunting horn from where it lay on the ground and had called his hounds out of the boxcar with one long, sharp note. They had rallied 'round him immediately, and now he fondly stroked a soft ear here and patted a head there. When he seated himself on a packing crate on the platform in his typically nonchalant fashion, they flopped down at his feet, tongues lolling happily as they rested. They were obviously glad to have their Huntsman back.

The same could not be said for some of the members of the Field. Kyra noted that several of them looked almost as uncomfortable at the turn of events as Oswald had. Almost without exception, they looked around for some means of escape but soon realized that there was nothing they could do that would not point the finger of suspicion right at them. Their only hope was to shut up and sit tight. But Kyra noted that Edna Harding in particular looked like a weasel that had suddenly found itself in a cage. Her sharp eyes darted from side to side with desperate calculation, and Kyra wondered what the woman would do next.

When Benny had disappeared over the crest of the hill, past the smoking mansion, Nathaniel rose to give Kyra a hand back onto the platform and said, "Now what was it that you figured out?"

"For one thing," Kyra answered, "I remembered that you've always admired your Grandfather Howard from the time you were a little boy. You often swore that when you grew up you'd be just like him. Your comment a few minutes ago about the escaped slaves is typical."

Nathaniel grinned slowly and sat back on the crate, saying, "Yes, I wanted to be like him, but there were no slaves to help to escape, so I didn't do much of anything until after my mother died. I realized then that the many thousands who had become addicted to opiates were as much slaves as the Negroes had been—no matter what the color of their skin. Together with my father, I vowed to do everything in my power to curtail the spread in opiate usage.''

"So when he got the current import legislation passed, you became the unofficial enforcer.''

"Yes." Nathaniel nodded. "The New York Customs Office has been known for its corruption since the early 1870s, and all official attempts at cleaning it up have failed. So I began a silent, underground campaign to discover the persons responsible and to stop them, unaware that my own brother-in-law was one of the most flagrant offenders." Here he turned to look at Melvin, whom Gerald had brought out from the passenger car, with his hands still tied behind his back. "I should have thought of him earlier, of course, since he was in the pharmaceutical business, but sometimes one fails to look in one's own backyard.''

"At the Daisy Hill Hunt, for instance," suggested Kyra, glancing at the Field.

"Yes, the Daisy Hill Hunt," Nathaniel said sadly, following Kyra's glance. "The very people I thought were my friends. It wasn't until this morning that I began to put everything together—but Kyra, you seem to have figured it all out better than me, so why don't you explain what's been going on.''

"All right," said Kyra softly, reacting to the genuine grief she heard in Nathaniel's voice. He was the type of person who wanted to believe that people were basically good, although perhaps sometimes misguided, and she hated to shatter that with what she was about to say— but there seemed no alternative. Before she could begin, however, there was an interruption while Juliette and Nadine, accompanied by Corrie, made their way through the horses. When Nadine saw Nathaniel, she flung herself into his arms, sobbing, "I *knew* you weren't dead!" Juliette was right behind her, hugging and kissing her brother ecstatically.

Tobias LaFarge tried to make use of this interruption to slip away from the group, but Senator Howard himself pushed through the horses and grabbed the Field Master's bridle. "I think you're needed right here!" the white-haired man declared with a hard smile.

When he saw that he was not going to get away, Tobias muttered, "This is a lot of fuss over nothing. I have things I need to get home for. My family is waiting for me."

Hearing this, Kyra said, "They may have to wait a lot longer than they expected, if I'm right about your involvement in this business."

"My hands are clean!" LaFarge exclaimed. "I've done nothing. I just invested some money with Melvin. Ask him. He'll clear me. Won't you, Melvin?" His voice had taken on a pleading tone that attested to his guilt more clearly than if he'd openly admitted it. As he spoke, even his horse put its ears back and moved restlessly under him, in spite of the senator's grip on its bridle.

Melvin stared contemptuously at him for a few moments, then shifted his gaze toward Juliette, who was still hugging her brother. His face showed the barest flicker of emotion, then he turned to Kyra. "Before things go any further," he said, "I want you to know that my company makes medicines for hundreds of thousands of people each year who would probably die otherwise."

"And some of them die *because* of your medicines!" thundered Thurston. "But I agree with my son: Miss Keaton—er—Mrs. McMasters is the one who should explain what's been going on."

"I think that what happened here," Kyra said to the group, "is that one person saw an opportunity to make a great deal of money by putting together a coalition, shall we call it, for importing and distributing opiates—isn't that true, Edna?"

"Well, I never! I know *nothing*, absolutely nothing, about anything like that!" The sharp-faced woman began; but seeing that Kyra was not falling for that, Edna abruptly changed her tactics and screeched, "You have no proof of anything! I dare you to show one scrap of proof!"

"I'll give you proof!" LaFarge interrupted, his voice thin with panic and his face redder than ever. "I'll give you all the proof you need if you make things easy on me. Everything was Edna's idea. She got the whole bunch of us involved. It's all her fault!"

At this, Edna Harding turned her horse with a vicious yank on the reins and would have galloped off like Oswald, had not Senator Howard loosed his hold on Tobias's horse and grabbed her horse by the bridle instead. In her blind panic she slashed at him with her hunting whip, leaving a welt across his face, and would have hit him again had not Kyra fired a warning shot over her head. At that, Edna froze, then slowly turned back toward where Kyra stood next to Nathaniel, Nadine, and Juliette on the platform.

"I suppose," Edna said proudly, her pointed nose stuck in the air, "that if I don't tell you what happened myself, someone like Tobias will give his own garbled version." She sniffed and continued, "When Oswald's inheritance from his fraternal grandfather proved to be smaller than we'd expected, we needed to invest it in something that would produce a fast return. Like everyone else, we were reading in the papers just then about Senator Howard's battle to raise import duties and restrictions on the opiate drugs. But unlike everyone else, I realized the potential there for making money. *And* I realized that Hopsworth would be the perfect place to hide shipments until they could be distributed—no one would ever suspect it, there was the convenient railway line, and I'd heard rumors of underground tunnels. So on one of my shopping trips to New York City, I stopped by the offices of Dickey Pharmaceuticals and proposed the idea to Melvin, who had the necessary contacts with the customs people. Ironically, he already knew about the Hopsworth tunnels, although he'd never thought of using them the way I suggested. But he was certain that none of his usual import concerns would want to get involved in such a scheme.

"But that was no problem for me. I remembered Jerome Cushing from business associations he'd had with my dear, deceased husband. Perseus had despised Cushing as an opportunist who would stoop to anything if he thought he could get away with it, but that was exactly what we needed. So I approached him about bringing in shipments of opium along with his Indian teas and Turkish rugs."

"She can't prove any of that!" This time the refrain was sung by Jerome Cushing, whose face had grown nearly as red as the Field Master's. His young wife, who sat on a horse next to him, poked him in the side with her crop and motioned for him to shush. He opened his mouth again but decided against saying anything more.

"Cushing was definitely interested," Edna continued, "so I put him in contact with Melvin. Together, they worked out a way of bringing the opium into Canada, then smuggling it into the United States using the same railway lines Nathaniel's grandfather had used to smuggle runaway slaves in the *other* direction. Then they hid the shipments here in a large room under the kennels, the irony being that it was right under the nose of the man who had been most responsible for imposing the import restrictions and increased duties."

"Well, I'll be!" interjected Thurston with a whistle. "I'd never have thought little Melvin had the nerve!"

Edna addressed her next remarks to Thurston and Nathaniel. "What neither of you realized was that the hounds' occasional restless night was caused by the loading and unloading of the drug shipments in the room under the kennels. And we always took the precaution of disconnecting your phone."

"I didn't know such a room existed!" Nathaniel exclaimed. "I knew about the passageways in the house, but I thought that's all there were."

"Ooooh," groaned Thurston. "When you and Juliette were just children I had the house passageways blocked off from the tunnels—I was afraid you'd find them and go exploring and get trapped by a cave-in. They did cave in sometimes."

"I found them anyway," Juliette chimed in unexpectedly. "I found the room under the hound kennels first, then the rest of the tunnels, when I was ten or eleven years old. They were my own private place, and I kept them a secret from anyone else. I used to go there to be alone and I kept my private diary there. The only person I ever showed them to was Melvin, after we were engaged—I thought that a woman should have no secrets from her man."

"You've certainly changed in that respect," Melvin said sarcastically. Juliette gave him a quick look but said nothing.

"I say!" interrupted Lord Randolph, who had finally found his tongue again. "This is all very interesting, but some of us have schedules to meet." He pronounced "schedules" in the British way—"shed-u-als."

"I was just getting to your part in the story," Edna said acidly. "Do you think I'd let you off?" She turned back to Kyra and added, "Lord Randolph and Lady Pandora became involved in our little business after it had been under way for some time. One of the reasons for the astounding success of their 'health' resorts has never been advertised but is well known among their patrons: it's the abundant supply of drugs, mainly opiates, provided by the resident doctors to those willing to pay the price. Thurston's new import duties were making many of these drugs prohibitively expensive: The Roseberrys had to underwrite part of the cost. Lord Randolph didn't really mind that, as the major profits came from the gambling casinos and the exorbitant fees people paid for room and board. But Pandora couldn't stand to lose even a penny—her poverty-struck childhood had made her extremely frugal, to put it mildly. So she came up with the idea of asking Melvin if he could get the drugs any cheaper than their regular suppliers. He thought about it for a while, talked it over with Cushing and me, and we decided to let the Rose-berrys in on the deal. We could make it twice as big as originally intended by using their money and that of a few other select investors, such as Becky Hollingshood, to help fund initial purchases.''

Here Edna turned to the Field Master and said, ''That's where Tobias came in. Several of his land deals had recently fallen through, and to avoid big financial trouble he needed to come up with a lot of cash fast. He had tried to interest Nathaniel in a scheme to develop Hopsworth, in the hope that the Howards would put up the cash he needed for other projects. When Nathaniel consulted with Melvin about the deal, Melvin realized right away what was going on and we decided to cut Tobias in on the import scheme in return for his cooperation with regard to some other matters. He immediately saw the potential for recouping all of his losses and invested everything he could get hold of, including some of the money Nathaniel had given him for initial research into developing Hopsworth.''

''This is an abomination!'' blustered Tobias. ''She's a lunatic! She can't prove anything she's saying!'' It was becoming a familiar refrain. ''I don't know about any of the rest of this; I simply made an investment in Melvin's firm. Certainly that's no crime, is it?''

''Yes, Mr. LaFarge has a point now, doesn't he?'' interjected Lord Randolph. ''I do believe none of us knew what Mrs. Harding and Mr. Dickey had afoot when we invested in his firm—it was simply a business deal to us, a way of diversifying, you might say. As for that poppycock about our health resorts—our resident doctors have limited supplies of medications for emergencies only. That's it.''

''Yes, that's it exactly,'' chimed in Tobias again. ''None of us knew what we were investing in—it was simply a paper transaction.''

Edna ignored these disclaimers and continued. ''With so many investors, we needed to bring in more drugs than could be accommodated by Melvin's Canadian routes, so he and Jerome Cushing decided to bring some shipments in through the New York Customhouse by bribing an official or two. But we needed a convenient place to store it. Ironically, Nathaniel owned a warehouse in just the right area, so Melvin decided that Cushing should talk to Nathaniel about leasing it. That's where we made our first mistake. Of course, we had no idea at the time that Nathaniel was pursuing his own investigations of the customhouse. But he was, and he got wind of the possibility that his brother-in-law might be evading the new duties. For Juliette's sake, he did not want Melvin involved in any big scandal when the authorities cracked down on evaders, so he took it upon himself to warn Melvin in what he thought was a discreet manner that did not reveal his own participation in the investigation. But Melvin was smarter than he thought. He immediately realized that Nathaniel must have been working with his father and that our whole import scheme was in jeopardy. If we were going to make the kind of money we intended to make, we had to work fast.

"Therefore, we arranged to transfer the drug shipment to a special train, so that they could be brought here, transferred temporarily into the storehouse while everyone was busy at the hunt ball, then put on another train out during the hunt itself. Meanwhile, we arranged for two large-scale sales of the drugs—one of cocaine to southern Negroes, the other of opium to San Francisco Chinese. A third portion went to the Roseberrys—enough to keep their resorts supplied for years. The proceeds from these sales would pay back everyone's initial investment plus a neat profit, as well as make Melvin rich enough to 'retire' to South America, where he intended to raise coca plants and export cocaine."

"But who tried to kill my son?" interjected Thurston. "And why?"

Edna looked truly baffled here and answered with a ring of truth, "We've been trying to figure that out ourselves all weekend—it wasn't any of us. We were just trying to make money; we're not murderers!"

"I believe you," Kyra interjected. "But I think you'll shortly see that your scheme *was* indirectly responsible for two deaths—Michael's and Egerton Harding's." Kyra's words caused a murmur of shock from the Field, none of whom had known about Egerton's death until that moment. "The same person who killed them also put a decapitated hound's head in Nadine's desk, drugged Juliette, and twice tried to scare me off the case, once by setting a trap in the steeplechase course, the second time by sending a man to my room to rough me up.

"As you must be aware, Edna," Kyra continued, "when you and your partners decided to bring all of the drugs here during race day weekend, each one reacted to the pressure. The biggest concern, however, was that Nathaniel or his father would find out what was going on before you could get the drugs out and distributed.

"In order for the transfer to work, the hunt on Sunday had to be an extra long one, and the hunts recently had been quite short due to unseasonable warmth that wore both fox and hounds out sooner than usual. The problem was solved when Lord Randolph suggested that he have his Indian groom dress as a woman, suitably veiled, of course, ride out with the hunt as his guest, then slip away and set a drag leading down into Killdare Ravine, where the hounds would scatter and take a long time to retrieve. This would be an easy accomplishment for the groom, as he had set many drags over rough terrain in India—and he also knew how to ride sidesaddle because he had taught riding to the maharajah's daughters.

"The only concern was whether Nathaniel would fall for the drag and not call his hounds off, but it was decided to risk that possibility. That is, everyone agreed to risk it except one, and that person already had his own vendetta against Nathaniel. Do you want to tell us about it, Oswald?" Kyra finished, turning in the direction of the replacement Huntsman, whom Benny had led back to the group a few minutes earlier.

"Oswald, be quiet!" ordered Edna with genuine panic

in her voice. "Don't say a thing! She's just guessing. She can't prove anything."

"No, Mother. I've listened to you long enough," Oswald said. "If it weren't for you, I'd have married the woman I loved long ago and none of this would have happened."

"You'd have been a poor, struggling clerk at the Library of Congress, barely able to support a brood of brats!" sneered Edna.

"And I would have been happy. I know that now, but I listened to you then and all of this has happened. Kyra's right. I *am* the one who set the trap for Nathaniel, not only to get him out of the way for Sunday, but to get him out of the way forever. So that Nadine would love me again. I knew that if he were just gone, she'd turn to me—and with the money my mother and I were getting from Melvin's scheme, I could support her in style. We could have a family and be happy." There were tears in his eyes as he said this. He stopped, wiped them away, then continued, "Nathaniel didn't deserve her like I did. I had loved her long before he did, and *I* never would have fooled around with . . ." Here he paused and looked at Becky Hollingshood. "With other women," he ended lamely.

At that, Becky flushed and urged her horse to the front of the group. When she had reached the platform, she looked up at Nadine and said loud enough for everyone to hear, "I want you to know that Nathaniel is absolutely innocent of any wrongdoing with respect to his marriage vows. I admit I tried to seduce him, but he would have none of it and put me soundly in my place. What you saw behind the barn was one of my attempts to ensnare him. I feigned a fall so that he had to help me up, which he did in the most gentlemanly way possible, even when I threw my arms around him in a provocative embrace. If you'd watched a moment longer, you would have seen him set me sternly on my feet and tell me to cut out the nonsense. You're a very lucky woman, Nadine, to have a husband who loves you that much—perhaps I would be different if I'd had a husband like that."

"Thank you, Becky," Nadine said softly, then looked at her husband with tears shining in her eyes.

Becky turned to go, but Kyra stopped her, saying, "While you're at it, what were you doing in Egerton Harding's room this morning?"

Instead of the guilt Kyra expected, Becky's face showed only confusion. "Egerton's room?" Becky asked. Then something clicked. "Oh! You saw me . . . ?"

"Yes, I saw you walking away from the East Wing."

"That was Egerton's room," Becky said in a stricken tone. "Oh my God!" she groaned.

"You didn't know it was Egerton's?" Kyra asked.

"I had no idea," moaned Becky. "Could I have helped him?" she whispered, adding, "He was my friend."

"No," Kyra answered simply. "He had been dead for hours by then. But why did you go to *that* room?"

"It was supposed to be my Uncle George's room—he hadn't shown up yesterday, so I went to see if he'd arrived during the night. I peeked in the window and saw someone else's head in the bed—Uncle George is bald and this head had hair—so I tiptoed away as quickly as I could."

"But you were upset . . ." Kyra said.

"Yes, Uncle George was going to help me to purchase hounds for my own pack. The Roseberrys can tell you that—he's their partner."

"Oh, dear yes!" exclaimed Lady Pandora. "George Christianson is our partner and chief medical officer, don't you know. He rang up last night to say he wouldn't be here, but with all the confusion I simply forgot to tell Rebecca. I'm so sorry, dear."

An embarrassed silence followed, until Inspector Drogan cleared his throat loudly and said in his best British accent, "I say, speaking of hounds and all that, why in heaven's name would Oswald put a deceased hound's head in Nadine's desk if he purports to love her so much?"

"That was a mistake," Oswald answered. "I had killed the hound shortly after Nathaniel and Nadine had had an altercation, which I overheard—I intended to put it in his desk as a warning. I just wanted to scare him, to make him feel bad, like he was making Nadine feel bad." As he spoke, an edge of insanity came through in his voice more and more clearly. "I waited for several days, until they were both out, then sneaked up the back stairway to their suite and put it in what I thought was Nathaniel's desk—at first I was going to put it on his bed, only there was a pussycat asleep there. But it was the wrong desk, so he never found it. I figured that out later. But not before . . . before she was . . . was . . . there, in bed, with her maid in the room. I knew it would start smelling soon, so I . . . I got one of the packets of sleeping powder my mother uses and when the tea trays were going up, I made some excuse to be around the kitchen and I put the powder in Sobie's tea. But the trays got mixed up somehow, and Sobie's went to Juliette's maid. Then I heard that Kyra had found the head and I knew she'd suspect me sooner or later. So I had double reason to scare her off the case. I'd already had my new man, Jones, dig the hole by the jump earlier, which hadn't worked, so I knew I needed something more direct. When I heard about Gerald's mare being about to foal, I knew what that was. I faked the call to get him away, then sent Jones up to scare Kyra. I didn't want him to hurt her, just give her a good scare, so that she'd go home and leave things alone."

"This is Jones?" asked Drogan, pointing to the ugly Chinaman by the carriage.

"Yes," Oswald answered. "Unpronounceable name, so I call him Jones. Quite old, but still strong and speaks good English—as good as any of them, at any rate—and cheap. That's why my mother hired him—he'll do anything I want him to do, without question, and he's cheap. He also translates letters from Chinatown opium dens ordering supplies."

"Why hasn't anyone seen him before now?" Kyra wanted to know.

Oswald answered with the simplicity of insanity. "I wanted to keep him to myself—I didn't want Nathaniel or any of the others stealing him from me, offering him more money. You don't know what it's like, living in Nathaniel's shadow all the time, practically another one of his servants. Not much better than poor Michael."

"Poor Michael, whom you killed," Kyra said.

"I feel very bad about that," Oswald said, tears filling his eyes again. "Michael was very good to me. I didn't mean to hurt him, only Nathaniel. Nathaniel was too proud. He had everything, and he *deserved* to be taken down a peg or two!" Here he paused and glared at Nathaniel with insane hatred.

"What about Egerton Harding? Did he deserve to die, too?" Kyra said.

"He was too smart. He figured things out too quickly, so he *had* to die. He was going to tell what I'd done and then Nadine would never love me." Oswald said this with utter seriousness, as if it were the simplest thing in the world. As if anyone could understand.

"What did he figure out?" Kyra wanted to know.

"That it was me who'd wired the fence," Oswald answered simply. "You see, he was writing a new novel, and he has something like that in there—only not on purpose—someone has wired a fence and a fellow tries to jump it without seeing the wire. At any rate, just the other day he came by to ask Nathaniel about how a horse would fall if caught by a wire like that—but Nathaniel was out for a ride, so Michael and I answered his questions. That's when I got the idea about wiring a fence for Nathaniel. It was almost certain to kill him—and it would look like an accident. But Egerton figured that out, as soon as the news of Nathaniel's death reached him in Washington. He rode out immediately and went to look at the fence. He came to me later during the ball and started asking questions about it—I knew that he'd tell you about it next, and I had to stop him."

"Those were *his* footprints then, that I saw on top of the rest," Kyra mused out loud.

"So you followed him when he left the ball?"

"Yes," Oswald said, looking surprised. "I heard him talking to Senator Howard, and I saw what room he was going to stay in—and I remembered the snakes. So I went and borrowed one from Tobias—he didn't even ask me why—and snuck into Egerton's room and slipped it under the covers."

Kyra glanced at the Field and saw from the looks on their faces that most of them now fully realized what could happen when a group of otherwise sane people become obsessed with a crooked scheme. The few who border on instability are driven to extremes that seem necessary to them in the situation—extremes that could include murder and in this case included murder twice. Edna Harding in particular had lost her haughty air entirely, her face crumpled into a mask of agony. "I did it all for him," she said over and over again. "I didn't know he'd do that."

"Why didn't you ask Oswald what he wanted the snake for?" Kyra asked Tobias.

"I . . . I'd had a bit too much to drink at the ball, and it somehow didn't seem odd at the time. There were so many strange things happening" was the reply.

"Yes," Kyra agreed, "so many strange things happening—but perhaps we've stopped that for now. You can all go take care of your horses, if you like," she continued, "but don't attempt to leave Hopsworth. We'll need to call in officials from the state capital and go over everything again." She sighed sadly, looking down at a group of people who should have been gathered together to simply enjoy themselves. People who had almost everything money could buy, but who just couldn't leave it at that. They had to have more—at the expense of others. That was the catch. She sighed again and took Gerald's arm to step down off the platform—it would be good to go back to their quiet life with the children.

As Kyra and Gerald walked back toward the smoldering mansion, they were joined by Inspector Drogan. "Quite a splendid piece of work, *quite* splendid," he said to Kyra, still affecting his British accent.

"Thank you," she said, and continued walking until they were out of earshot of the rest. Then she added, "I suppose neither you nor the Roseberrys wish to have your part in this investigation disclosed to the general public."

Drogan gave her an astonished glance, then laughed heartily. "I should have known we wouldn't fool you," he chuckled, "but how *did* you figure out that they were working with me?"

"Your accent," she said with a smile. "It was certainly good enough to fool the ordinary American, though it would never have stood muster with a real Englishman—or woman. But there you were, talking to them in Juliette's room and even sitting next to Lady Pandora at dinner, with never a curious glance from either of them. That's when I began to suspect a connection."

Drogan nodded his agreement, a twinkle of admiration in his eye, and Kyra continued, "The final clue was your revelation that you had been working on the opium import problem for some time when it has been under tariff restrictions in the United States for only a few months. The British, however, have been trying for years to soothe relations with China by curtailing opium trade. Also, some members of the British aristocracy had vowed as many as twenty years ago to combat opium eating and smoking, which had reached almost epidemic proportions in England. The Roseberrys were among them. With their international chain of health resorts, they would have an excellent excuse to travel anywhere and associate with anyone, especially those interested in selling them nostrums for their clients. Then they could quietly pass the names of opium dealers on to the British agents with no suspicion coming to rest upon them.

"They would naturally work only with the most reputable detective agency in America—Pinkerton. And of all of the Pinkerton agents, you would be the natural choice for a liaison because of your background as a chemist—not to mention that you're the best private detective in America, which is how you came to be hired by Thurston as well," Kyra concluded.

"I may be good, but I'm not good enough to fool one other detective that I know!" exclaimed Drogan.

"Thank you, Philip," she responded with a smile. "But I would never have put it all together without this." She reached into the pocket of her riding habit and pulled out the telegram. "It came for you this morning, but I didn't have an opportunity to give it to you—so I read it myself, in my bunk on the train."

Drogan took it from her hand and read it silently.

"That was the final piece to the puzzle," Kyra said when he'd finished.

"Yes," said Drogan, "but it's only a small part of the worldwide puzzle."

"I'll leave the rest to you, the Howards, and the Roseberrys," said Kyra. "I assume that you'll be working together, now, instead of separately. As for me, I've had enough detective work for a while. And enough foxhunting, too. Can we go home, Gerald?"

"Of course," Gerald answered immediately. "I rather miss the children myself."

About the Author

TEONA TONE is a Ph.D. in nineteenth-century English and American literature and is a former private investigator. She lives with her husband and their infant daughter on a cattle ranch in the Santa Ynez Valley, California, where she has ridden with a local foxhunt for the past four years—chasing coyote and wild boar, instead of foxes. She also has a son in college who enjoys riding to hounds when he can spare the time.

Teona has written one other mystery, *Lady on the Line*, which features Kyra Keaton investigating a telephone company intrigue in 1899. She has also co-authored a non-fiction book entitled *Housemates: A Practical Guide to Living with Other People*. Both are published by Fawcett.